STRANGER ON THE SHORE

marilyn brant

Twelfth Night
Publishing

(Mirabelle Harbor, Book 4)

DEDICATION & THANKS

For my family, my good friends, and my amazing readers & early reviewers—I appreciate you all so much! And for my mom and her sisters. This story is for the three of you. My deepest gratitude goes out to my wonderful critique partner and friend, Laura Moore, for her notes on this manuscript, and to another talented friend, Karen Dale Harris, for reading the opening chapters of this book in one of its earliest drafts.

Last but not least, much love and thanks to my husband for introducing me to the beauty of Sarasota, Florida. I know why you love visiting there, Jeff... Thank you for sharing those long walks along the beach with me & for teaching me where to look for the prettiest shells.

OTHER BOOKS BY MARILYN BRANT

According to Jane

Friday Mornings at Nine

A Summer in Europe

The Sweet Temptations Collection
~On Any Given Sundae
~Double Dipping
~Holiday Man

The Perfect Pair
~Pride, Prejudice and the Perfect Match
~Pride, Prejudice and the Perfect Bet

The Road to You
The Road and Beyond (expanded edition)

All About Us (novella)

The Mirabelle Harbor Series
~Take a Chance on Me
~The One That I Want
~You Give Love a Bad Name
~Stranger on the Shore
~Going For It (bonus Kindle Worlds novella)

Wanderlust in Suburbia and Other Reflections on
Motherhood (nonfiction essays)

NOTE FROM THE AUTHOR

STRANGER ON THE SHORE is Book 4 in Marilyn Brant's Mirabelle Harbor series, but this story and all of the contemporary romances in this series can be enjoyed as stand-alone novels.

Also, please note that this story takes place during the same summer as THE ONE THAT I WANT (Mirabelle Harbor, Book 2), so Chance and Nia from Book 1 (TAKE A CHANCE ON ME) are already together, but Blake and Vicky from Book 3 (YOU GIVE LOVE A BAD NAME) haven't met yet.

"Sit in reverie, and watch the changing color of the waves that break upon the idle seashore of the mind."
~Henry Wadsworth Longfellow

"Today is a smooth white seashell; hold it close and listen to the beauty of the hours."
~Unknown

CHAPTER ONE
Nautilus and Conch

I scanned the nearly empty living room and picked up my favorite clock—a peachy conch shell, tough on the outside, a delicate pink on the inside, with slightly scalloped edges and a circular clock face with hour and minute hands implanted into the center of it. My sister Ellen had given it to me years ago, a gift from Florida's Sunshine Coast.

It read 3:42.

Huh. What could be a more unremarkable time in the middle of an unremarkable day, week, year and, let's face it, life?

But I'd saved this clock until the end for a reason. Its ticking had kept me company and, now, it played the role of the marker for my final task.

In spite of myself, I felt a heady zip of excitement rising inside me as I rolled up the clock in bubble wrap, nestled it into the center of the very last of the cardboard packing boxes, and taped the top shut. Sealing the flap of that box was like slamming the door on all four decades of my existence until now. The past tucked safely, firmly inside.

Most everything here, shell clock included, was to be transported to the storage facility this afternoon. Only my one large suitcase, my oversized purse, and my frayed windbreaker would be stuffed in the trunk of my car and would make the trek to Ellen's Florida bungalow with me. God willing. The engine of my nine-year-old Civic was about as reliable as one of those mystery vehicles from Louie's Used Car Lot at the edge of town. But, still—it was *my* mystery vehicle.

I heard a honk from the driveway. Ah, they were here.

My good friend Olivia Michaelsen waved from the passenger seat before hopping out of the moving van. Her husband Derek slid out from behind the wheel, and two of his brothers—Chance and Blake—jumped out of the backseat. All of them grinned at me as I stepped out of the front door to welcome them.

"The Michaelsen moving crew is here," Olivia announced.

Chance nodded and immediately flexed his muscles, which were sizable, owing largely to the fact that he was a professional fitness trainer at the local gym. And Blake, who was a DJ at 102.5 "LOVE" FM in town, mocked his kid brother by imitating him with the muscle flexing, then pointed to his own biceps and said, "Just look at these guns."

Derek snorted. "Lightweights," he said, striking a weightlifter pose.

Chance, the quiet one of the family, raised a dubious brow at both of his brothers.

Olivia rolled her eyes in feigned exasperation before turning toward me. "Marianna, please point these charming Neanderthals toward all the things you wanted loaded into the van and consider it done. And, oh!" Olivia reached back into the vehicle and pulled out a paper bag and two large to-go coffee cups with plastic lids. "These are for us. Just a couple of Greek pastries from The Gala, compliments of Chance's girlfriend Nia." She winked at me. "And Mocha-Cocoa Lattés from Not the Same Old Grind. I figured you probably already packed your coffeemaker and mugs."

It was so like Olivia and her family to be extra thoughtful. Not only volunteering to help me move my furniture and boxes to the storage facility, but to stop by Mirabelle Harbor's popular coffee shop to bring me a gourmet drink and send me off with baklava, too. I felt a deep pang of loss, missing my friends already.

The guys got to work right away, loading up the van with my many boxes and the few large pieces of furniture I hadn't sold, given away, or tossed out. Meanwhile, Olivia prattled sweetly about all the fun I was going to have this summer and how refreshing it would be to get a break from the usual Midwestern scenery and have a Floridian adventure.

"And that *gorgeous* beach!" she enthused. "I envy you the white sand, the time to stroll along the shore, the many new people you'll meet…and maybe even some hot and very tanned men, who'll bring you Mai Tais while you dip your toes into the blue Gulf waters."

We laughed together, drinking our steaming coffees on this unseasonably cool June day.

I listened to her optimistic spin on my circumstances with appreciation but, admittedly, few words. What was there to say, really? *You've painted such a nice fantasy, my friend. Too bad I'm not a big believer in fairy tales anymore…*

As the Michaelsen men carted away my belongings, I took a deep breath and studied the living room in all its bareness and vulnerability. So strange to be doing this again—making a real move—especially after all of these years.

Only twice before did I have to pack up all of my belongings this way and leave home. Both times it was summer. Both times I knew where I was headed. Both times I'd shared the journey with someone else.

When I was five and my sister was ten, our parents

moved us from our two-bedroom apartment on the south side of Chicago to a sturdy house in the upscale suburb of Mirabelle Harbor. Nice neighborhood. Good schools. Time proved this was a smart move.

Then, when I was eighteen, just a week after high-school graduation, I moved again, this time with my boyfriend Donny, also eighteen (at least chronologically—his maturity level hovered somewhere around age twelve), into his parents' basement, two days after our secret elopement in Atlantic City. Time proved this was *not* such a smart move.

I'd gotten our daughter Kathryn out of the marriage, though, and that was worth something. Quite a lot, really.

But Kathryn was going to college in Michigan now—thankfully on scholarship, smart girl—and the upkeep of a house was too much. Especially being all alone and with no source of income. So, I found myself packing up all of my belongings and moving once again.

Like the first two times, it was summer and, for seven weeks at least, I knew where I was headed. Unlike the first two times, I was not sharing the journey with a single soul.

I could still hear the faint ticking of the conch-shell clock, even trapped as it was in the last packing box by the door.

Time. It did have a way of pressing forward whether I was ready or not, didn't it?

"So, after we unload everything at the storage place, you're going to drop off the house keys at the realtor's office and then...what?" Olivia asked. "Drive directly to Sarasota?"

I nodded. "That's the plan."

"Isn't there anyone en route that you might want to stop and see? To break up the long trip?"

"I don't think so," I murmured, taking a final sip of my latté and setting the cup down on the ticking cardboard box.

Olivia was the type of person who was forever visiting

people and inviting others to her house. She was beautifully, generously, and relentlessly social. Once upon a time, I was more like her. Now, not so much. The demise of both my marriage and, more recently, my job had drained me of some of my former extraversion. These days, I was like a sea mollusk, happiest when hiding in my shell.

I rubbed my hands together, contemplating the best way to try to explain this change to my friend. We'd talked about it before, of course, but with Olivia, these reflections never quite seemed to sink in. My fingertips caressed the spot where my wedding band had once been, but there was no longer any visual trace of it. Didn't mean I'd forgotten it, though, or stopped mourning the loss of the more innocent, hopeful girl I'd once been.

Before I had a chance to say anything else, she brightened and, literally, snapped her fingers as if a big idea had just popped into her lovely head. "You remember Abby Solinski, right?"

Vaguely.

"The name sounds sort of familiar—" I began.

"She's Chandler's ex-girlfriend, and I'm pretty sure she lives in the Sarasota area now. You should look her up when you get there!"

"Look up your brother-in-law's ex?"

"Yes," Olivia insisted. "Abby's a sweetheart. Blond hair, late twenties, warm smile." She lowered her voice. "Between us, I think Chandler was a numbskull to let her go. And I'm not the only one. If you ever want to get Chance talking—" She motioned toward the picture window, where they could see the Michaelsen men working together to get a chair into the van, "just start asking him about what a fool his twin was when it came to Abby. Chandler strung the poor girl along for, like, five years, and dragged her all over the country. No wonder she finally had enough and just stayed in Florida."

"Well, maybe—"

5

"I think Shar might have her current number. I'll get it from her and text it to you." Olivia rested a gentle hand on my shoulder. "You never know when you might need a Mirabelle Harbor friend, right?"

It was hard to fight the persistence of one of the Michaelsens. I didn't know Derek's (and Blake's and Chance's and Chandler's) sister Sharlene particularly well, but I knew she and Olivia were ridiculously close as sisters-in-law and that they shared a similar determination.

"Right," I whispered. "Thanks."

My good friend took our empty coffee cups to run them out to the overflowing garbage bin, and I had a brief moment alone.

With my heart beating in metrical synchronicity with the conch-shell clock's second hand, I wandered into the kitchen to peer out the small window above the sink at the yard and at my favorite sugar maple tree in the back. The trees, flowers, and muggy atmosphere outside of this now-sold house were no more mine than the paint-chipped walls and dented floorboards. They, too, seemed to be waiting for me to leave the Midwest and Mirabelle Harbor behind for a summer. To see if anything at all awaited me a thousand miles—and a world—away, before I had to return to face the chill of fall and a nearly blank slate in a couple of months.

Oddly, I felt so light with my possessions pared down, I was almost buoyant. For maybe the first time in the three years since Donny ran out on Kathryn and me, I felt genuinely unshackled. It was a hopeful thing.

So, I raised an imaginary wineglass and toasted the house, the yard, the boxes one last time: *Here's to the past, with all of its good and its bad.*

And, while I couldn't quite bring myself to make a toast to the uncertainty of my future, I managed to raise my make-believe glass one final time: *Here's to new beginnings.*

6

CHAPTER TWO
Bungalow 26

"Here's your key," Mr. Niihau, the elderly proprietor of the Siesta Sunset bungalows, said to me, handing over a plastic keychain in the shape of a golden nautilus with a single key on the end. "It works for the laundry room, too."

I nodded and tried not to look as unenthusiastic about the idea of doing laundry as I felt. As hard as it was selling the house and, with it, the washer and dryer that I'd scraped together enough cash to buy the year after Donny left me, I couldn't say I was going to *miss* the appliances all that much.

"Here are bath towels to get you started." He placed an assortment on the counter between us. "Garbage bags and a roll of paper towels." He added those and pointed in the direction of the narrow parking lot. "There should be extras of everything in your unit. Garbage pickup comes on Tuesdays. Throw your bags in the green dumpster at the end of the lot. And there's a big bin for recycling, too. Fresh towels and linens on Thursdays. Any questions?"

I inhaled and held the breath deep inside my chest for a moment. I was almost forty years old with no husband, no home of my own, and no paying job. My most pressing question was "Seriously, what am I gonna do with my life?" but I did not ask Mr. Niihau this.

"Looks like I'm all set," I told him instead. "Thank you."

He smiled kindly, the corners of his eyes crinkling even further. The sun-weathered skin had seen seven decades at least, but he looked as though if someone were to say, "Surf's up!" he'd grab his board and race them to the water. My sister Ellen had told me he was born in Hawaii and still had the heart of an Islander. Having met him now, I totally believed that.

"Your sister's unit is number twenty-six," he reminded me. "Let me know if there's anything you need during your stay."

I assured him I would then meandered down the outdoor walkway. The early June humidity was so oppressive—good God! A person would be crazy to think Mirabelle Harbor was muggy by comparison. I felt wrapped in a tight wool blanket, the sweat being squeezed out of me, until I got to the shaded canopy of the bungalow that Ellen and her husband Jared bought as a vacation unit over a decade ago.

With the exception of a few weeks every winter, my sister and her husband rarely visited this property. They just rented it out through the year with the help of Mr. Niihau and his staff—often to an assortment of regulars and to some others, mostly families, who were looking for a place to stay on their beach holiday.

But not this summer.

For seven weeks, Ellen kept the reservation book clear for me. A gift for which I had no earthly idea how I might ever repay.

The door to unit #26 creaked as I unlocked it. I twisted the knob, pushed my way in, and stepped inside a photograph.

I remembered this image exactly from a snapshot Ellen

had sent one winter: A lush floral sofa with pretty buttercup throw pillows dominated the living room. A glass coffee table was parked in front of it. A small spotless kitchen was just beyond the front seating area with stainless steel appliances and a circular dining table jutting up against the main kitchen counter. A hallway could be found beyond that, with speckled tile floors throughout, an occasional throw rug, and stark white walls dotted with a few small seascapes to break up the monotony.

The only difference between the photo in my memory and this room was that, in the former, my smart, successful older sister was lounging on the sofa, drinking from a 24-oz. ceramic mug of extra-strength coffee, and glancing up from her collection of work pages scattered on the glass table in front of her.

I had no such papers in my own bag, just an invisible, ever-growing list of differences between Ellen's life and mine. My sister's ability to do work while on vacation was only one of them.

My loafers click-clacked against the ceramic tiles as I strode down the hall to where the bedrooms were hidden. There were two available: One with a queen bed and one with a double. I opted for the larger of them—well, heck, why not live large, right?—and tossed my suitcase, purse, and jacket in the corner. The only items I retrieved from my bag were my flip-flops, which I slipped on after kicking off my travel loafers. Much like the way Mister Rogers changed his shoes at the start of his famous show when I was a kid, I felt the need to do the same.

I smoothed down a few wrinkles from my short-sleeve shirt and shorts and inhaled. Yes, I was about as comfortable as I could get under the circumstances. Ready to enter the Neighborhood of Make-Believe.

I squeezed the plastic nautilus keychain in my fist and pivoted toward the door, but the phone rang.

I don't know why, but that intrusive sound just

paralyzed me. I stood there for several seconds, my heartbeat racing to fill the gap between rings. *Who would call here? What disaster is waiting to befall me now?*

Finally, I snapped out of my inertia and grabbed at the beige phone on the wall.

"Hello?" My voice sounded tinny and unsure, even to my own ears.

"Marianna!" came the energetic, good-natured growl on the other end, signifying my sister. "Welcome to Sarasota!"

I glanced out the front window, straining to spot Ellen's wiry frame, her sharply defined jaw, her mischievous brown eyes. I didn't see them. "Are—are you *here?*"

Ellen laughed. "No, silly. I'm home in Connecticut." She paused, no doubt enjoying making me wonder and squirm, as always. "I asked Mr. Niihau to email me after you checked in. That's how I knew you'd gotten there." I could hear Ellen's laptop keys clicking and the distinctive echo-y reverberation that indicated she'd switched me over to speakerphone already. Ah, my big sister, Queen of Multitasking. "So, what do you think?" Ellen asked. "Do you love it already?"

At this, I couldn't help but grin into the receiver. "I arrived ten minutes ago, Sis. The Gulf looked very pretty from the car window—I caught a few glimpses of it on the interstate. But I haven't been to the beach yet."

Ellen half smothered one of her involuntary huffs of disapproval, but I still heard it. Much as I loved my sister, the woman was not known for her patience and, admittedly, I found myself relieved not to have to deal with her face to face. Was it too much to ask not to be judged for one day? By anybody?

"You should go out and walk around," Ellen commanded. "You can call me back after you've taken a look." She paused but not long enough for me to explain that this was exactly what I'd intended to do. "You like the bungalow, though, right?"

"I do," I said truthfully. "It's just perfect. Everything I need, and nothing I don't. It's simple. Uncluttered. Like Miss Garwood's private cabin at Camp Willowgreen, only much nicer and without all those snot-nosed little kids and pesky teen counselors knocking on the door, asking annoying questions."

My sister found this description very funny—laughing in delight, and even pausing (albeit momentarily) in her typing to get all sentimental about Camp Willowgreen and witchy camp director Miss Garwood. "Oh, man, those were the days," Ellen said, as she waxed fondly over memories of tipping canoes and mosquito bites. Ellen had, apparently, forgotten that I didn't share her love affair with summer-camp adventures, and it never did any good to try to explain to my sister that I'd been more ambivalent than not to those long weeks away.

However, Ellen had blithely given me the kind of gift worth the weight of Mr. Niihau in gold. My heart almost burst open in appreciation of it but, at the same time, being in Florida felt like an exercise in procrastination. Like I'd been sent off to summer camp when everyone else was busily working on something more productive. I wasn't sure how anything I might do in Sarasota would help me when I got back to my *real* life in Mirabelle Harbor, any more than learning to play water polo, roasting marshmallows over a fire, or weaving placemats were skills of much use to me in high-school geometry or world lit.

"I envy your summer," Ellen concluded on a sigh.

I rolled my eyes, glad my sister couldn't see me. Once again, I told Ellen how grateful I was for the use of the bungalow.

"Then why the hell don't you sound happier?" Ellen demanded.

What to say to this? Up until my senior year in high school, my sister had always been five years ahead of me. Thanks to our birth order, that was a given. I'd never thought for an instant that I'd catch up to her. Not really. But, if I were to be honest, I guess I'd hoped our experiences would eventually even out.

And, for a time, they seemed to. After my impromptu marriage, right around the time when Ellen, by contrast, was in the process of getting her very practical CPA, I almost felt *more* experienced. I was a married woman and then a mom, living an adult's life, even if it was in my in-laws' basement. Ellen, meanwhile, was still a student, living single with Mom and Dad at home.

But that soon reversed again—in Ellen's favor.

When Ellen moved out, started dating Jared, became a tax partner, and began jetting off on international vacations to exotic locales like Bali, Ixtapa, and Prague...our five-year age difference seemed magnified to ten. And when Ellen and her man relocated to New Haven, Connecticut (Jared had once been a Yalie before his work took him to Chicago), had a lavish wedding, and moved into a McMansion overlooking Long Island Sound, the gap between us felt like decades. Ellen was a mover and shaker in her world, up in the stratosphere, while I was...well, nowhere close. And that always seemed to scratch at my insecurities. Which was something I sure as heck didn't need right now.

So, I took a deep breath. "I don't know if you'll understand this because you're so...so *good* at everything," I began, knowing this would probably be interpreted by my sister as "whiny" even though I was trying hard not to be. "You have a husband who loves you. A beautiful home. A career you excel at." I frowned. "I mean, I'm sure your life isn't *totally* perfect." Although, to me, Ellen's life had always seemed that way. "I'm sure you get tired of working so many hours sometimes and you need a break. But my being here isn't fun like that. It's not a *vacation*, you know? It's a delay tactic." I slowed my speech in hopes that the truth might sink in. "I failed at *everything*, Ellen. I have to start *all over again*. This isn't a 'happy' kind of thought."

There was a long pause on the line. Oh, damn. Maybe I was finally getting through to my sister, but I was managing to offend her in the process. "Sis, I'm sorry," I added. "I don't mean to sound ungrateful because you've been wonderful to me. But I'm just—just—"

"Scared," Ellen supplied. She exhaled. A long, slow breath. I could hear the air streaming out of her like a deflating balloon and knew I was the one responsible for puncturing Ellen's good mood. I was a lousy little sister.

When Ellen spoke again, her voice had that clipped businesswoman tone to it that I always heard her use when speaking to clients on her iPhone. "Well, explore a little and get to know the area. Sarasota is pretty different from Mirabelle Harbor, so your first visit to Florida ought to be an eye-opening experience. Even if it isn't *a vacation*."

She was mocking me now. Great. I rolled my eyes again but succeeded in uttering a very cordial, "Okay."

"And stop being so hard on yourself," Ellen said, evidently unable to turn off the bossy big-sister gene for more than ten seconds. "You did not fail at *everything*. From what my niece tells me, you're not even an *entirely* dreadful mom."

At this, I laughed. I'd cheerfully strangle Ellen sometimes, but my sister *was* funny. Plus, I knew Ellen loved me. And Kathryn. That counted for more than a little.

"Anyway," Ellen said, "we all need a fresh start sometimes. Regardless of our age or how successful people *think* we are." I heard the rapid-fire clicking again and was so preoccupied trying to calculate how many words-per-minute my sister must've been typing—I was almost positive I was a hair faster than Ellen at *that*, if at nothing else—that I almost missed Ellen's last sentence. "No one wants to stay in a rut forever," my sister murmured. "Not even a gold-plated one."

❁❀❁

A mix of cerulean with teal for the furthest watery depths.

A dabbling of silvery sunlight, whiting out patches of sea and sand like a spotlight.

Gil Canton studied the shoreline with the practiced eye of an artist. Which was what he was, he reminded himself. Never mind the low, deep voice from decades' past that told him otherwise. That told him he should be using his powers of observation on "a worthier, more lucrative cause."

Bullshit.

A faint blend of burnt umber and goldenrod in a subtle line underscoring the crisp cottony tufts of rolling waves.

A flash of gray and green as the sunfish tangled with the seaweed just below the surface.

Anyone with a heart knew the creatures of the ocean were as *worthy* as anything out in the world. That the Gulf was not only a visual feast for a painter, but it was a composer's symphony, a poet's playground.

Anyone with a heart...ahh. But that was the problem, wasn't it?

Gil grimaced. Calf-deep in the warm water and strolling languidly along the Siesta Key shoreline, he picked up his stride to outrace that old, familiar voice. It didn't work. It never the hell worked. But he turned his attention to the passersby in hopes of a distraction.

Shades of skin color in a palette of creams, tans, bronzes, chocolates and, sometimes, sunburned reds.

The fascinating discordance of fabric hues and textures and patterns, draping the wearer in a manner that left no question as to whether the individual wanted to be noticed...or wanted to blend into the seascape.

He knew he looked at the beach differently than he had

when he'd first moved here twenty-six years ago. And, unlike the appreciative but unobservant gazes of the bikini-clad tourists, he needed to distinguish between the various ranges of blues and greens, the buffet of multicolored accessory images and the differing degrees of whiteness from the sand to the bungalows—for the sake of his passion. His paintings.

Why was it so easy, so natural for him to be both loving and discerning in one area of his life but not in another?

With a canvas, he could step back and assess it. If he saw he'd done something wrong or, more frequently, had neglected to do something completely right, he would be able to see the problem area with the help of a few feet of distance and, then, correct it.

With relationships—parental, romantic, professional or otherwise—it was never that simple. Stepping back was harder for the other person to accept. And it tended to create more damage, even when the objective was to do just the opposite. To achieve a fresh perspective. Clarity.

Art and life? Not so much the same.

He kicked lightly at a broken conch with the tip of his water shoe. Even with a chunk of its shell missing, it was still beautiful. There was almost heartbreaking beauty on this shore.

Seagulls squawking above and around him in a flying dance of circles and landings.

Children splashing and frolicking, often with a battalion of siblings and water toys.

An old woman dressed all in white, someone he'd seen many times, stood several yards from him, chatting with an attractive younger lady—an obvious newcomer. He couldn't help but check out the new woman. She was a tad overdressed in her pinkish t-shirt and navy shorts. Untanned and pensive. Awed by the Gulf setting in that mystified tourist sort of way. The coast was full of visitors like that. Nothing wrong with them, he supposed. His business depended on them, after all. But it was hard to get to know many people well in such a transient environment.

With a shrug, he returned his focus to the water—the rhythmic breaking of the waves trying their darnedest to drown out his father's voice once and for all until, a few minutes later, a sound he couldn't ignore pierced his concentration.

The white sand enveloped my feet.

It was so powdered-sugar like that my poor toes, unprotected in flimsy pink flip-flops, weren't safe from the thousands of granules of warmth that attacked them and my heels with every sinking step on my trek to the water's edge. Warm sand, yes, but not scorching. That surprised me.

Ellen was right. Sarasota was not Mirabelle Harbor. And the Siesta Key beach was not remotely like a visit to the chilly, rocky shores of Lake Michigan. I felt myself to be a stranger in a strange land.

I'd barely had a chance to register this thought when, in spite of the jarring differences between my home state and this all-natural water park, I began getting caught up in it.

The colors grabbed me first. Had I not known better, I would've sworn they were fake. I gazed out into the Gulf and that blue was so vibrant, so very *azure* that I was sure it'd been dyed. Nothing in the real world could possibly look *that* blue. I recalled photos of tropical places I'd seen in magazines like *National Geographic* and always figured they'd been touched up somehow. Tinted, so as to make the landlocked Northerners envious.

But I could see now that—no—reality actually could be this stunning. This utopian. And that the photographs were only able to capture the images, not the pervasive scent of sand, salty water, and sunscreen. Not the sound of the squawking seagulls and chattering beachcombers. Not the feel of the hot sand granules, the sweat beads sliding down my arms, neck, and spine. Not the shocking warmth of wading into the Gulf, like sinking into the most amazing Jacuzzi ever.

A giggle rose in my throat, and I was that five-year-old girl again, discovering the world freshly after our move to Mirabelle Harbor. How magically different my new home had seemed to me then…as this one did now.

With a degree of impulsivity I hadn't felt in a while, I kicked off my flip-flops and carried them, stepping along the undulating seam where the waves lapped rhythmically against the shore, caressing it. Every stride was a brand new stitch, connecting me, however tenuously, to this exotic, amphibious fabric of a place.

The further I walked, the faster my blood pumped. I could feel my heart rate increasing, and not just from the exercise. My pulse was matching the heartbeat of the sea—the ebb and flow of the Gulf's ever-shifting tide—marking the passage of time like a ticking grandfather clock. The waves were a swinging pendulum of seconds, beating the minutes, hours, days, and reminding me of years that had passed, of relationships that had come and gone, of emotions I'd once felt and now ceased to feel.

And then the harmonious unity of my footsteps in flawless synchronicity with time came to a crashing halt.

"Ow!" I squealed aloud, the pain in the sole of my right foot too sharp to ignore.

Admittedly, I hadn't been looking at where my feet were landing, but I knew I'd have to remember not to lose focus in the future if I wanted to keep my toes.

I spotted the offending object jutting out of the water-packed sand. The jagged edge of the twisting shell was serrated enough to cut flesh. I inspected the bottom of my foot for blood. None, although there was an indentation where I'd stepped on that thing. I rubbed my sole for a moment then reached to pick up the shell. On first instinct, it reminded me of a funnel cloud, like a palm-sized Midwestern tornado. I dipped it into the seawater, shook the sand and grit from it, and held it up to the light.

It was beautiful.

I'd seen shells like this before in shops, but I never imagined just finding one in the wild. On closer inspection—save for the broken ridge I'd stepped on—the shell was so perfect, it was almost edible. Brown lines drizzled dark color down the cream and gold sides, like chocolate syrup over a vanilla and caramel cone. The top swirled into a point, managing to make it look at once both delicious and dangerous. Tempting enough to wish I could take a bite.

"That there's a lightning whelk," an old lady's voice informed me. "It's unusual to find a nice one like that this late in the day. Best shelling is in early morning."

I shaded my eyes against the sun's glare and squinted at the woman. She was probably about the same age as Mr. Niihau but, unlike his dark hair and deeply bronzed, weathered skin, this woman was a study in white. Her hair was as snowy as Mrs. Claus, worn in a bun and covered with a wide-brimmed sunhat. Her milky complexion was textured with dry, pale wrinkles, and her swimsuit and wrap were varying shades of ivory. Standing next to her in the burning midday sun reminded me that I desperately needed to buy sunglasses, a beach hat, and more sunscreen. SPF 50 at least.

"Thanks," I said brightly. "I didn't know its name. It's pretty."

The woman nodded. "You looked like an out-of-towner, girlie." She pointed further up the beach. "If you get out here at five or six in the morning and keep walkin' about a half a mile that a-way to the rocks, you'll find some real stunning ones." She motioned toward my flip-flops,

"And you'll wanna put them back on or get yourself some Beachwalkers like me." She lifted up a foot to show the only dark piece of clothing she had on—slip-on water shoes, like the kind marine biologists or serious snorkelers might wear.

"I will," I promised her, glancing behind us, surprised to see how far I'd already ambled down the coast.

The older woman caught my gaze and stabbed her bony index finger at the hotels in the opposite direction. "Walk that other way another mile or so and you'll find yourself at some pretty ritzy hotels and bungalows and such. But you don't need to be rich to enjoy the beach." She flung her arms out on both sides, as if to capture the air. "The beach is free for everybody."

"I'm not rich," I murmured, pondering for a split second what it must be like to feel comfortable like that. Never having to wonder where the next rent payment or doctor's fee would come from. Never having to make a choice between buying a much-needed coat for yourself or new school clothes for your child. Never having to worry about selling your house because you can't swing the mortgage or the insurance or the utilities...

"Me neither, girlie." She tapped her chest with the flat of her palm. "I'm Vivian, by the way."

"Marianna," I told her, as the woman stuck out her hand to formally shake mine. Vivian's grip was strong and sure, grounding me to the present.

"I walk all the way down Siesta Key beach and back, twice a day. Two and a half miles each way," Vivian informed me proudly. "So, I'm sure I'll see you again. And you just ask me if you have any questions 'bout anything, you hear?" She patted her chest again and grinned. "Fourth generation Floridian. Not one of them newcomers."

I grinned back. "Thank you," I whispered, a lump rising in the back of my throat for a reason I couldn't begin to justify. When had the simple act of a stranger being kind to me reduced me to tears?

Vivian waved and was on her way, and I was left swallowing back an emotion I was too anxious to let myself fully feel. But I did eye the people on the shore a little more closely now.

There were lots of women in bikinis with perfectly even tans and trim bodies—showing off their butterfly tattoos on their shoulders, their silver or coral anklets, their diamond-studded belly piercings—and hard-muscled men jogging along the shore with shades and waterproof watches. The youngsters frolicked like water nymphs, and even the older people had a lean, outdoorsy look about them.

I felt frumpy in my t-shirt and shorts. A pale-faced tourist in paradise, carting only my bungalow key, a pair of flip-flops, and a shell. A simple existence, really.

I spied a family with three or four...no, *five* kids under the age of eleven or so. The youngest ones were a set of twin boys—a handful from the looks of them—about four years old. Probably similar to what Chance and Chandler Michaelsen had been like at that age. These young boys were racing each other to the water as fast as their brown little legs could carry them, giggling, with maniacal expressions on their faces like Thing One and Thing Two from *The Cat in the Hat*. Their beleaguered mother was calling after them, but she had the three older kids hanging off of her. Literally. One of them was pulling at the straps of her swim top.

I heard her shout, "Steve! Get them!" in an exasperated tone, motioning toward the adult male nearby, ostensibly the twins' father, who was occupied blowing up a beach ball for the siblings. He dropped it and began to chase the little terrors into the Gulf.

I found myself mildly amused by this scene—half relieved, half wistful at having those parenting days long behind me—and I couldn't help but reflect on what it might have been like for me, Donny, and Kathryn if there had been other children in our little family. Kathryn had always been such a quiet little girl, only starting to emerge from her room and explore the world more once she got into high school. The blow of her father leaving when she was just sixteen stunted that growth for a time, but she soon found more consolation from her friends than from me. Maybe all teens did. Certainly, Kathryn now preferred her new college pals, her boyfriend, and her exciting university life to another dull summer with her mother.

Again, I felt the lump of emotion rising in the back of my throat and forced it down once more. There was no use crying. I just needed to regroup. To take a few deep breaths. Get back into the swing of things. And slog away even harder this time. That strategy had worked in the past and, by God, I'd make it work again.

I felt a splash on my legs and the sudden hot breath of Thing One as he raced past me, deeper into the water. Quite a few yards away, the father had nabbed Thing Two and was holding him firm with one arm and waving wildly at me with the other. "Please stop him!" he shouted.

So, I threw my flip-flops and new seashell on the sand and plunged deeper into the Gulf after the boy. But he was fast, and I...was not. He zigzagged in and out of the water, in between people, around clumps of seaweed, giggling demonically the whole way. I reached out to grab him on the shore but, just like some hapless adult in a kids' sitcom, he slithered out of my grasp and I slipped in the wet sand, falling to my knees.

"Ow!" I cried, not sure what jagged object I'd landed on this time, only that everything out here—be it on land or sea—seemed to be conspiring to cut or bruise me.

I heard a deep, throaty laugh (not maniacal, not demonic) and a voice beside me that said, "This one yours?"

I turned to face the sound and stood up, brushing the sand from my limbs and spotting a collection of cat's paw shells in a heap where my knee had been. "No—" I began, but then I focused on the man and, for a moment, found myself actually tongue-tied. He was holding up the four-year-old as easily as I'd hold up a coconut…if it had legs and were kicking.

This was not what was remarkable about him, though.

The Sunshine Coast, while full of heavenly bodies in varying states of undress, had presented me with someone wholly unexpected. Although roughly my age, the man had jet black hair—slicked back—full lips, twinkling baby-blue eyes, and a tanned, toned frame, like he'd just stepped out of a late-1960s beach movie. There was just no other way to say it: He looked like Elvis Presley in some film like *Clambake*.

I blinked at him. "Do you sing?"

"What?" he asked above the noise of the still-squealing kid.

"I, um—" I swiveled around in frantic search for Thing One's father and, suddenly, he was there.

"Sorry, sorry," the dad said to the Elvis lookalike and to me. "Thank you for grabbing my boy." He snatched the kid from Elvis's capable hands and the giggling and squealing came to an immediate stop. As the father marched the child back to his family, Elvis chuckled and said, "I do not envy that man."

I laughed. "Or his wife."

"Agreed."

We shared a fleeting smile.

"Thanks for catching him when I couldn't. I slipped…"

"I noticed." He squinted at my feet. "If you're going to run on the shore, you should get some Beachwalkers."

"I know, I know. You're the second person to tell me that today." I noticed he was wearing some very sporty-looking black water shoes with red stripes to match his long swim trunks. "Do you know a good place to buy some? I just got to Sarasota."

"Yeah, you looked like an out-of-towner."

My awe at his resemblance to The King began to wear off and a splinter of irritation took its place. "Do I have a sign on my back or something?"

"Nah. It just takes one to know one. I'm not a native either, but I've lived in Florida for a long time." He checked his watch (waterproof, I was sure) and added, "I've got to get to work, but the best beachwear outfitter around is just a few miles down the road in St. Armand's Circle on Lido Key. Take Tamiami Trail to 789 North and follow the signs. The shop is called Castaways, and it's on John Ringling Boulevard, just past the circle. They've got clothing, bathing suits, snorkel gear, footwear—everything you need for your visit. Lots of other great shops on the block, too. The Beaded Periwinkle and The Golden Gecko are a couple of my favorites and they're right next door. You should check 'em out."

"Hmm," I said, noncommittally. "Thanks."

"You're welcome." He paused, flashed me one of his twinkly grins and waved like he was The King himself. "See you around."

I waved back and watched him stride down the beach, finding it hard to believe our paths would really cross again. He had the gait of someone who didn't spend a lot of time idling on sand drifts and talking to frumpy divorced women, despite how even his tan was or how effortless his manner.

But, then, people always said insincere things like that to each other. Probably even more often in a beach-culture environment such as Florida, where the population fluctuated with the tide.

I grabbed my pink flip-flops and new lightning whelk— both half buried in the sand—patted my pocket to make sure my key was still there and, finally, began my trek back to the Siesta Sunset bungalows. Where the rich people stayed. I knew I didn't belong there, but I was getting attached anyway.

Such simplicity. It struck me freshly again and again.

What a contrast from the crazy complexity of my life with Donny, his kind parents (when they were still living), and Kathryn as a baby. What a contrast from the quieter life of just me and Kathryn alone, when my daughter was a teen. This summer life felt almost *too* easy.

And, yet, as I approached #26, my pulse started racing again. Not like the rush of rejuvenation I'd felt at the exercise of walking along the stunning beach. No. More like a return to the combination of fear and indistinct emotion I'd felt after talking with Vivian. More like the misgivings I'd tried to express to Ellen at having come to Florida at all.

With simplicity abounding—so much daily clutter cleared away—it was shockingly apparent when there was a big problem sitting in the middle of the room. Like, oh, my entire nebulous future.

I sighed and pushed open the door to the bungalow. It was precisely how I'd left it and, for some reason, this brought with it a fresh wave of sadness. I swiped away any remnants of sand and sea from the shell and placed it in the middle of the glass coffee table. My first decoration.

It wasn't even three o'clock in the afternoon but, suddenly, the two days of driving, the tension of moving, the odd sense of displacement I'd felt since getting here, and the endless stretch of the unknown all mingled inside of me to create only the certainty of exhaustion.

I curled up on Ellen's cushiony floral sofa—a buttercup pillow under my head—and closed my eyes. I needed to call my sister back soon, but for the next hour, I could let myself drift into sleep and away from all anxiety-producing things.

The day might not yet have ended but, tomorrow was still another day. I figured I had more than enough worry and angst to carry over into it. For the time being, though,

I'd burrow deeper into my borrowed shell, pretend the ocean was a melody designed to lull me to sleep, and dream about my longest-held fantasy—the one I pointedly refused to name aloud.

CHAPTER THREE
Connecticut Disconnect

Ellen Slater had always prided herself on being a strong woman. A warrior, even. In the tax world. In her marriage. Everywhere. No one questioned her ability to do her job extremely well, reel in new clients, get thirteen things done at once—and all brilliantly. And they damn well *shouldn't* doubt her. She was forty-four, clever, experienced, and at the absolute top of her game.

Which in no way explained why, after doing nothing more challenging than having a ten-minute phone call with her longtime client, Gage Bartholomew, Ellen had sequestered herself in the far left stall of the women's restroom—the one on the fifth and highest floor of the New Haven, Connecticut branch of Palmer, Jacoby and Slater—and was trying desperately to breathe deeply and keep her hands from visibly shaking in front of her.

She stared with increasing horror at her fingers, her nails polished with a tasteful rose-red sheen, but each digit trembling as if she were afflicted by some sort of palsy. Her heart raced, she found herself wicked short of breath, and she was sweating straight through her cream-colored silk blouse. Disgusting. She figured she was either dying or—

worse—going through early menopause.

What the hell was happening to her?! She'd just had a comprehensive physical in May, and her doctor had pronounced her in good health.

So much for what *he* knew. Stupid asshat.

Ellen had every intention of telling off Dr. Joseph Cole when she spoke with him next...once she could stop quivering long enough to dial his number on her cell phone. It would, however, be a far less effective rant if she were, say, incapable of speaking above a whisper. Like she was at the moment.

She leaned against the cool ceramic tiles on the wall, letting the chilled smoky-blue squares ice the back of her neck, and debated whether or not to call 9-1-1. The fact that she could still "debate" made her less inclined to initiate such a call. Besides, the symptoms of whatever she was experiencing seemed to be lessening—at least she wasn't feeling quite as lightheaded or nauseated as she'd been back in her office fifteen minutes ago.

Her office... Oh, Christ. She was supposed to have a conference call with her client Carole Grayson this afternoon. In twenty minutes. That just wasn't going to happen. She'd have to ask her secretary to call Carole and reschedule. This illness—or whatever it was—was effing up her day, big time.

And it was going to take all of her strength just to keep news of her potentially imminent death from her husband Jared. The man might be smart, well-connected, over-educated, and affluent, but he couldn't even make a grilled cheese sandwich by himself without detailed instructions and/or a step-by-step flowchart. What would he do without her?

Hire a live-in cook, Ellen supposed. Or find himself a new wife.

Crap.

She swiped the beads of sweat off her forehead with a

bit of tissue, her breathing starting to come a bit easier now.

No, she definitely could not meet with Carole. And she would rather not tell anyone—not Jared and certainly not her whiny little sister—that she wasn't in such great shape these days. They relied on her to be their rock. Jared was juggling a dozen projects at work, and Marianna had always been such a catastrophic thinker when it came to anything, especially other people's health. The way she clucked like a little Mother Hen whenever Kathryn had the sniffles or her in-laws were sick...ugh. Always trying to make up for that bastard of a husband by being such a dutiful mom and daughter-in-law. The woman must have spent two decades in the Land of the Worrywarts after she married Donny the Freeloader. No way was Ellen going to give her sister something new to fuss over. Marianna had enough problems.

Ellen forced out some air and inhaled long and slow.

She slipped her hand beneath the neckline of her blouse and placed her palm on the bare skin above her heart. Still pumping furiously. *Too* furiously, considering she wasn't running a 500-meter dash or sprinting up a flight of stairs.

What did they always say to do if you thought you were having a heart attack? Chew on baby aspirin?

Well, she didn't have any baby aspirin. She didn't even have any ibuprofen—at least not with her. Then again, it wouldn't be the worst idea in the world to check with her secretary to see if she had anything like that on hand. That, of course, would mean admitting she was sick, though. She cringed at the thought, but if she was going to leave early, she'd have to tell *someone*. Might as well be Selena, whom she at least liked a little and felt to be somewhat loyal.

Ellen splashed a bit of water on her face, blotted with a paper towel, and tried to tidy up her appearance as best she could. But, really, there was no way around it. She no longer looked like a tax partner. She looked like one of those unfortunate women who'd had their brains half eaten by rabid zombies in the latest horror flick. No one would doubt she had some terrible bug. Maybe it was a kind of summer flu? People got weird things like that, with symptoms like hers, didn't they?

When she got back to her office, her secretary eyed her with concern. "Ms. Slater, are you all ri—" Selena began.

"No," Ellen said. "I'm coming down with something. Twenty-four-hour...hmm, maybe forty-eight-hour flu, I think." She watched as Selena nodded sympathetically and leaned a few inches back from her.

"I'm sorry to hear—"

"Please reschedule my call with Ms. Grayson for next week, and cancel all of my appointments for tomorrow," Ellen interrupted. "I'll call in if I think I'll be gone longer than that."

"Of course, Ms. Slater," the secretary said promptly. "I hope you'll feel better."

"Thank you." Ellen escaped into her office, gathered her laptop, her phone, a folder of paperwork to be signed and a handful of peanut M&Ms. No, they were not exactly *baby aspirin*, but she'd changed her mind about asking Selena if she had any of that. And, besides, Ellen could tell her heart rate really had returned to normal (almost), and it was foolish for a person to take medication they didn't need. Especially if chocolate tasted so much better.

When she was safely in her silver Lexus, though, she called her doctor's office. "Yes, this is Ellen Slater. I need to speak with Dr. Cole at once." She waited as the receptionist transferred her to Dr. Cole's nurse, who then asked her to describe her symptoms.

"Why can't I speak with Dr. Cole directly?" she asked instead. "Where *is* he?"

"He's with another patient, Ms. Slater," the nurse replied. "But if you'll please tell me what you've been experiencing, I'll be happy to—"

Ellen clicked off her phone.

She'd overreacted by calling in the first place. She was *fine*. Really.

She'd go home, rest up, and be her normal self by tomorrow or the day after at the latest. And everything would return to the way it was.

Whatever had happened, it was just a fluke. She was sure of it.

Nevertheless, she stopped at a corner pharmacy on the drive home and picked up a bottle of chewable baby aspirin—that chalky orange-flavored stuff she'd hated as a kid—and forced herself to take a couple of tablets, along with a few swigs of Evian. She washed both down with a small pack of almond M&Ms (she liked to strive for variety in her snacking—*everyone* knew how different almonds and peanuts were from each other—and, besides, nuts were *good* for you) and ordered some freshly rolled sushi for dinner from Tasty Tokyo's "lite menu." There were heart-healthy Omega-3s all over the place with that meal. Although, maybe not so much with the side order of fried calamari.

She was fine. Totally fine.

When the doctor's office called and Dr. Cole himself left her a personal message on her cell's voicemail, Ellen ignored it.

Instead, she picked up her carryout, drove home and crashed on the sofa.

But not before changing out of her cream silk blouse, so revoltingly drenched in sweat that she doubted even the drycleaners would be able to get the stains out. *That* she threw in the trash, wrapping it in a plastic bag first so Jared wouldn't see it.

She had other blouses she liked better anyway.

CHAPTER FOUR
Lobster

I slipped into my beach-life routine as effortlessly as I slipped into my bathrobe.

Morning shifted into afternoon. Afternoon slid into evening. Evening dissolved into night...and then, magically, the hot Florida sun rose and it was morning again.

A couple of days passed like this, with me going nowhere but to the beach and back. I dutifully wore sunscreen to avoid the lobster-red sunburns of my youth. (My sister forced a vow from my lips: "Repeat after me— 'I, Marianna Gregory, promise to apply *and* reapply SPF 50 sunscreen every day I'm in Florida.' I wanna hear you say it. *Now*," she insisted in her bossiest voice.)

I walked further toward the extreme edges of the available shore, making it all the way down to the southern rocks on my next trip. And then, on the following visit, going all the way up to the northern ritzy high-rise resorts. My circle was ever-widening, like those ripples that formed when you threw a pebble into the water and watched the expanding waves.

After a few meals consisting of only what I could

scrounge from the laundry room's vending machine, however, I ventured on foot to the corner grocery mart—a little family-owned store about a block away—and found a treasure trove of mini cereal boxes (Froot Loops, Cocoa Puffs and Trix, oh, my!), milk in quart bottles, all-veggie frozen pizzas, and iced tea mix. They had sunscreen, too, thank God—I was running low already—cheap sunglasses, and postcards from all around Sarasota and the Sunshine Coast. I noticed one for nearby St. Armand's and studied it.

Pretty place. Palm trees lining the streets. Restaurants. And lots of stores. It would be an interesting area to window shop.

But, still, a visit there would require me to actually get in my car and drive a few miles from the bungalow. It would also most likely require that I spend money I didn't have. So, I decided to stick to my explorations on the free beach for the moment. And, anyway, there were still so many things to discover right there on the shore...

After unloading my groceries and reapplying my sunscreen yet again, as best as I could alone (how did anyone get their mid-back by themselves?), I trekked down to the sand and water in my navy one-piece swimsuit with a built-in skirt, relieved to have the extra cover up when I saw the skimpy bikini-clad girls again.

Turned out I was half right in my prediction about running into beach people. While I didn't see The King again, I'd crossed paths with Vivian every day like clockwork, and today was no exception. As usual, the older woman was dressed from head to toe in white, which made her easy to spot.

I waved to her, and we chatted for a few minutes about her exercise routine ("Been speed walkin' on the sand for a half hour already," she told me with pride) and the unrelenting summer heat and humidity.

As we were talking, I tried to keep pace with Vivian, who was clearly not kidding about the speed walking thing.

However, when she saw a pelican alight on the beach, she stopped abruptly and I immediately halted, too, managing, of course, to step hard on another shell.

"Ow!" I cried out.

"Girlie, if you're not gonna watch where you walk, you need to get yourself some water shoes." Vivian took the tone of scolding camp director Miss Garwood, but it didn't suit her. She was way too Earth Mother to pull it off.

I laughed, despite the pain in the soft arch of my bare foot, and said, "Yeah, yeah. I know."

The older woman scowled at me.

I rubbed my foot then scooped up the new shell and handed it to Vivian. "Here. Take a look at this one. I know you'll be able to identify it, and I have no idea."

"Lace murex," Vivian said, as instinctively as if I were asked to differentiate between dark, milk, or white chocolate. She bounced the shell in her palm then ran her thumb along the perfect architecture of the shell's dome. It was spiked on the side in a way that reminded me of the head of a triceratops. "You wanna add it to your collection?" she asked.

I shook my head and watched as Vivian shrugged and pitched it deep into the Gulf. The woman had a good arm.

"I'm trying to leave most of what I find here on the beach," I explained, "but I really love that lightning whelk, and I'm sure I'll want to keep a special shell every now and then."

Vivian nodded approvingly, all trace of the scolding camp director having already dissipated. She walked along the shore with crane-like steps, careful and angular, yet—similar to the bird—still very much at one with nature. She and Mr. Niihau both seemed to be descendents of the beach life. It was as if their human bodies had been formed, like Adam and Eve, from sand, mud, and water…built on the shore as a sand sculpture and, then, touched by the divine.

"So, you're stayin' the summer?" the older woman

asked, tilting her big sunhat to block out the most direct rays.

"Yes. Until the end of July or beginning of August, anyway."

"What d'ya do up North before you came here?" She studied my face silently for a second and drew a surprising conclusion. "Salesgirl?"

"No. Secretary."

Vivian squinted at me. "Really? Typing and filing stuff? Did'ya answer phones, too?"

"Lots of typing. Lots of filing. Not so many calls. I was with an insurance company for sixteen years, but the man that hired me—my *real* boss, Mr. Morris—was let go around Christmas. The new management—" *The evil fiends!* "They, uh, started bringing in their own people after that, and the few of us who remained were seen as expendable. So, I, um, lost my job last month."

I tried to gulp down the bitterness that rose at those words. A decade and a half of my life spent working at the insurance offices on Carraway Street, and only two weeks' severance pay and ten minutes' notice that I was being laid off this spring. I remembered that horrible early day in May. Cleaning out my desk with the new secretary posted at my door, arms crossed, assigned to "watch me" so I didn't steal or destroy anything as I packed up.

"Huh," Vivian said. "I'm real sorry to hear that, girlie." She cocked her head and scrutinized me again. "But you don't look like someone who'd be happy just typin' and not talkin' much. You're too…interested in people."

I didn't know how to respond to this. "I—I *did* get to talk to people," I explained, "just not constantly. It was more of a break-time thing." And, although I didn't say this aloud, I had to admit to myself at least that those were by far my favorite times. The interacting with others. The laughter and even the tasteless jokes. The funny expressions my coworkers would make while small-talking. It gave me a sense of family while at work.

"Huh," Vivian said again. "Well, what'cha gonna do now?"

"Look for another secretarial type of position in Illinois when I get back," I told her. I could hear the forced conviction in my voice as I said these words. The steely determination of them, which I'd artificially inserted, of course. I just hoped they didn't sound as hollow as they felt. "I'm sure some company or firm will want me somewhere in the Chicagoland area," I stated, continuing with the chin-up optimism. And, though I didn't verbalize this, I mentally added: *I'm reliable, personable, a really fast typist. I have a solid associate's degree and an unblemished work record. Just because I didn't find a job right away in my first month of looking doesn't mean I won't when I start searching again in August.* My well-rehearsed internal monologue, bordering on a mantra.

Vivian smiled kindly. "Well, then, it won't kill ya to get yourself some decent Beachwalkers while you're here, so you can relax good and proper without getting yourself cut and scraped. Don't want you settlin' down to your new job with bandages on your feet. Right, girlie?"

In spite of myself, I had to laugh. "Fine, Vivian. You win. I'll go shopping for some water shoes tomorrow." And because I was certain I'd see Vivian soon and would face a stern lecture from the Earth Mother if I didn't follow through, this was a promise I knew I'd need to keep.

We parted ways for the afternoon and, a few hours later, when it began to downpour like crazy and I could no longer justify staying away from the silent tomb of the bungalow, I returned to #26 and begin to make the place my own.

I dried off, flicked on a few lights, turned the TV on, and flipped channels until I got to some loud game show. To the comforting sounds of a squealing woman, who was playing for a $25,000 cash prize, a new Honda Accord and, possibly, a trip to the Caymans.

As I changed into a fresh t-shirt and shorts, I imagined how loudly *I'd* squeal if I won the cash and the car. I already had Siesta Key Beach, though, so I supposed I could probably live without the Caymans.

I WILL find a job. I'm reliable, personable, a really fast typist, I reminded myself again.

Then I rooted around in the kitchen, trying to decide on the meal option that appealed most at the moment: kiddie cereal or frozen veggie pizza?

I got as far as dumping one mini box of Trix into a bowl and considering adding another half box of Froot Loops, just to see what that would taste like (complementary flavors, yes?), when I heard a melody that was, at once, very familiar but, also, discordantly clashing with the beeping coming from the game show.

Ah, my cell phone.

I hadn't used it much since I'd arrived in Florida—it was a wonder I'd even remembered to keep it charged. I'd already spoken with both my sister and my daughter this morning from the landline, and they both knew better than to call my cell phone if I had another option. So, who could it be? Olivia Michaelsen, maybe?

I raced into the bedroom to grab it, clicking to answer even though the number on the display wasn't Olivia's or anyone I recognized. "Hello?" I said, just a hint breathless.

"Marianna?" a man's voice said, and I had to sit down. Immediately. Good thing I happened to be right next to a bed, huh?

"Uh, Donny?"

There was a pause. "Yes." There was another pause. "I heard you sold the house."

There was no preamble to this statement. No working up to it with niceties and polite chitchat. No mention of the *twenty-seven months* that had passed since last I'd heard from him. Then again, Donny had always sucked at foreplay.

"Yes, I did." I refused to make any apologies for this. The house had been mine to sell.

Since he'd cleared out our bank account when he left us—and moved to the West Coast, for God's sake, to surf and sell Camaros to the ultra wealthy—ownership of the house was the only bargaining chip he'd had. The only thing he could give his ex-wife and daughter to get the divorce lawyers and the judge off his back when, in violation of having never made a single child-support payment, my attorney (a genius woman and friend of Ellen's) finally managed to track him down and confront him. He claimed he wasn't making much money selling cars yet, so he couldn't afford child support. And being out of state and having moved a lot in California, no one could pin him down long enough to enforce it.

But the lawyer got him to sign over the house to me. I had the legal documents in a safety deposit box with his autograph on every freaking page.

"That was my parents' house, Marianna," he whined. "My childhood home." I heard a sharp intake of breath on the line, as if he was barely holding back a sob.

"Been taking acting classes in Hollywood?" I asked, biting down on my bottom lip so hard, I drew the metallic taste of blood.

Unlike a lot of people I knew, I had no nasty in-law stories to report. Donny's parents had been nothing but loving and generous toward me, teaching me to play backyard croquet, showing me how to grill the perfect cheeseburger, and sharing their deep love of classic movies. They even sold us their small three-bedroom house a few years after our marriage for thousands less than the market price because we'd given them Kathryn, their beloved granddaughter. Donny's folks—God rest their souls—had been committed to making life easier for us.

Their son, unfortunately, hadn't been nearly so

committed.

Donny's voice on the phone turned cold. "Look, when I gave you that house, it was all I had. I didn't think you'd sell it. That you'd cash in on my family's legacy." I could almost hear him spit out the words. "What are you gonna do with all that money now, huh? Live the high life in Florida for half the year like that rich bitch sister of yours?"

In that instant, I saw several shades of red—the full spectrum from scarlet to crimson to burgundy—before I could even focus on the soothing calm and fluff of the bedroom. I grabbed one of the puffy pale-blue pillows on the bed and squeezed.

The real-estate market was still depressed, so I knew I was incredibly lucky to have sold the house at all, let alone as quickly as I had, even at a loss. I'd priced it to sell, though. Most of the money from the sale was already spoken for—paying off years of credit card debt and setting aside a chunk to help Kathryn with some of her college costs not covered by her scholarship or her summer job. The rest I knew I'd need as a tiny cushion against the possibility of not immediately finding work when I got back home. To pay my expenses while I was in Sarasota, and to rent a small apartment in Mirabelle Harbor this coming fall.

"First of all, don't insult my sister," I managed to tell him, struggling not to raise my voice. "And, second, how did you know the house was sold and that I was in Florida?" There was a long pause and, in it, my head cleared enough to make the proper deduction. "Oh, wait. Let me guess. You're still in touch with Vince Jordy, aren't you? Still spying on us through him? I take it he hasn't found anything better to do than watch the neighbors through his mother's attic window and play 'Dungeons and Dragons' online with his imaginary playmates."

"They're not *imaginary*," Donny said with a huff. "They're *real* people. They just live in different cities."

"Uh-huh."

"There's no reason for you to get all judgmental. Just because Vince likes an activity you don't approve of, it doesn't make him a bad guy."

This was one of Donny's old refrains: That I "looked down" on his friends. That I was hypercritical. That the people in his neighborhood weren't up to the standards of my old neighborhood. The first two were true (Donny had a talent for choosing scumbag friends and I'd stopped keeping my opinions about them to myself a decade ago), but the last one was a blatant falsehood that always pained me to hear.

"Donny, I don't care about the virtual games Vince plays. But I guess it always bothered me that your best buddy from the neighborhood is a voyeuristic thirty-eight-year-old man that *never* held a full-time job, despite his parents paying for his college education more than once—" Vince switched majors five times, "—and who still sponges off his elderly mother."

He sniffed. "I've known Vince since we were kids. And stayed his friend even in hard times. Guess I can't expect you to understand lifelong friendship. You came into the neighborhood, lived in my parents' house, and never really appreciated it 'cuz you just compared everything to *your* parents' neighborhood. Not that they ever cared about you or visited you or even remembered you in their will. So now you've got to grab onto *my* inheritance instead."

Donny knew how to rip at my old scabs but, unfortunately, this was another half truth where the untruth part of it really wounded. But so did the truth part.

To say my parents were displeased by my marriage to him would be a gross understatement. They thought I was short-circuiting my future, told me so and, basically, left me to sink or swim after I moved into his parents' basement. My mother and father were snobs to a degree, yes, but that was some of what I'd thought I was running away from in marrying him. And they were dead wrong about Donny's parents and their neighborhood. Sure, it was slightly more rundown and not as ritzy as their side of Mirabelle Harbor, but there were lots of people with hearts of pure platinum who lived on the block—including Vince's mom. Donny's parents were at the top of that list, too—generous, caring, thoughtful, and compassionate. I'd loved them as much as any blood relation.

My parents' assessment of Donny, however, was sadly correct.

Dad didn't live long enough to witness the collapse of my marriage, but Mom watched—from the distant sidelines—and she had the satisfaction of seeing all of her dire predictions about my life come true before she, too, passed away.

"I'm making dinner now," I informed Donny, still slumped on Ellen's queen bed and squeezing that poor pillow. "I need to go."

"Oh, no, you might burn something," he remarked sarcastically. "Don't want you to ruin your lobster tail. Or is it filet mignon tonight?"

I didn't bother to answer. Kiddie cereal with skim milk was always a good choice, but it wasn't exactly on par with fresh lobster or filet. Honestly, I couldn't even remember the last time I'd eaten either one.

"I think it would be *decent* of you to just agree to share some of the profits from the sale of the house with me," he said. "It'd be easier than going through the lawyers. That would cost us both extra money, and we don't need them now anyway. I think twenty-five percent would be fair, don't you? I mean, after all my parents did for you, can't you finally be the one to be a little generous?"

After his parents sold us the house and moved into a retirement condo, Donny often left me with the job of scrounging up the money for our monthly mortgage payments, and I'd supported him on and off for years while he quit one stable job after another in search of the latest get-rich-quick scheme. There was that t-shirt business he started and abandoned. There was that one delivery service he got into with another bum friend. There was the memorable year when he and Vince tried their hands at inventing the perfect marshmallow roasting stick. Then he left me and our daughter—taking every penny of our savings—to go to L.A., to live in the sun, and to sell sports cars to celebrities. Guess that didn't turn out so well for him, huh?

"I've been plenty generous with you already," I said, my voice dropping to a whisper.

"Oh, c'mon, Marianna," he pleaded. "I need a little help. It's a tough economy. I don't want to have to chase you around with lawyers and paperwork. Fifteen percent. You owe me...and the memory of my parents...at least that."

For a second I considered his threat—that he'd get the lawyers involved. That I'd have to deal with him again on a regular basis until he got what he wanted. That he might really have the power to take away what little I had left.

But, no. Damn him. *No.*

The legal documents we'd signed were ironclad, which was why he was trying to guilt me into giving him the money instead of going through lawyers. He knew he wouldn't win that way. And somewhere deep inside of him, he knew even his parents would agree that he didn't deserve another red cent.

Furthermore, I'd mostly played by the rules for thirty-nine years. Except for one stupid act of teenage rebellion—my "escape" into marriage, or so I'd thought at the time—I'd been a good girl growing up. Almost always reasonable. Not too demanding at home or at school. Loyal at work. I did my job and then some. I'd been a dedicated employee, wife, daughter, sister, mother.

And still the company let me go.

And still my parents didn't forgive me for my single foolish, childish mistake.

And still Donny left me.

Well, I couldn't get my old job back, and I wasn't sure I really wanted it again anyway. My parents were dead. For Kathryn's sake (the one true blessing I'd gotten out of all of this), I stayed cordial to Donny and didn't openly bash his character in our daughter's presence. I didn't yell at him or swear at him, even when I thought my head and heart would explode.

I'm almost forty, and where did this good behavior get me?

"Screw you, Donny," I said, enunciating very clearly. "I don't owe you anything. And don't you dare call or threaten me again, you lying parasitical louse."

Then I flipped the phone shut, buried it under Ellen's pale blue pillow, and raced into the kitchen. My hands were shaking so violently I couldn't pick up the milk to pour it on my dry cereal without fear of dropping the plastic bottle, so I shoved the bowl to the back of the counter and just stood there. Motionless. Listening.

It was hard to hear over the sound of the TV and the rumbling thunder outside, but the cell phone rang a few times. It stopped. Then it rang again. I turned up the volume on the game show and paced by the sofa until my legs were tired and I ceased to hear the phone anymore.

But I couldn't flipping *stand* it. This aimlessness—like a piece of driftwood floating on the water's surface. This frustration at feeling so helpless against the current. And waiting, waiting, always waiting for the next storm. For something bad to happen. Not being in control of *anything*.

Next to the DVD player, there were books and magazines in a neat stack. I rummaged through them until a picture of a decorative dinner plate heaped with shrimp scampi caught my eye. Yum. It was a local dining guide with a list of restaurants in the vicinity. I still didn't want to go out—least of all to a restaurant by myself—and I knew better than to splurge on pricy carryout.

But this was a special occasion, I decided. My independence day from Donny. And I'd be wholly and completely fiscally responsible again come tomorrow morning.

I chose the least expensive restaurant in the guide that offered delivery and dialed the number from Ellen's landline. "Hi, I'd like to order dinner. Just for one. Your Wednesday early-bird special, please. Yes, that's right, the lobster…"

CHAPTER FIVE
Man in the Mirror

Gil sautéed half a pound of fresh shrimp and, as always, enjoyed watching the color shift in the skillet from uncooked grayish blobs to invitingly plump pink crescents.

He smacked his lips and turned to Nancy. "I know how much you love having shrimp for dinner, my sweet," he told her. "Yours is already waiting. We'll eat together after I finish fixing mine, okay?" He tossed in a few handfuls of sliced red and green pepper, diced onion, and fresh Portobello mushroom. "Too bad veggies aren't your thing. They're so gorgeous. So colorful."

Nancy opened her mouth but didn't utter a sound. A second later, she glanced away.

"Oh, don't worry," he reassured her. "I'm not being judgmental." He squirted some teriyaki sauce into the skillet and checked on the wild rice, bubbling on the back burner.

Nancy returned her attention to him and blinked, a slight air of accusation in her gaze.

"I'm *not*," Gil insisted. "Geez, what is it with you females? Always jumping to conclusions. Seriously. Just look at the range of hues right in front of us. This pan is like a painting. It only needs a hint of..." He stirred his shrimp and veggies a few times before adding the last ingredient on his memorized recipe—drained pineapple tidbits. "Yellow," he murmured, pointing out the cheerful addition to Nancy who was, at last, studying the skillet with interest. She took a few steps toward it.

"Ah, no you don't, darlin'." He scooped her up in his palm, stroked her back from the tip of her sleek amphibious head all the way down to her long black tail, then he blew her a kiss, which she didn't return. "I love ya, Nancy. You are the most beautiful fire-bellied newt to walk the earth. Or at least my kitchen counter." He stroked her back again. "And one of these days you'll tell me you love me, too, right?"

Nancy looked dubious.

He laughed. He loved the feel of this petite living thing strolling across his palm. The slow, graceful padding of her tiny feet stepping cautiously toward his forearm. The licorice swizzle of her textured tail swishing behind her. To Gil, proof of God lived in the existence of the world's smallest creatures. There might not be a lot of things he believed in—lasting marriages, for one...supportive parents, for another—but he had faith in newts. And in salamanders, seahorses, and starfish.

If there was any good in the universe, it would be found in them first.

He lifted Nancy carefully—her red-speckled underside visible only when he gave her belly a quick look—and he gently set her back into her tank, letting her loose on a sturdy flat rock. She'd been out of the water for only ten minutes but, clearly, she reveled in being wet again. She splashed herself greedily as he reached for her specially formulated newt food. He fed Nancy her everyday pellets most of the time but, on the occasions when Gil made shrimp for himself, he gave her some of the "newt treat" shrimp flakes. It was kind of like sharing a meal with a friend.

Then he washed his hands and fixed his own shrimp plate.

He'd only managed a couple of bites when the phone rang. His mother.

"Hiya, Ma." He stifled a sigh. Calling at dinnertime was rarely a good sign. "Everything okay?"

"What? I can only call my son when there's a problem?" she asked, her voice that distinctive brand of indignant he knew so well.

He grimaced. Now he knew for sure there was a problem. Only question was how long she'd chitchat before she'd reveal it. "Of course not," he said. "What are you doing tonight?"

"Watching golf on ESPN. There's a tournament."

It was Florida. There was always a tournament. "Sounds great," he managed, striving for a sliver of enthusiasm. "And you're feeling fine? Is there anything you need me to pick up for you? Your blood-pressure medication? Some groceries? A few new books from the library?"

She huffed. "I'm sixty-eight, not ninety. I can get my own damn books." She paused, mumbling something about the joys of owning an eBook reader. "But, um, there *is* an event coming up that you could drive me to tomorrow afternoon. If, um, you're not too busy."

He rolled his eyes, grateful only Nancy could see him. He loved his mother but some days... "I'll make time, Ma. Where do you need to go?"

"Just to Tampa for a few hours. You know I don't like driving long distances."

He knew. Even though Tampa/St. Pete was just an hour away from Sarasota, driving much further than the local Publix grocery store always flustered his mother. She was very forthcoming with the location of the event (a bridal shower at Minerva's Tea Room for her friend JoAnn, age seventy-eight, who was getting married for the third time) and the time of the event (one p.m. sharp) and tomorrow's weather forecast (hot and sunny). Too forthcoming. Which meant there was something else she wasn't telling him.

"So, I'll plan to pick you up a few minutes before noon, Ma. I'll make sure to get you to the Tea Room on time. And then, when it's over, you can just give me a call on my cell and I'll—"

His mother cleared her throat. "Well, actually, Gil…"

Here it comes.

"…it's one of those *couples* showers. You know, both the bride and groom will be there. So, you don't have to leave. There are going to be *lots* of people. Men and women. Even some younger folks your age. Why, JoAnn's niece is going to be driving down from Tallahassee, and you know, JoAnn and I were talking about how you two both like *artsy* things, so you might want to meet—"

This time Gil didn't try to stifle his sigh. "Ma," he interrupted. "Thanks, but no thanks. I'm more than happy to drive you up to Tampa, but I don't want to be set up with anyone. Not with JoAnn's niece. Not with your hairdresser's sister. Not with the daughter of the clever man who did your taxes last year." God, she'd tried every single one of them on him and more. "I'm sure she's very nice—"

"Veronica," his mother interjected.

"I'm sure Veronica is very nice," he said, "but I am not going to a couples shower."

"We could all get together for some coffee after the shower," she suggested. "Then you wouldn't have to actually go to the—"

"Ma, no. But thank you for thinking of me. I'll be in your driveway at eleven fifty tomorrow."

"You're a commitment phobe," she said, and not for the first time. "You're forty-two years old, Gil. Who are you savin' yourself for? Stop spending your life just *observing* everyone. You need to get out there and date! You need—"

"I need to finish my dinner and get some work done tonight, Ma, so I can take off tomorrow afternoon."

She exhaled heavily on the line.

"Love you," he added before she could take another breath and continue expounding upon his, apparently, never-ending list of needs. "See you tomorrow."

His mother begrudgingly rang off. Not that she wouldn't return to this particular tirade at the earliest opportunity, especially since they'd have two full hours alone together in the car the next day. He steeled himself for the fun he knew was coming.

He poked at his now-cold shrimp as Nancy ignored him—either out of indifference or pity, he wasn't sure. Her tail was a fascinating thing. He let its movements hypnotize him for a few moments as Nancy used it to propel herself around the tank. Her skin, too, was a kind of miracle, just porous enough to require moisture, but also water-resistant enough to allow for a semi-aquatic life.

On more than one occasion he thought of how similar this was to being an artist. That a special type of membrane was necessary to deal with rejections of one's work and the slings and arrows of public opinion. And yet…yet…an artist's skin still had to be thin enough to let in new experiences, new people. To let life affect a change, when it might be beneficial, significant, constructive, and possibly even inspiring.

Maybe—though he'd never admit this to her—his mother was right. Maybe he was too detached. He did look at life like an observer, after all. He dated a fair bit, but he did resist commitment. As a bachelor for over four decades, though, and given his observations of family life, it would take an extraordinary woman to get him to feel a real relationship was worth the risk.

"And present company aside," he said aloud to Nancy, who swam blithely in ignorant bliss, "I don't have a non-related female in my life who fits the bill."

CHAPTER SIX
Under Pressure

The second time it happened, Ellen had to rush out of an executive board meeting, effectively truncating a two-and-a-half-hour discussion on recent state-initiated tax law changes by a full twenty minutes.

She instinctively ran to the same fifth-floor restroom stall, but had a harder time convincing herself that she was *just fine,* even after the episode was (mostly) over.

When she was able to return to the boardroom, she apologized to her startled colleagues, claimed a relapse of her flu, shot a handful of rapid-fire instructions at her secretary, and didn't even bother with the medicinal peanut M&Ms.

No. Not this time.

This time she drove straight to the doctor's office in the stout gray building next to the hospital. She'd be right by the emergency room if she needed it. No wasting precious minutes with preliminary phone calls. No ordering of carryout. Apparently, she looked so dreadful, so near-zombie-like when she stumbled into the clinic, that not even the nurse or the receptionist dared to patronize her with stupid small talk.

"I need to see Dr. Cole," she told them. "Now." And they believed her.

Dr. Cole appeared within two minutes of her arrival, escorted her to a private examination room and listened attentively as she detailed her symptoms from both this episode and the last one. He even took notes. Then he fiddled around with his stethoscope for a few minutes more, checking her heartbeat and blood pressure and such, before delivering his diagnosis.

Ellen couldn't have been more stunned.

"What do you mean by 'panic' attack?" she said, staring at Dr. Cole with as much incredulity as she could muster. "That's for people who are *scared* of things. Anxious, cautious, unassertive, passive people." People more like her sister. Ellen crossed her arms and glared harder at the doctor. "I'm not one of *those* types."

"Ms. Slater," he began in an infuriatingly patient tone, "I'm not implying in any way that you're weak. Panic attacks can be caused by many factors, not the least of which is cumulative stress over time." He paused to level a significant look at her. "I know from our prior conversations that you have an intense relationship with your job, and there's a possibility that it may be a contributing factor."

"What *are* you implying, then? That I'm a workaholic?" she asked, hearing the challenge in her tone, the defensiveness.

"Not necessarily," he said, consulting some papers in her medical file. "But, given that your recent lab work on May fifteenth was entirely without abnormalities," he held up one of the lab sheets and pointed to it like it was Exhibit A in a legal investigation, "there are some causes we can already eliminate from our list. For instance, you appear to have no thyroid issues. No anemia. Those are both medical conditions that can sometimes trigger an attack."

"Really?"

He nodded. "Of course, there are others, so we need to be comprehensive. I'd like to run a few blood tests again, along with a couple of new ones. Plus, I'd like to take a chest x-ray and have my colleague, Dr. Whiteman in Cardiology, take a look at you more closely. We want to rule out any heart-related concerns."

"So, if this Dr. Whiteman decides that it's not my heart then, chances are, I'm probably not dying?" Ellen asked, equal parts relieved and curious.

"Probably not, Ms. Slater," the imposing doctor said with an almost-smile on his pale, dry, authoritative lips. "But panic attacks can make you feel like you are. Many sufferers experience palpitations, sweating, accelerated heart rates, blurry vision, trembling, shortness of breath, nausea, dizziness, confusion, some areas of tingling or numbness—"

"My vision was fine," Ellen insisted. "Totally fine. The whole time. And I don't remember any tingling or being confused." Well, she'd been confused about what was happening to her, but not about anything else.

Dr. Cole looked interested. "But you're saying you had *all* of those other symptoms?" When she nodded curtly, he said on a sigh, "Let's begin by just doing these other tests first. It's standard procedure when cardiac conditions may be a factor. But, I'll be candid with you. I suspect my initial diagnosis is correct, and I would highly suggest you consider reducing your trigger behaviors. If you're unable to do that on your own, we can certainly look into medications later that might help you control your reaction to those triggers."

"What trigger behaviors?" she said. "All I was doing both times was…work."

Again, he sent her one of his significant glances. That annoying, know-it-all bastard.

"That's right, Ms. Slater. So, something at work, or something you were thinking about while you were there, may have been the trigger. Can you recall what was running through your head prior to both episodes?"

She couldn't.

"Well, a few things to consider then," he said. "Heredity, for one. Did any of your family members suffer from panic attacks or take medication for anxiety?"

"Not that I know of," she said, thinking back. *Had they?*

"Also, environmental factors, such as one's parents' espousing an overly cautious worldview during one's childhood, or the stress of one's work situation building up over time, have both been found to be closely correlated with panic attacks. Were family issues or, perhaps, demanding work commitments in your thoughts this afternoon?"

Ellen tried again to recall what was going through her mind during the board meeting. She remembered thinking about her parents and her sister. That "overly cautious worldview" thing fit her family to a tee. Her parents, especially, had been suffocating when she was growing up. Cold, demanding, and unforgiving people. Thinking about their attitude made her throat tighten and gave her that familiar jolt of wanting to get far away. To be elsewhere. But it didn't cause her to *panic*.

As for her job, she loved it. Sure, it had its stressful days, but she thrived on activity. She still had no idea what could have set off such a crazy reaction, not to mention all of that sweating. And this time she'd ruined a blouse she really liked. This bizarre illness or condition—or whatever the hell it was—was wreaking havoc on her wardrobe.

"I really just don't have a clue," she admitted.

"That's all right," Dr. Cole said, sounding unnervingly competent and reassuring. "We'll figure it out and get you back to one-hundred percent in no time." She was trying very hard to still hate the man but, unfortunately, not succeeding as well as she'd like.

She watched as he filled out the lab request form and called over to cardiology to set up an appointment for her. While her next two days would be filled with decidedly un-fun tests and procedures, the discomfort ahead wasn't what was worrying Ellen as she walked down the long corridor to get her blood drawn.

It was that she was going to have to talk to Jared about all of this soon. That something in their idyllic little world—a world they'd painstakingly crafted for themselves and polished through years of tiny adjustments until it was just perfect for the two of them—was going to have to change in some way. Jared really wasn't fond of change.

And she wasn't either. Not when it wasn't a change of her own making.

CHAPTER SEVEN
In the Circle

Thursday morning dawned bright, not a trace of the tempest that raged the night before or a drop of rain left on the baked concrete in front of the bungalow.

I considered a quick stroll along the beach but didn't want to chance running into Vivian until after I'd fulfilled my promise to go shopping for better beach shoes. It was time to finally venture out to St. Armand's.

Armed with an E-Z map from Mr. Niihau—who'd looked at me like I was insane to need directions, but he kindly gave them to me anyway—I drove the nine miles from Siesta Key, the barrier island just offshore from the city of Sarasota, down the lengthy Tamiami Trail and followed the signs north and west until I got to the John Ringling Boulevard exit. Breathtaking views of the beach abounded in this region of Florida. And crossing the bridge onto Lido Key made me feel as though I was on a grand adventure for the first time in a very long time.

Even at ten a.m., this neighboring island was bustling with shoppers. I had to hunt for a parking spot. As I whizzed by the palm-tree-lined streets of St. Armand's Circle, I was reminded of a confetti cake. The buildings and tourists were like handfuls of cheerful pastel swatches, tossed in the air and swirled together as if in celebration.

I finally found a space and parked. Then I wandered into the heart of the party.

"Wanna try a fudge sample?" a teenage girl in a Fudge Fantasia apron asked me. The girl had slices cut up and waiting on a tray in front of her, just steps away from the fudge shop's entrance, and she held out a little plate. "Turtle is our special of the day."

I swallowed in anticipation just looking at it: Dense, dark fudge topped with pecans and curlicues of caramel. "Thank you," I said. Then, after taking my first bite, "Ohhh, wow."

The girl nodded knowingly. "Yeah, I love it, too. On sale today for twenty-five percent off per pound." She pointed at a placard with the reduced amount listed.

"I'll think about it." I knew this wasn't an outrageous price for high-quality fudge, but I also knew my limited budget and that I'd want to come back later and explore the delectable displays inside the fudge shop. "It's delicious."

"We've got Oreo Crumble and Peanut Butter Swirl today, too," the teen added with more than a hint of devious temptation in her tone.

I laughed. "Seriously, I *promise* to return." Maybe I could afford a quarter pound. Or even a half pound.

"Good." The girl glanced to either side, handed me another little plate and winked. "Take one for the road."

The teen was going for the hard sell, but it was effective. As I gobbled down my second piece of Turtle fudge, I knew for certain I'd be back.

For the next hour or so, though, I simply meandered down the streets surrounding St. Armand's Circle in delight and amazement. The postcard I'd seen at the corner grocery store hadn't succeeded in convincing me that there were would be *this many* cool shops and restaurants assembled in one relatively small space. The area had a high-end, bazaar-like atmosphere that I immediately connected with and appreciated.

I peered into a number of sophisticated stores, exotic boutiques, and artsy galleries, appreciating the beautiful, handcrafted work of the artisans—many based in Florida, but quite a few from destinations around the globe. I couldn't help but run my fingers across the expertly tooled leather handbags, admire the ceramic birds and dolphins, marvel at the crystal wave sculptures, and enjoy the color fusion of clothing, paintings, and jewelry. Such a remarkable array of shades and textures.

Eventually, I spotted The Golden Gecko, which was one of the shops the Elvis guy mentioned, and I wandered inside. Like many of the others, it was an assembly of fascinating crafts, this time with a special focus on decorative lizards and amphibians for yard and home. In the window, there was an enormous wrought-iron alligator. Near the door, I found a painted wooden iguana in the shape of a child's chair. And, of course, there were clay, ceramic, glass, and bronze geckos throughout the shop—sitting on tables, perched on shelves, hanging on walls.

I saw several paintings, too. These weren't primarily of slithery creatures, although I did catch sight of a few baby lizards in the corner of one canvas. No. The focus was on the waves and the water. They were seascapes, brightly, beautifully painted in vivid acrylics. Like a visual love letter to the stunning beaches of the Sunshine Coast, and very much like my first impression of walking to the shore: The unbelievable blues of the sky and the Gulf, the clarity of the water, the powdery whiteness of the sand, the surprising burst of color in the form of a swimmer's bathing suit or a child's pail and shovel, the small but perfect shells.

I collected these images, as if carrying my own bucket of sea treasures, and kept them with me as I moved onto the store next door. Castaways. That was the place that should have my water shoes in stock.

From my view on the sidewalk, it looked to be busy inside—a good sign. And to the other side of it was The Beaded Periwinkle, which appeared to be some kind of shell shop. Interesting. I plunged into the beach outfitters first, deciding to explore them in order.

Castaways had a motley assortment of very weird stuff.

But, I had to admit, Elvis was right. There were tons of clothing items, water gear, shoes for the beach, and shoes for the water. I found the Beachwalkers in the snorkel section without a problem and was both pleased and relieved to see that they were reasonably priced. But, after I grabbed a pair of those, I was inspired to sift through some of the shop's other wares and, goodness, what an amalgamation of items they were.

Stacks of extra-large, extra-loud towels covered one row of shelving. One of the towels featured thick strands of purple, orange, and green swirled strangely together like some kind of '70s tie-dyed creation. Next to it was a huge sky-blue one that was covered with hot air balloons. Another was an unusually artistic one that looked like a picnic on the beach, with a picture of a towel on the real towel and a basket filled with goodies in the middle that was half unpacked.

There were adult-sized goggles with leopard-print designs, flippers that were painted to resemble a duck's webbed feet, swim trunks for men dotted with images of tropical fruit—pineapples, coconuts, mangos and…wow. Nothing like a large banana right on that front zipper, eh? I stifled a laugh and forced myself to look away.

My gaze landed on a wall crammed with t-shirts with bizarre sayings like, "Shelling is easy. Explaining the increasingly expanding spiral of a Nautilus without using differential calculus is hard."

Huh?!

Most of the other shirts were a little easier for me to

understand, but still very original, smart, and funny. Maybe if Donny had been half as creative with his t-shirts, he would've been able to make his business take off.

I spied a set of paintings in this shop, too, and they appeared to have been done by the same artist whose work was in The Golden Gecko. Again, beautiful, vibrant shades of teal, sapphire, cerulean, indigo, emerald, and lime—and that was just the water and sky. I studied one canvas up close and noticed it had a very loud beach towel in it. Made me wonder if the artist's work was influenced by seeing the towels in this shop, or if the shop's owner bought that particular painting because it had the towel in it.

I managed to inch my way up to the busy counter, pay for my purchases, and step out of the store into the insane midday mugginess. The Beaded Periwinkle was next on my list of visits, but the stirrings of hunger and thirst took priority.

After finding a sandwich shop and picking up a tuna wrap and a lemonade, I collapsed into a chair in the air-conditioned corner of the deli and enjoyed my lunch. The flurry of passersby and the call of seagulls I heard every time the door opened was entertainment enough.

Afterward, I even allowed myself to wander back via Fudge Fantasia, where I waved at the teen girl who was still working there. The girl had lured a young couple into her net and was busy giving them the details of the sweets sale, but she still took a second to grin at me and say, "I knew I'd see you again!"

Inside, it was as irresistible as I'd expected, and I walked away with a half-pound splurge of Turtle fudge and a large sample pack of some of their most popular dessert creations. This way, I'd get to try the Oreo, peanut butter, dried fruit, raspberry, caramel, French vanilla, hazelnut, almond...etc. They would make for a great dessert for weeks—if I could get them back home before they melted.

I window-shopped a little more en route and began to

feel the edges of exhaustion—the combination of the humidity and the visual overload took its toll—and I knew I ought to head back to the bungalow soon. But, when I finally entered The Beaded Periwinkle, I was glad to have saved it for last.

I was struck at once by the sheer number of shells packed into this small space and the gazillion unique uses for them. There were picture frames made of shells, wind chimes, hall mirrors, lampshades, nightlights, an array of shell-encrusted furniture and, oh, jewelry. So much jewelry. Earrings, bracelets, necklaces, even belts. They were so imaginatively designed and well-crafted that I was mesmerized.

Hanging from a tall spinning case were a hundred pairs of shell-and-bead earrings of various styles, shapes, lengths, and colors. The ones that caught my eye first were made of six calico scallops—three on each side—with the smallest shell on the top, followed by the medium, and then the largest. When jostled, they jingled like angels' bells. But it wasn't just the sound and shape that grabbed my attention. It was the starbursts of soft pink, rose, and lavender that zigzagged across each shell. The expertly fastened sterling fishhook gave the dangles the finished sheen of a professional piece. The natural symmetry of the ridges and ripples. How gorgeous.

"You should try 'em on," a petite dynamo of a woman in her mid-thirties said, a hint of Texas lingering in her voice. "You'll find a mirror just over there." She crooked her thumb at the shell-framed oval mirror hanging on the wall behind me.

I pulled out my small, mother-of-pearl teardrop earrings, and I slipped on the scallop-shell ones. Staring at my reflection, I couldn't help but think that, until yesterday, it had been a long, long time since I'd purchased anything for myself that wasn't a dire necessity. I realized another thing, too. That even a change in my appearance this small could make me look and feel like someone else.

And I happened to quite like this new someone.

"They are really lovely," I told the woman.

"So thrilled to hear you like 'em," the shop lady replied. The delight in her voice and the hawk-like gaze of the woman snagged my attention, and I immediately suspected the other woman's heightened awareness might be more than just interest in a potential sale. There was more at stake here.

"By chance, did you make these?" I asked, motioning toward the earrings I was wearing and then toward the entire twirling jewelry stand.

The shop woman grinned and nodded. "I make everything in here." Her focus strayed to a small table in the far corner where two other women were sitting and poring over some shells, decorative beads, nylon strings, and various metal hooks. They were so absorbed in their task, neither seemed to see or hear anyone else. "Well, *almost* everything," she clarified with a laugh. "My friends over there are helping me with a special project."

When I raised my eyebrows in curiosity, the energetic jewelry lady motioned me closer. "C'mon. I'll show you," she said.

The two new ladies, one about my age and one a decade younger, glanced up and smiled as the jewelry lady and I approached them.

"Hi, there," the tall brunette said, her Southern origins evident in just the softness of these two syllables.

"This is Lorelei," the jewelry lady told me, pointing toward the brunette, who had a very intelligent expression and had to be in her early forties. Then to the blonde, who was shorter, rounder, younger, and very sweet-looking, "And this is Abby. My best friends." She beamed at them. "They're also my rescuers. I don't know what I'd do without them this week." She turned back to me and stuck out her palm. "I'm Joy Canton, owner of this shop and—"

"A recovering Texan," Lorelei interjected, with an arch of her thin, dark eyebrow.

"Someone who hasn't yet learned to say no," Abby added, her amused tone not remotely Southern.

"Oh, put a sock in it, y'all. I was gonna say I'm always glad to meet visitors. Maybe I should say I'll be glad to get some *new* best friends." She mock glared at the other two women.

"Nope, you're stuck with us," Lorelei said to her, then she winked at me.

Abby picked up a long nylon string and snapped it in Joy's direction. The jewelry store owner laughed.

I felt a sudden bolt of envy at their warmth and sense of community, but I smiled and shook the hands of all three women. "Marianna Gregory," I said. "Very nice meeting all of you."

"Nice to meet you, too, Marianna," Abby replied. "Midwestern, yes?"

I nodded. "I'm from a northern suburb of Chicago, Illinois—Mirabelle Harbor—but I'm in Sarasota for—"

"WHAT? You're from Mirabelle Harbor? So am I!" Abby beamed at me. "Wow. Small world."

Something tugged at the edges of my mind. "Oh, my goodness, wait. Are you Abby Solinski, by chance? My good friend Olivia mentioned—"

"Olivia Michaelsen?" Abby interrupted.

"Yes."

The younger blonde paled just a little, but she recovered quickly. Probably not quickly enough to escape the notice of her friends, though.

"Yeah," she said. "I'm Abby Solinski. And I know the Michaelsen family, uh, pretty well."

Because she'd been Chandler Michaelsen's girlfriend for five years, I remembered. Oh, poor lady. Those Michaelsen men could be heartbreakers. But I didn't say that.

"You're right. It's a very small world," I told her instead. "And Olivia said wonderful things about you. She was hoping we might meet."

"Thanks," Abby murmured. "Olivia was always really nice to me. Any friend of hers is a friend of mine." She paused. "How long are you in Sarasota, Marianna?"

"Just for a few weeks."

"Yeah, that's what I thought, too, when I first got here, but it's turned into a few years." Abby chuckled. However, I couldn't help but detect a note of sadness just beneath the laughter.

"I hail from Tallahassee," Lorelei said, successfully turning our attention toward her, maybe as a way to give Abby a break from her memories. "My husband's job got us transferred down here about a decade ago. Fell in love with Sarasota."

"And I'm originally from San Antonio," Joy told me. "I've been in Florida since I was in junior high, but—"

"She *refuses* to let go of her Texan ways," Lorelei teased, motioning me nearer as if to share a deep confidence. "I am *sure* she does it just to torment me." She drew out her vowels extra long for emphasis and fluttered her hand like a fan by her face, as if she was in need of reviving.

Joy rolled her eyes, her lips twisting in an unsuccessful attempt not to grin. "Hi, ho, there, Mrs. Lorelei Beck. Don't you take that pomegranate tone with me or I'll be fixin' to get even."

The other two women chuckled in delight, but I was perplexed. What the heck was a "pomegranate" tone? Maybe it was an expression native to Florida...or to Texas. All I knew was that I never heard it before.

I was still debating whether or not to show my ignorance and ask, when Joy said, "What do you think of their bracelets? Beautiful, aren't they?" She pointed to a shelf right beside Lorelei and Abby that was strewn with jewelry—mostly bracelets, but also a few necklaces and earrings—and I was struck by the thoughtful combination of small shells and beads that comprised their designs.

"Yes," I replied, reaching to pick one up. "They're really lovely." The one I was holding was made of white slipper shells, pierced and strung in an alternating pattern with delicate pale-pink beads and an occasional indigo-silver swirled bead. In the middle of the bracelet was a single sterling butterfly charm. But there was no price tag. "Are you selling these?" I asked, knowing I shouldn't buy more of anything, especially since I was already planning to get the scallop earrings, but this bracelet was just as pretty in its own very unique way.

"Not yet, but we will be," Joy said. "They're for the special project I was telling you about—B.E.A.D.S.—Bracelets for Endangered And Defenseless Species. All of our donations will go directly to help Florida's most endangered mammals, birds, insects, and marine life. We're selling the bracelets for the first time this weekend at the Annual St. Armand's Craft Festival."

"And, because Little Miss Texas has been talkin' them up in her shop all month, we have a list of advanced orders and have to make at least a hundred more pieces by Saturday," Lorelei complained, digging for a clamp and arching her eyebrow again.

"Well, what was I supposed to do?" Joy cried. "Not show the customers the new charms when they came in? Y'all know how cute they are."

"They are the cutest," Lorelei admitted, putting the finishing touches on the bracelet she was working on by attaching that final clamp.

Abby glanced at me, noting that I was still clutching the bracelet with the butterfly, and she smiled. "Let's show them to Marianna. I think she'll like them, too."

Lorelei nodded and tipped over a small black canister filled with sterling-silver-shaped creatures. "See this one here?" She pointed to a butterfly charm just like the one in my hand. "That's the Schaus' swallowtail butterfly. It's been threatened since 1976 and endangered in these parts since 1984." And then she rifled through a few more and pulled out a chunky sea animal of some kind. "This one's a manatee."

"Oh!" I'd heard of them, of course, and I knew they were endangered, but I'd never seen a charm shaped like one before. "What other animals do you have?"

The three women hunted through the pile until they found a representative charm of every type—seven in all. In addition to the swallowtail butterfly and the manatee, there were also charms for the shortnose sturgeon, the American crocodile, the peregrine falcon, the Florida panther, and the green sea turtle.

"All endangered," Joy said, frowning, the change in expression creating a crease just above the bridge her nose. "Even before the big oil spill, but that sure didn't help. The Florida Fish and Wildlife Conservation Commission does what it can, but it's a never-ending battle. They can use every penny we send them. Aside from subtracting the cost of materials, we donate one-hundred percent of what we make from the jewelry."

"So, you three came up with this idea?" I asked, reaching for my wallet and pulling out a couple of twenty-dollar bills. Yes, yes, I vowed there'd be no more unnecessary spending, but I fully intended to help support this cause. A world without butterflies and sea turtles wasn't a place I wanted to live. Definitely worth cutting back on a few carryout dinners and fudge treats.

"No, Joy came up with it," Lorelei said, "but we were enthusiastic supporters."

"Well, I'd really like to help, too," I said. "Is there any chance I could buy just three bracelets early? This one for me—" I held up the one in my palm. "And two others? I'd like to get one for my sister and another my daughter. I know they'll love them. Plus, I'd like to make an additional cash donation."

Joy glanced at me speculatively, and I noticed Lorelei and Abby exchanging a look that I didn't immediately understand. In a surprise move, Joy lurched forward and grasped my hand. Her slender, cool fingers were very gentle, but it was still a little…odd.

"She's very turquoise," Joy informed her friends. This comment took the moment past "a little odd" and deep into the territory of "rather strange." Then she released my hand and broke into a grin. "No," she said brightly.

I blinked at her and thought back to what I'd originally asked. "You're saying, no, I can't buy the bracelets early, or, no, I can't make a donation, or both?"

"You can't buy *that* bracelet," Joy told me, referring to the one in my hand, "because I'm giving it to you. You can buy the other two, if you'd like, but not until this weekend. You said you'll still be in Sarasota, right?"

I nodded, sensing a catch coming.

"Good. Then come to the Craft Festival and get 'em on Saturday. Ten a.m. to five p.m., right here in the Circle. And if you want to make a cash donation, I won't stop you, but I'd much rather have you make a *time* donation." Joy wagged her index finger at Lorelei and Abby, who were unsuccessfully trying to suppress their amusement. Then Joy added, "What are you doing this afternoon and evening, Marianna?"

"Um, I don't have any particular plans but—" I began.

"What about all day tomorrow?" Joy asked. "I know it's a Friday, so maybe you've got a lunch date with friends or family? An evening get-together? "

I smiled at her, taking guesses at what the jewelry lady might be up to. Hoping I was right in what might transpire next. "Nothing, really. Not today or tomorrow. I'm here in Florida alone." This was true, of course, but I felt a rare fluttering in my chest and a surprising surge of excitement in hopes that my status might change.

"So, yay! You're free then. Now you're ours!" Joy concluded, clapping. "Excellent." She swiveled around. "Let me grab another chair."

Abby laughed at her friend's quick-moving form. "I knew she'd reel you in somehow."

And Lorelei got up and motioned for me to put my belongings in the backroom. "Honey, you're gonna be here a while. Get comfy."

Joy returned with a chair for me and an irrepressible grin of triumph that I suspected was as much a part of her nature as her liveliness, her sun-streaked light-brown hair, her freckles, and her blue eyes. "Ready to make some jewelry?"

CHAPTER EIGHT
Illuminations

Gil was not able to escape meeting Veronica. His mother and her longtime friend JoAnn were both far too crafty. They'd cornered him in the parking lot when he returned to Minerva's Tea Shop to pick up Ma.

"So, what'd she look like?" Carter, Gil's animated college-aged employee, asked when he finally got back work that evening. "A little cute?"

Gil shrugged. "Yeah, she was fine. It wasn't about her looks." Actually, if he were perfectly honest, she was pretty hot for a thirty-something divorcee. "But I could tell she was just going through the motions, too. The four of us chatted by the car for fifteen minutes. I think she checked her iPhone about two dozen times during our conversation."

Carter appraised him, a speculative gleam in his eager brown eyes. "You know, my mom has this friend who's about forty and single. She's real pretty. Blonde. Just moved to the area from Orlando and—"

"Jesus, Carter. Not you, too?"

"I'm just sayin', there are a lot of pretty women out there. I don't think my mom's friend even has a smart phone."

Gil stared at him then slowly shook his head. "Seriously, man. It's not about the phone, either."

"Well, c'mon," Carter said. Then, lowering his voice, "You've gotta be able to get, like, a *ton* of action. You're a cool dude. You've got your own place. You're, um, experienced at picking up the ladies."

In spite of himself, Gil laughed. He remembered what it was like to be in his early twenties and still thinking that a night spent with a woman was like finding the Holy-effing-Grail. He supposed that, to Carter's way of thinking, he was squandering a lot of opportunities. But the appeal of mindless one-night stands wore off after a few years. Even for reputably cool dudes with their own place.

"Hasn't there been someone you've been attracted to in the past week? The past month?" Carter persisted. "I'm, like, hot for new girls every day. Sometimes, you know, I see, like, six or eight in a row that I'd totally jump...if I could."

Gil was about to shake his head but, then, he remembered that funny tourist lady at the beach. She seemed nice enough. A little clueless about Gulf Coast life but pretty cute. And she'd been trying to be helpful when it came to catching that preschooler. But the most memorable thing about her was that, when she spoke to him, she wasn't distracted by other possible conversations. She may have looked at him oddly at first, like he was a yellow-eyed alien, but she paid full attention to what he was saying, and that was an increasingly rare trait.

"Yeah, okay," Gil admitted. "I met a woman I sort of liked in Siesta Key a few days ago. But, you know what it's like around these parts. Half the people you see aren't here to stay for longer than a week or two."

Carter was forced to nod in agreement on that point, but the kid still managed to find a silver lining. "Yeah, but then there are no strings, right?"

He punched the tall, skinny young man lightly on the bicep. "You got me there, Carter." No strings, no commitment. Given his lack of interest in the latter, Gil felt this thought should have cheered him more than it did.

But the kid grinned as if he'd just cured cancer, put an end to world hunger, and solved the problem of peace in the Middle East in one fell swoop. "I'm here for you, dude," he said.

"I know you are, Carter. That, I know for sure."

After three hours of work, we finally broke for dinner.

Joy, a vegetarian, I soon discovered, ordered us garden salads and a spaghetti-marinara feast, while Lorelei ran out to grab a bottle of red wine to accompany the meal. But, though my hands were aching and I'd developed a weird crick in my neck from hunching over, I wasn't tired at all. Truth be told, I didn't want to stop working.

Being here, in the company of these women, made me happier than I'd been in a long time. My loneliness of the past few years was acutely obvious by comparison. Aside from Olivia Michaelsen and her family and, perhaps, a few former work colleagues and kind neighbors in Mirabelle Harbor, I had a hard time thinking of anyone who'd cared enough to talk or laugh with me lately. My sister, sure. My daughter, on rare occasion. But I'd had more in-depth conversations with Vivian at the beach than I'd had recently with most of the acquaintances who'd been a part of my life when Donny and I were still married.

I inhaled the scent of delicious food and good wine, and realized it was more than that, even. This feeling created a strange and wondrous dichotomy. Being around people I liked, and who seemed to like me, made me calmer, more grounded, and content.

But there was yet another layer to it.

At the same time, I felt myself becoming more curious, more alive, and more adventurous. Those two layers swirled within and through me simultaneously—like standing knee-deep in the ocean and feeling both the current of the sea and the waves lapping above it. If I weren't afraid these women might think I was too needy, I'd camp out overnight on a chair in Joy's backroom, so I could be rested, ready, and the first one at the shop tomorrow morning.

When Abby unveiled some of her homemade apple cake—the delectable aroma of cinnamon, pecans and buttered apples enticing us all—I jumped up suddenly, remembering something.

"I have fudge," I told them, wanting to share my specially purchased dessert treat with my new friends far more than my earlier desire to parse it out in bits to myself over the next month. I wanted to show them my deep appreciation for their immediate acceptance of me into their little circle. Their generous sense of inclusion.

"Oh, yum!" Abby said, spotting the logo on the bag. "I love Fudge Fantasia. And, obviously, it loves me." She patted her curvaceous hip. "My favorite is their Oreo one. Any chance you have some of that?"

I nodded.

Abby hooted in delight. Joy hunted for a knife to section the fudge into pieces we could all sample, and Lorelei poured everybody some more alcohol. "Well, it is a dessert wine, you know," she said wryly. We all laughed and chatted some more.

It was this ease of simply being in each other's company—not trying to hide anything, not trying to prove anything—that I found so very endearing about this trio of women. And about myself when I was with them.

After a while, Lorelei rooted through her bag to unearth her cell phone. "Got to call my boys," she said. "My husband has a work dinner, so they've been left to their own devices all day. Just want to make sure they haven't blown up the sunroom or anything yet."

Abby grinned and shook her head. "Teen boys... My brother and his friends were always 'experimenting' with rockets and homemade explosives. Did I ever tell you about the one time when they—"

Lorelei covered her ears with her palms. "No! Don't wanna hear it. You've already scared me plenty." She race-walked into the backroom to make her call.

"She's never going to forget that chemistry lab story you frightened her with last year," Joy told Abby. "Or the one about how your family went on that beach vacation and your brother made baby Molotov cocktails."

"Allan and his friends definitely had pyromaniac tendencies. Especially his best buddy, Rick Zimmerman. We used to call him 'Rocket Rick' behind his back," Abby said. "He was, quite possibly, even more dangerous than my brother when given free reign with science equipment."

"His name sounds really familiar," I said. "Rick and Allan both went to Mirabelle Harbor High?"

"Yep. The guys were in the same grade, two years ahead of me. Remember when there was a fire in chem lab at the high school about a decade ago? Thousands of dollars in damage and a large hole that burned straight through the wall into the geography classroom?"

My jaw dropped. "That was them?"

"Oh, yeah." Abby shrugged. "You understand what I grew up with now, right?" She laughed and glanced at her watch. "Oops! I need to check on something at the agency." She grabbed her keys and raced toward the door. "Be back in fifteen minutes," she called over her shoulder.

Joy explained, "She works part time at Floriday Excursions—it's like Florida plus holiday—an agency that specializes in local vacation packages. It's just a block away. And she also works part time here with me." She paused and smiled so warmly. "Marianna, I'm so glad you were able to stay this afternoon."

"Thanks," I replied. "Me, too." I got up, helped Joy throw out the carryout bags, paper plates, and plastic utensils. It felt wonderful to stretch and, also, to be able to talk to Joy a bit just one on one.

In the flurry of getting swept into the bracelet making, I hadn't had the chance to look around The Beaded Periwinkle as much as I would have liked, so I took this opportunity to conduct a more thorough investigation. As with the other shops nearby—The Golden Gecko and Castaways—there were paintings of the seashore that had the distinctive look of that one artist. Same vivid colors. Same gorgeous seascapes. But a few more weird elements this time. I noticed a canvas in Joy's shop that featured a salamander on the sand wearing a beaded necklace, and there was a shell-rimmed clock face that was baking on a rock nearby. The salamander seemed to be slithering toward it.

"This is a really...interesting painting," I told Joy. "The colors are just stunning, and the water is as beautiful as I remember it." I paused.

"But?" Joy asked, and I could almost hear the giggle behind the word.

"I—um, I'm not sure I quite get the salamander and the clock," I admitted. "Although, I'm pretty sure I've seen this artist's work in a few stores, and I really, really like it." I peered at the canvas up close and spotted the initials GC in black at the bottom right.

Joy was openly laughing at me now. "My brother Gil painted it. He's a fan of Salvador Dali, you see. It's his response to *The Disintegration of the Persistence of Memory*, which he's gone to gawk at a bunch of times at the Dali museum in St. Petersburg." She strode up to me, still energetic, even after all of these hours of racing between helping customers and helping the three of us with the beading. "Gil owns the shop next door and is an artist as well. He loves having his work praised, by the way, so I'll have to tell him you like it—in spite of the watch and the silly salamander." She studied the painting, as if seeing it for the first time. "It's all scrambled eggs and burnt toast," Joy said in a dreamy voice. "Very crunchy on the edges but melty in the middle."

I desperately tried to make sense of this statement. To see what Joy saw. I felt as though I could only approach knowing what she meant, though, not completely get it. And there was a persistent fear running through me like an electrical circuit that, perhaps, I was missing something super huge. I'd never studied art history during the two years I'd worked on my associate's degree. I'd tried to keep up with new ideas by reading, watching the news, and catching programs on the Discovery Channel whenever I could (at least back when I could afford cable), but I hadn't traveled the world like my sister or had time to visit museums or go to cultural lectures. Not as much as I'd wanted to. Certainly not with a child at home, a deadbeat husband, and a full-time job. All of which were gone now.

So, was the problem that I just wasn't comprehending this? Or was the gap between my level of education and Joy's as large as it was between mine and Ellen's?

"What are you thinking?" Joy eyed me carefully, the dreamy tone now gone.

I cleared her throat. "I'm thinking that you have a really poetic way of viewing the world," I told Joy truthfully. "I'm not sure I know enough about art to call it crunchy or melty, and I don't know what was pomegranate-like about Lorelei's voice earlier or what you think is turquoise about me. But you've been very kind to me today, and I...I really wish I understood everything better."

I felt a sudden squeeze, and it took me a moment to realize Joy was side-hugging me. Oh, God, when was the last time anyone besides my daughter had hugged me?

Ellen, when she visited for a weekend at Christmas. A few colleagues on my last day of work in May. Vince Jordy's mom and a couple of neighbors the day the "SOLD" sign went up in front of my old house. And Olivia, of course, when I left for Florida. Few and far between, though.

I slowly reached around and side-hugged Joy back. It felt like such a foreign motion.

"There is not a thing wrong with your understanding," Joy said, letting go and gesturing, her palm making a circle near my head. "I'm the one that's kinda different, Marianna. My senses are jumbled. They always have been. It's called *synethesia*."

"Oh?" I'd never heard of this. "All of your senses are mixed up?"

Joy shook her head. "Many, but not all. Some synesthetes have perceptions I don't have. Their way of thinking about numbers, for instance. To them, the integers have personalities, like the number three is a bald, cranky old man with bad breath and a cane. Or their mental number line isn't straight or from left to right—it loops in unusual spatial patterns within their brain. That doesn't happen to me. But, I have a friend I got to know in a group online who tastes triangles when she eats broccoli. And smells the scent of chocolate when she hears a D-minor chord. For me, my synethesia is closer to that. The letters of the alphabet and days of the week have colors. Some images and sounds have tastes and textures. And people I meet have auras that I can usually see or feel." She laughed. "It's a little odd, I know."

"It's fascinating!" I said, truly intrigued and, okay, equally relieved that it wasn't that I was stupid. "I wish I could do that. Taste chocolate when I hear music. See pink when I think of the letter M."

Joy exhaled. "No, you don't. I mean, now—as an adult—I have fun with it. I can be myself around my friends and they don't blink when I say June is a golden caramel color or that their voices sounds like fruit flavors. But you try doing that when you're a little kid in Texas with some family members who don't understand you. Not to mention living in a conservative neighborhood and going to a private school. You tell your teacher Wednesday is green or that her outfit tastes like a lemon lollipop and see what happens. Say enough things like that and people start to think you're awfully strange. They judge you. They call you names."

Hard to imagine anyone thinking harshly of Joy. Her name fit her. She was so vibrant and such a gentle being but, clearly, the memory of ridicule still made her flinch. I caught her shivering despite the Florida heat.

"Well, I think it makes you wonderfully unique. And I think you should ignore anyone who says otherwise," I told Joy. "Your way of perceiving has to add to your gifts as an artist because your designs are so lovely and so original." I fingered the scallop earrings I was still wearing. "I'm buying these, you know. I've seen some really nice pieces today in other shops, but your jewelry is by far my favorite."

The other lady nibbled on her lip for several seconds. "I knew there was a reason I liked you," she said finally. "Plus, you're turquoise, so..." She let the thought trail off.

"What does that mean exactly?"

Joy chuckled and opened her mouth, but Lorelei emerged from the backroom. "Well, the boys are still alive," she informed us. "Praise the good Lord and all the angels on high."

And a heartbeat later, the front door swung open and Abby returned. "Are we ready to work again?"

"I'll explain another time," Joy whispered, nudging me toward the back table. "For now, just know it's a good thing."

It occurred to me that I never doubted it would be. Obviously, I wasn't any kind of synesthete, but I could feel the waves of kindness radiating from Joy. If I were to give that warmth a color, it would be the orangey shade of autumn leaves from when I was a kid. If I were to give it a texture, it would be the downy comfort of the scarf Donny's mom knit for me during my first winter as a young wife.

As we all got back to the making of the bracelets, I found myself opening up to the women even more than I had before. I confided a little about my life to them. Not all the sad details, of course, but enough so they knew I was staying at my sister's bungalow on Siesta Key, that I had a daughter in college, an ex-husband, and no real plans for the summer.

"Not true," Lorelei informed me. "You have very important plans tomorrow and through the weekend. Don't even think of tryin' to get out of helping at the Craft Festival now. We need you. Truly."

I laughed. "Oh, I wouldn't dare skip out on you guys." But I was stunned by how grateful I felt to be needed. Even if it was just for a weekend.

As the light faded from St. Armand's Circle and night arrived with the softness of a caress, I rubbed my eyes. All of me was bleary, but it had been worth it.

"Okay, time to wrap up, y'all," Joy said. "The beads'll be waitin' for us in the morning." She glanced at her watch. "Nine thirty, can you believe it?"

Lorelei stretched her tall frame. "My back is a believer."

Abby helped me wrap up the remaining fudge and what was left of the apple cake. I offered her the last bit of the Oreo sample. "One for the road, Abby?"

"Thanks." Abby popped it into her mouth with a satisfied grin and then reached out to grasp my shoulder in a quick squeeze of gratitude. "I keep expecting it not to taste so good after a while, but that just never happens." She filled my Fudge Fantasia bag with the extras then added her wrapped-up cake leftovers to it. "You keep the rest of this. I don't want to be tempted to nibble any more tonight."

Before I could protest, there was a knock at the door. I shot Joy a puzzled look. She'd locked the shop to customers hours ago. Who'd stop by now?

Joy skittered across the room to answer it, peeking through the window first to check who it was before swinging open the door and chitchatting with her usual friendliness to the person outside.

"Hi, there," I heard her say.

A male voice replied, "Hi, back. I was just working on the computer, adding up expenses, and I saw your light still on. Everything okay?"

I glanced over at Abby and Lorelei. "Boyfriend?" I mouthed to them.

Abby shook her head, and Lorelei mouthed back, "Brother."

Ahh. The interesting painter.

I bent down to pick up a crumpled paper napkin that had fallen to the floor. When I stood up again, I heard Joy say, "C'mon in, Gil, and say howdy to the girls." But when the man stepped through the door, I felt the napkin slip from my hand and my jaw drop.

"Oh, my God," I murmured. "It's Elvis."

CHAPTER NINE
Hearts of Gold

Abby and Lorelei smothered their laughter, and I hoped neither Joy nor her brother could overhear them. I didn't think so, not even when Abby whispered, "Yeah, there's a resemblance."

Elvis—er, *Gil*—stepped further into the room, his gaze zeroing in on me with immediate recognition. "Ah, we meet again," he said, striding toward me and, also, greeting Lorelei and Abby by name. "Did you finally get yourself some Beachwalkers?"

"I did," I managed to say. "Just today. At Castaways." *His shop*, I suddenly realized. "Oh, Joy told me it was your place. That was clever."

"Sneaky of me, wasn't it?" He laughed heartily. "But what kind of salesman would I be if I didn't believe in my own products?"

Joy was staring at us, incredulous. "Y'all know each other already?"

"We ran into each other a few days ago at the beach," he told his sister. "She was chasing after this wild kid who'd escaped his parents, but—"

"But your brother—who, of course, I didn't know was

your brother until now—was the one who actually caught him," I explained to Joy. "I tripped and the little boy got away." I felt my cheeks flush a bit hot at the memory. It was embarrassing to think back on my klutziness in the face of someone so...agile-looking.

Joy's lips twisted upward in suppressed delight, but she didn't immediately comment. She just glanced back and forth between her brother and me. And I couldn't help but notice a few things. The siblings' hair colors were different shades. Their complexions were different tones. Their heights were very different as well. But their twinkling baby-blue eyes were identical.

Joy's brother extended his hand. "We haven't been formally introduced, though. I'm Gil Canton."

Somehow, I managed to say my own name and shake his hand. His dwarfed mine, but it was warm. "Nice to officially meet you."

Joy finally decided to speak. "We were just finishing up with our work here for tonight, Gil. You locking up soon, too?"

"Yep. Was thinking about it. Carter is opening for me at nine tomorrow, so I don't have to get up early." He stifled a yawn. "It's been a long day."

Joy nodded. "For us, too. But Marianna is helping with the B.E.A.D.S. project now, so I think we'll actually finish before Saturday." She beamed a grin in my direction.

Gil seemed to take in all four of us women, one at a time, no doubt reading our faces and assessing our level of exhaustion. I didn't know if he'd also picked up on the shimmer of excitement just beneath the surface, at least in my case, but I felt his gaze trained on me. Studying me. Drawing conclusions.

"Well, you ladies ought to get some shuteye then," he said. "I can walk you all out to the lot."

"Oh, we didn't park there today," Joy told him, glancing at her two good friends.

"I picked up Abby and Joy at their condo complex this morning," Lorelei explained. "And we parked just a few steps down Ringling Boulevard. It was so early, there were still a bunch of spaces when we got here."

"What about Marianna?" Gil asked, turning his inquiring eyes back on me. "Did you park near them?"

"I don't know," I confessed, trying to remember where, exactly, I'd found that spot for my car all those hours ago. "It was on a little side street. Off St. Armand's Circle. Sort of near Fudge Fantasia."

The others exchanged a look, and Abby said, "Nope. That's nowhere near us. But we can drive you to your car. It shouldn't take us long to find it with it being this late and everything being so empty now."

"Or, I'd be happy to walk you there," Gil suggested. "I'm parked in that vicinity. Just give me a couple of minutes to close up my shop."

I was rendered momentarily mute by his offer. No one had cared enough to see me to my car in a dozen years at least. Donny had never been thoughtful that way, and there had been only a handful of friends and no lovers since he'd left.

Joy shot me a cryptic glance. "Marianna needs to get her stuff regardless, and I have to grab a few things from the backroom. We'll be back in a sec." Joy motioned for me to follow her. "I noticed you got really quiet," she whispered when we were alone. "This is totally your call. I can vouch for Gil being a gentleman and, well, he's my brother. I know he's a good guy. But if you don't feel comfortable having him walk you to your car, we can overrule him. Just say the word, and we'll drive you to where you parked instead."

I realized my new friend had completely misinterpreted the reason for my silence. "It's okay if he walks me," I managed to say, my pulse kicking up a notch at the prospect of getting to chat with Gil alone for a few minutes.

"I trust your feelings about him. He seemed to be a really good guy when I met him at the beach, and now knowing he's your brother...well..."

I didn't have a chance to finish the thought before Joy interrupted. "Oh, good!" Joy snatched up her tote bag and her keys. "Because I can tell he'd like to talk with you for longer. You must have made quite an impression on him when you first met."

She could *tell* he'd like to talk with me for longer? How could she tell?

I opened my mouth to ask, but all that came out was, "What color is he, Joy?"

She laughed. "Very aquamarine," she said immediately, then paused. "That's complementary to turquoise, you know. Not just the shade but the aura." Then she dashed out of the room before I could question her further.

"Ready?" Abby asked.

Joy nodded and jingled her keys in the air. "Okay, y'all. We're set. Gil, you can walk Marianna to her car. Lorelei and Abby, same time tomorrow morning?"

Lorelei piped up. "I'll be in front of your building at seven forty-five."

Abby grabbed her purse. "Works for me."

"Great." Joy turned to me. "I know I roped you into this for tomorrow, too, and I'm not letting you off the hook," Everyone laughed. "But, you don't have to show up here at the crack of dawn either. We'll be around from eight a.m. onward. If you want to come at eight thirty or nine or even nine thirty—"

"I'll be here at eight as well," I said decisively. "You can count on it."

This earned her another heartfelt smile from Joy. Abby clapped. And Lorelei said, "Thank you, honey."

As for Gil, I was too self-conscious to glance at him in order to gauge his reaction, but I sensed positive vibes coming from his general direction.

As Joy locked up The Beaded Periwinkle, her brother disappeared into Castaways to close up for the night, too. He emerged in less than three minutes with a tan leather briefcase, one of the shop's plastic bags, and a large sketchpad.

Everyone said their goodnights. Then Gil and I began strolling away from the other women, toward Fudge Fantasia.

It was a pleasant evening. Still hot by Midwestern standards, but I'd begun to appreciate that about being here. I liked that it felt different. Tropical. Reminded me that I wasn't living the same old, same old—however temporarily.

"So, when you were in the backroom with Joy, the ladies told me that you all had just met today. That you came down from Mirabelle Harbor for the summer."

"That's right," I replied, but something about the way he phrased the question snagged at my memory. I couldn't quite put my finger on why it poked at me.

"Do you have family in the area?" he asked.

I shook my head. "My sister and her husband live in New Haven, Connecticut, and my daughter is up in Ann Arbor, Michigan going to college. My ex-husband is somewhere in California," I added, trying to drain the natural tension that crept into my voice at the mere mention of that asshat. "That's the only family I have left."

Not that I really considered Donny my *family* anymore, of course, but I was aware of wanting to let Gil know that, once upon a time, albeit a long while ago, someone had wanted to marry me. And that, despite surviving the hellfire of divorce, I was also strong enough to have weathered it. That I'd now moved beyond it and, maybe, was even on amicable terms with my ex. Joy's brother wouldn't have to know the whole truth. Wouldn't have to fully understand how the demise of those illusions of everlasting love still ripped my heart to shreds. And, honestly, I wouldn't be in

Florida long enough for it to matter.

"Ah," he said, not unkindly. "Most of my family is here now. Sister in Sarasota, as you know. Our mom, too. A few relatives back in Texas." He shrugged. "It's easy to keep track of the important ones when there are only a few."

I nodded in agreement, but didn't fail to notice that he didn't mention a wife—past or present. I also noticed there were no references to a girlfriend. Interesting. I never would have imagined someone so attractive would be single.

"A couple of my employees have a bunch of siblings and at least a hundred cousins. I have no idea how they deal with that family craziness over the holidays." He smiled as we strolled by the fudge shop, and he pointed down the street. "You still further down the block?"

"Yes," I said, finally recalling both the general area of my parking spot and the odd thing about his phrasing. Unlike Joy's style of talking, there were no "y'alls" in his speech. And the way he pronounced his words didn't sound remotely Texan either. That was odd. "Joy has more of a Texan accent than you do," I observed. "It's not an overwhelming drawl in her case, but it's noticeably there. Did she live in Texas for longer than you?"

He eyed me carefully with those curious baby blues, taking several long strides before he spoke. "Our parents divorced when she was eleven and I was eighteen," he explained. "She was a minor, and I was a legal adult when our mom moved us to Florida. So, I actually never went back to Texas, whereas Joy was shuttled back and forth to San Antonio for seven more years."

I tried to process this new information, conscious of the fact that there had to have been details he left out. He'd *never* been back to Texas…in over twenty years? Did he see his father only when the man came to Florida then? "So, uh, does your dad still live there?"

There was a lengthy pause yet again as Gil made a

show out of scanning one of the side streets for parked cars. He was *stalling*. Fascinating! I couldn't help but wonder why.

Finally, he glanced over at me and nodded. "Yes, from what I hear," he said briefly, not allowing time for follow-up questions. He cleared his throat and with an abrupt change of subject said, "I have a present for you." He thrust the plastic Castaways bag at me.

I squinted up at him as I took it. These Canton siblings were very generous people. I'd gotten more gifts from Gil and his sister that day than I'd gotten from anybody other than Olivia, Ellen, or Kathryn in several years. "Thank you," I murmured.

"Open it."

So I did. Inside, under a layer of tissue paper, was the beach towel with the picnic scene on it. "Oh! I was admiring this one today," I told him. "I loved it. It's so creative. But, um—" I paused. "You really don't need to give me—"

"Marianna," he interrupted, his voice strangely stern. "I'm the owner of the store. I can give away whatever I want, to whomever I want, whenever the mood strikes me." Even in the dark, I could see his blue eyes glinting and his attractive features forming an expression of amusement. "I'd sort of tricked you into visiting Castaways. If you'd come in there while I was working, I would have insisted on giving it to you then, just for taking a chance on my place. New customer special."

He stopped at the next corner and waited as I glanced down the side street in search of my Civic. "I appreciate that you took my advice that day at the beach. That you bought something you needed at my shop. And that you've been kind to my sister. She seems very open but—actually—she doesn't take easily to many people," he said. "I like seeing her happy."

"Joy is wonderful," I told him with feeling, finally

spotting my car and pointing to it. He followed me as I turned to walk toward it. "And so are her friends. I've never met people so warm and welcoming."

He assessed me silently as we sidled up to my car. "She'll be thrilled to hear that you think so." He paused. "I know people are supposed to say nice things about their sisters but, in Joy's case, I happen to mean them. You won't find a more kindhearted person on the planet. Or a more artistically talented one."

This was refreshing to my ears. Incredible, really. To be around a pair of siblings who loved and respected each other this much. Who genuinely seemed to want to build each other up in the eyes of the world. I loved my sister but—let's face it—I didn't always like her. And vice versa.

I nodded at the sketchpad he was carrying. "Joy's pretty impressed with your artistic talents as well," I told him. "And so am I. I truly enjoyed looking at your paintings today in several of the shops, and your sister is awfully proud of your work. I could tell by the way she talked about you."

I noticed Gil swallowing, and I saw an expression I couldn't identify flashing across his face. At first I thought it was pleasure, but I soon realized it was more than that. It was gratitude.

"Well, thanks," he said. "I like to paint seascapes with some surrealistic images. It's relaxing for me."

"How many have you painted?" I asked him. "Just the ones at the shops I visited today—yours, your sister's, and The Golden Gecko? Or are there a lot more?"

He laughed. That deep, throaty laugh I remembered from our meeting at the beach. "Oh, I've got a bunch. If you're coming to the Craft Festival this weekend, you won't be able to escape seeing them. I'll have a box of my painted greeting cards in the same booth as Joy and her bracelets. And she'll outsell me a hundred to one." He arched a dark eyebrow. "So, if you were only being nice by complimenting my artwork, you're stuck pretending to love it. At least through the weekend."

I laughed in return—feeling younger, suddenly, as if two decades had just melted away and I was a nineteen-year-old girl again. My daughter's age. Talking on a hot summer night to the charming lifeguard at the community pool. Daydreaming secretly about what it might be like to date someone smart and funny like him...someone so different from Donny...even though I was already a married woman back then and not free to act on those fantasies. A window to a world of brand-new possibilities had been flung open for me on that long-ago night. But, after my quick peek out into that exotic landscape, the blinds were snapped shut again.

Then, I remembered something rather significant.

I was no longer that young girl. I was also no longer married. I was free to fantasize about any foreign world I wished to imagine. Without embarrassment. Without restrictions. Even one inhabited by The King, who was apparently alive and well and living in Sarasota.

"I'll definitely be seeing you and your paintings this weekend," I informed him, proud of how confident I sounded. How calm and sure. "And I promise to disguise how dreadful I think your artwork is." I feigned a bored shrug. "I mean, I'll tell everyone I meet what a talentless hack you are, of course, but only behind your back. To your face, I'll be sure to fake it *really* well."

He grinned at my obvious sarcasm. "I guess I deserved that. I should have left it at 'thanks,' shouldn't I?"

I grinned back at him. "Yes," I said, unlocking my car. "And thank you, Gil, for the coolest towel I've ever owned and for walking me here. I appreciate it." I slipped into the front seat and he shut the door for me. A gentleman, just as Joy had said.

We waved good night and I drove—no, I floated—away. Back to the mausoleum of silence that was bungalow

#26, which, for the first time since I'd arrived in Sarasota, I didn't mind at all.

❁❀❁

Gil strode back to his car and sat in it, mentally painting a portrait.

Honey-blond hair with streaks of light chestnut—wavy, mid-length, braided hastily. The flyaway strands that escaped were like wispy baby hair. Uncurled ribbons.

Creamy skin, merely a shade darker than it had been when they met. Sun-kissed on her cheeks, perhaps, but still a Snow White level of fair.

Hazel irises with curious tints of gold, green, and cinnamon. Smile lines at the outer corners of her eyes, but faint, as if not often used.

Lips...falling somewhere between dusky rose and cerise. Soft and sans lipstick. Who'd kissed her last?

She had a grown-up daughter, he reminded himself, which she seemed too young to have. And an ex-husband, which always equaled baggage. But then, who at thirty-five or forty didn't have a shitload of that, whether they'd been married before or not?

He wasn't pleased to admit this to himself, but he liked her, dammit. A lot. And the strength of his attraction surprised him, especially given their whole twenty or maybe thirty minutes of acquaintanceship. Being around her had even brought out a few college-boy feelings in him. Carter would be so proud. But Marianna wasn't quite as transient a visitor as he'd initially thought. She'd be in Sarasota for much of the summer.

Huh. Didn't know if he should be more excited or worried by this.

Though Joy liked her—that much was obvious. For his sister's sake, he hoped Marianna might stay even a little longer than expected. For his own sake, well…it was far too early to say.

His cell phone rang.

"Speak of the devil," he said to his sister, grinning into the receiver. Although, really, in Joy's case it was more like "speak of the angel." He hadn't been exaggerating one iota when he told Marianna what a good person his sister was.

"You were talking about me to Marianna?" Joy asked, unable to disguise her delight. "Is she still there? Are you two going out? Should I hang up?"

He snickered. "You and Ma use slightly different tactics but, really, you are the same sneaky animal."

There was an offended huff on the other end of the line. "You *offered* to walk her to her car, Gil. I didn't suggest it. And, anyway, the difference between Ma and me is that I know when I'm right."

At that, he burst out laughing. "I stand corrected, Sis. You are far, far worse than even our mother. And, no, Marianna is not still here, and she and I are not going out." *At least not tonight*, he added to himself. Hey, he wouldn't rule it out. "But she's very nice, and she said several sweet things about you. I'm glad you have a new friend."

"You two share a color vibration," Joy said smugly. "You should know about it. The two of you go together like peanut butter and cucumbers."

To anyone else, this would sound incredibly unappetizing, but Gil knew his sister well. It was one of her favorite food combinations.

"Enough with the matchmaking, Veggie Girl. I've had my dose for the day already." He relayed all the gory details about their mother's event up in Tampa that afternoon. "Next time, she can pick on you. Try to set you up with her chiropractor or her lawn guy or whatever barista made her latté that morning."

Joy groaned. "You think she hasn't tried that already?

But don't worry. I'll escort her to whatever event comes up next. I just…I just wanted to say thumbs-up, Gil. I think the summer is going to be more fun now—for both of us—with Marianna here. Don't you?"

"Maybe," he said. "Maybe not. Your instincts are usually on target." He paused. "Except when it comes to food."

His sister laughed, just as he'd hoped. It always made his heart dance a little whenever he managed that. She'd lived in sadness for too long, and he'd never tire of seeing her basking in the light of levity and acceptance. It was good for her.

As for him? Well, life had just thrown something intense and interesting his way, but he'd reserve judgment on whether it was good or bad for him until he saw what happened next.

I was not prepared for the blinking red light of the unit's landline indicating a message awaited me. Nor was I expecting the intermittent beeps of my cell phone, which I'd left to charge on the kitchen counter, telling me there were voicemails on that, too.

I checked the number of messages. Five unanswered calls on the landline. Three on the cell. My first impulse was, naturally, one of fear: *Who died? Or was it just Donny again with more threats?*

I listened to the first landline message and discovered it was my daughter, Kathryn. Parental concern immediately intensified. *Oh, no. What could be wrong?*

"Hi, Mom. It's about noon. I need to talk with you. Can you give me a call right away? I'm at home until three."

She didn't sound panicked, just in need of something. My anxiety lessened a tiny bit.

The next message played. Kathryn again. "Did you get my call, Mom? It's two forty-five."

Then, "Mom, it's *six o'clock* and I haven't heard from you yet. I'm at work now. Call me here. Please."

Two more calls on the landline, one at seven thirty and one at eight fifteen—both hang-ups.

On the cell, all three were from Kathryn, and the last one, time-stamped at 9:27, simply had my daughter asking in a shrill voice, "Where. Are. You?"

I checked my watch. It was already after ten p.m., but Kathryn and I were in the same time zone, so I had no doubt my little night owl would still be awake.

I dialed Kathryn's cell phone and she answered on the first ring. "Jesus, Mom, where have you been?"

But I didn't answer this. I had questions of my own. "Kathryn, honey, what's wrong? Are you hurt? In trouble?" *Oh, God. Hopefully nothing serious...*

"No, Mom, I'm just mad." She huffed on the line, so much like my sister that it scared me a little. Once upon a time, Kathryn had been a shy and quiet girl. Now it was like having Ellen II around to railroad me all over again.

"About what?" I asked. Although I had to admit to feeling a tiny bit guilty for having left my cell phone at the bungalow, I hadn't expected to be gone nearly that long and, obviously, I hadn't expected a crisis to pop up on a random Thursday while I was out window shopping and buying fudge and water shoes. To discover my daughter was, thankfully, only *mad,* and not hurt or in trouble, took away some of my initial panic, but it also made me feel a bolt of resentment at having my unusually good mood shattered.

"I've been trying to reach you for *hours* about this, and you've been ignoring my calls."

"Kathryn," I said, exhaling very slowly, "I was not ignoring you. I was just out for the day and—"

"Whatever," she interrupted. "The problem is with you

and Dad. He's so pissed off with you that he's called me three times this week just to rant, and he almost never calls. He kept me on the phone for *an hour* this morning, asking me questions about the sale of the house. Why did you have to argue with him again? I thought you said all of that was over. You *promised* me it would be over."

The accusation in her voice hung in the airwaves between us as I tried to process this latest betrayal by my ex. As always, when it came to the harebrained things Donny did, I saw shades of scarlet. I had to blink all of the red away and swallow twice before I could trust myself to open my mouth and begin to construct some kind of an answer.

"Sweetheart," I began, "what did he want to know about the house?"

My daughter forced out another puff of air. "Oh, like how much it sold for, exactly, and what extravagant things you've already purchased with the cash, and some stuff about my scholarship. I really don't know many of the house details, and I told him that. I just—I just don't understand why you two can't get along. And share things. Can't you just give him some money from the sale? He said he'd help *you* if *you* were desperate and in need."

This felt like being stabbed. Damn him.

I'd spent nearly two decades being the responsible parent. Being the one who set limits on our daughter's behavior and her bedtimes. Who saved for her braces and took her to orthodontist appointments. Who had to say "no" to getting the puppy we couldn't afford to take care of and "yes" to a reasonable curfew in high school. Who signed her permission slips and went to parent-teacher conferences. I was the one who, on principle, wouldn't badmouth the girl's father—just because *he was her dad*—even after our divorce. Even when I knew, from his infrequent phone calls to our daughter, that he'd never offer me the same courtesy.

This, however, was an example of Donny going way too far. I always figured Kathryn understood the truth without my having to say anything specific. That she knew he couldn't be trusted. He'd left *both* of us after all. Maybe I should have been clearer, though. Maybe my days of trying to protect his image with our daughter were over.

Well, actually, there was no *maybe* about it.

I took a deep breath. "Sweetie, do you remember when you turned twelve and you got that locket from Aunt Ellen and Uncle Jared? It was your golden birthday, so they gave you a golden heart locket on a gold chain?"

"Yeah. So?"

"Remember how a few months later it disappeared? At first, I thought you'd lost it at school, but you insisted you had it when you came home on Friday afternoon. That you took it off in your room and put it in your jewelry box as always, but you couldn't find it when you wanted to wear it the next week."

"Yeah, I remember cleaning my room really well, but it never turned up." She sighed. "What does that have to do with anything?"

I squeezed my eyes shut, dreading having to tell my still innocent daughter the rest of this particular story. "It was a 24-carat gold locket and chain, Kathryn. About a week or so after you told me it was missing, I was doing the laundry and I found the receipt from the pawn shop in your dad's jeans pocket." I paused to let this understanding sink in to my daughter's mind, and to let myself have a moment to swallow back the bitterness of that discovery over seven years ago. It wasn't just Donny's theft of the necklace that made me realize it was the beginning of the end for us. It was also the lack of respect toward his daughter, his wife, and even his in-laws that this act demonstrated, underscoring our marital problems. Not to mention his stunning lack of remorse when I confronted him about it.

"She's a kid," he'd said dismissively, even though I'd been in tears over the incident. "She won't miss it, and we need to put food on the table." Only it wasn't food he'd used the money for. It was drink. Specifically, *his* drinks—and Vince Jordy's—at Pritchett's Pub, a place an hour away from Mirabelle Harbor, near the dog-racing tracks.

"That...that can't be true," Kathryn whispered.

"I wish it weren't," I told her. "But I swear it is. I even kept the slip. I could prove it to you." The necklace was gone when I went to the pawn shop to try to find it. Not that it would've mattered. The damage had already been done as far as I was concerned. But I'd hoped, even then, that I could save Kathryn from this pain of his betrayal. "I've reached my limit with your dad's irresponsible behavior. With trying to cover for him when he does something foolish or underhanded. I'm sorry to have to say this to you, but your necklace was just the tip of the iceberg. I'm not giving him any more chances."

There was silence on the line for a full fifteen seconds and no further comments from my daughter on the subject—at least not at the moment. But I knew her. Knew she needed time to assimilate this information. To remember all the other incidents from her childhood that didn't quite make sense before and to wonder if there had been anything else her father might have lied to her about. No doubt, Kathryn would think of several possible occasions. More questions would invariably come later.

In an attempt to lighten the mood, I inquired about her job at the campus store selling books and sweatshirts to students during the summer school session. (Answer: "Fine.")

I then asked about her college friends in general and, specifically, about her two roommates. (Answer: "They're good.")

Finally, I asked about her boyfriend Sid, a young man Kathryn had been dating for five or six months.

Exclusively. (Answer: "He's really great. He's just so wonderful to be around. And smart. And funny.") Kathryn all but gushed, speaking of the boy using multiple—albeit short—sentences. This could only mean one thing: They were desperately in love and sleeping together.

Heaven help us all.

But, of course, I could hardly give my daughter decent relationship advice, and I'd already mentioned a few times that I thought she and Sid were getting serious *way* too fast. I didn't dare bring it up again. From what I could sense, my baby girl was already teetering on the brink of cutting her annoying mom out of her life as it was, and Donny the Idiot wasn't helping matters. I didn't want to push my daughter away or close down the lines of communication, however thin. I didn't want Kathryn to rebel against her parents like I'd once rebelled against mine. Look where that led?

"I love you, Kathryn," I said before we hung up.

And I enjoyed the minor victory of hearing my daughter reply, "Yeah. You, too, Mom," before clicking off.

But it was hard to know how Kathryn would react to this new information about her dad once she'd had a chance to think deeply about it. I suspected I'd still be blamed for it in some way, at least in part. For not being able to stop him from doing dishonorable things. For not being a stronger, more assertive woman. For not leaving him—and for letting him, instead, leave us. For not telling Kathryn a few truths about him much sooner.

I had to face it. I blamed myself for all of these. Why shouldn't Kathryn blame me, too?

I set down the phone, finally, and closed my eyes. I could hear the crashing of the surf outside, and I let the waves wash in—and then out—all of the day's memories:

My excursion to St. Armand's Circle, visiting shops, buying fudge and beach-walking shoes.

Meeting Joy, Lorelei, and Abby, making jewelry with

them, and experiencing the camaraderie of a group of women friends after such a long drought.

Seeing that man from the beach and finding out that he was kind, generous, funny…and a little insecure about his artwork…and a little weird about his father. Which kept him from being too perfect.

Everything in the Circle was so new and charming.

Then having the past collide with the present on the shores of my mind—talking with my frustrated daughter, hearing news of my cheap and childish ex, being reminded of the uncomfortable realization that this time down in Florida was just an escape from my old and un-charming daily life.

It was like reading a hot romance novel or watching a humorous chick flick. When the book ended or the houselights went up or the summer vacation at your sister's bungalow was over, it was back to reality. I had to face that as the truth. No use getting too attached to anything here. It would all disappear, like Cinderella's fancy gown and carriage, just as soon as six more weeks were up.

I flipped on the TV, suddenly in need of noise. There was news, some weird music videos, a really tasteless sitcom, and a talk show I'd never seen.

"Christina Chats!" the placard behind the wild-looking woman proclaimed.

The Christina in question was about twenty-five, had purple streaks in her long dark hair, and was wearing what looked to be a zigzag-patterned body suit—in shades of fuchsia and lilac. I tilted my head and stared at the screen to get a different angle. Gotta wonder how a person like Joy might describe the talk-show host if, even to me, the woman looked like some kind of bizarre fusion between a zebra and a bunch of Concord grapes.

"We're talking with my girls—Tatiana, Brandy, and Jenni," Christina said with an enthusiastic shimmy that should be banned in at least forty-seven states. She added a fist pump, which set her abundant chest jiggling, more noticeable than ever in that skintight outfit. I wondered idly what the woman's mother thought of Christina's television wardrobe.

"Starting over at *thirty*. That's our topic tonight!" Christina all but shouted from her faux-hardwood-floor stage as the three guests sat awkwardly behind her on a faux-brown-leather sofa. "These wonder women gave it a shot and are stoked to share their results."

Not sure I wanted to watch this. Well, actually, I was absolutely positive I *didn't* want to watch this…but I was even less inclined to watch news reports from a war zone, a dumb sitcom, or Lady Gaga singing anything.

"Jenni, I know there was tremendous heartbreak in your past." (Cue the maudlin background music as a twenty-second video clip played on the screen just behind them all.) "You got fired from your job, your boyfriend cheated on you, your brother was incarcerated, your great aunt, who was like a mother to you, died suddenly, and even your pet Rottweiler was taken from you and put in a shelter—all within just six months," Christina said, furrowing her thinly tweezed brows with faux concern. ("Faux" was big on *Christina Chats!*) "Can you tell us your story?"

Jenni, a perky little blonde, went on to describe her sad tale in well-rehearsed sound bites, ending with how she began getting, and I quote, "life coaching lessons from this awesome surfer from Pasadena" and was now planning their beach wedding for August. "It totally just took the power of positive thinking and finally finding the courage to get that cute flamingo tattoo I always wanted," Jenni confided, flashing her lower calf where the lanky bird was etched in dark pink just above her ankle. "'Cuz the tat shop was where I met my surfer man."

"And *that*," Christina added sagely, "was when you realized you could stand on your own two feet—or even just on *one*—and you went to work on *you*."

The studio audience clapped wildly at this insightful connection. Jenni giggled in a series of surprised little bursts and said, "Oh, my God, I never thought of it like that!" And I found it impossible to watch even a minute more of this dreck.

Maybe Lady Gaga wasn't so bad.

However, I managed to find my own courage and clicked off the TV instead. Then I began sifting through Ellen's and Jared's books on the shelf next to the DVD player.

I'd already rifled through the magazine stack, but there were novels and Siesta Key guidebooks still left unexamined. I set aside anything that might include fun and inexpensive daytrips around this region of Florida and turned my attention to the other books: A couple of Jared's legal thrillers; some serious women's fiction tale about friends and death; a series of historical romances set in Scotland, featuring hunky, shirtless men (wielding swords) on the cover; a few Jane Austen-inspired stories, including this odd one where the heroine has the ghost of Jane in her head, giving her dating advice; a number of nonfiction books on sailing; a collection of essays on shells; and a memoir or two.

I picked up the essay collection—*Gift from the Sea* by Anne Morrow Lindbergh—and flipped through it, reading random passages. Anne wrote lyrically, though with utter clarity, on topics such as how shells were the homes of various sea creatures, but how the structure of those shells fit them individually and perfectly—at least for a time. How the different shells could represent different stages in a woman's life. How Anne herself managed to find peace and some small measure of serenity on the shores of her beach. Reflecting on her life experiences, with all of their gifts and challenges, in solitude.

I was too tired and not in the mood to read the book cover to cover that night, but Anne's thoughtful musings inspired me to reach for my lightning whelk and roll it in my palm. What creature belongs in a shell like this one, and why did its original inhabitant leave? I felt as though I'd spent the past week trying to shed my old shell once and for all, but I couldn't shake the uncertainty of not knowing where I belonged now that I'd left my old life behind.

Perhaps it all depended on the kind of creature I really was…or, rather, the one I was becoming. I knew I wasn't the same woman I'd been at age eighteen, or even at twenty-eight, but starting over at almost *forty*—was that really, truly possible?

Somehow I doubted the producers of *Christina Chats!* would think so, but I also suspected—if Anne were alive and knew of my circumstances—that the wise lady would have been encouraging. That she might even have confidence in my ability to find my way. Probably more than I had in myself.

CHAPTER TEN

So Close, Yet So Far

There was no other way to say it: These changes sucked the big one.

On Friday afternoon, Ellen dug around in the kitchen for a snack, frowning at all of the things Dr. Cole had informed her she shouldn't eat.

No caffeine, since it could worsen panic attacks. *Say goodbye to those morning hazelnut lattés.*

No alcohol either, for the same reason. *Skip that glass of Pinot Grigio with dinner.*

Limited sugar and fast foods. *No M&Ms—dammit. And no more easy carryout for meals.*

She didn't happen to smoke cigarettes or take illicit drugs but, hey, those were off limits, too. Shocking. As if a line of blow was on par with a handful of Raisinets and a vanilla-caramel cappuccino.

Ellen rubbed her temples with the pads of her fingers and halfheartedly examined the cut-crystal bowl she'd filled with fresh pears, apples, mandarin oranges, and plums. She didn't want to eat any of them.

Once the cardiologist and lab technician had sent in their reports, Dr. Cole basically said, "I told you so," only not in those exact words. He was his usual very professional self and managed to speak to her without any overt snarkiness, although Ellen was sure it lurked just beneath the surface.

He informed her that she "needed to make some lifestyle changes immediately" or the attacks would most likely keep happening, and maybe even intensify.

Step One in the smug doctor's Get Well Quick Handbook involved extra rest, dietary alterations, and stress management. If that didn't work, they'd have to move on to Step Two, which included prescription meds and a psych eval. Ellen wasn't too keen on getting promoted to Step Two.

"If you have any vacation days coming to you," the doc had said, "you should consider using them."

Ellen laughed aloud at this. She'd been working almost nonstop since she was twenty-three. She had about four years' worth of vacation days coming to her, and she told him so.

"That's very fortunate," Dr. Cole shot back. "Then you have the time available to go somewhere relaxing for a week or two. Learn yoga. Or T'ai Chi. Add in forty-five minutes to an hour of aerobic activity every day. Perhaps do some walking, biking, or swimming. Maybe take up a craft—like knitting."

"Knitting?" she'd sputtered. "Are you joking?"

From the unsmiling look he gave her, apparently not.

She'd returned home with a bunch of organic produce (what the *hell* did people make with *kale?*) and a brand new "T'ai Chi for Novices" DVD. She was not, however, ready to do anything daring with either.

3:51. Or so read the digital clock in the kitchen. Jared was finishing up at an onsite meeting with a client and said he'd be home early today. Probably by four. She sighed and studied one slightly speckled pear more closely. Went so far as to pick it up, roll it in her hand, squeeze it, and sniff it. Hmm. Maybe if it were poached in rum and drizzled with a nice dark-chocolate sauce...

But it wasn't, and she knew the time had come to finally talk with her husband about all of this. No doubt he'd wonder at the sudden appearance of pears and plums on their countertop otherwise.

Ellen set the fruit back in the bowl the second she heard the squeal of the garage door opening.

"Honey, I'm home!" Jared said when he walked through the door a few moments later, posing by the banister with his briefcase in one hand and his umbrella in the other. Waiting for her to laugh, as was their custom, at his delivery of this line. "How was your day, dear?" he added for good measure, knowing this would earn another chuckle from her.

"Wonderful, darling," she responded promptly and with TV-show sincerity. "The meatloaf is in the oven, and I'm fixing homemade mashed potatoes and gravy right now." *With a side of kale.*

Jared's laugh rang out as he stashed his umbrella in the closet. He'd grown up with "two dads" in a western suburb of Boston. His family life had been far closer to *La Cage aux Folles* than *Leave It to Beaver*—but no one could have been more comfortable with that than he was. Jared did, however, get an insatiable kick out of playacting traditional roles, so he added, "Will there be corn on the cob, too? Some freshly made apple pie with whipped cream, perhaps?"

"Why, of course, dear," she said cheerfully. "Let me just fix you a dry martini first and grab your slippers."

At that, he dropped his briefcase, strode into the kitchen, wrapped his arms around her, and said with a grin, "You're cute. What are we really having? Leftover Thai? Maybe sandwiches with those Swiss slices and the garlic roast beef from the deli? Or do you want me to make a reservation at that new Italian place?" He eyed the pears in the bowl warily. "Did somebody at work give you a fruit basket?"

She hugged him tighter and buried her head against his firm chest. He was a successful corporate accountant with a Harvard MBA who'd gone through a weightlifting phase when he was a teen that had lasted, maybe, two weeks. He wasn't one of those big bulky men, but he was taller than she was and his chest was broad enough to make her feel reassuringly safe when she rested her head against it. "No. I went, um…grocery shopping," she admitted.

"You did what?" His eyes danced with amusement as he pulled back from her and placed his palm against her forehead. "Running a fever or something?"

She glanced up at him, but then had to look away. Damn.

"Hey, Ellen." The joking came to an abrupt halt. He caressed her cheek until she turned back to meet his gaze. "It's okay. Tell me what's going on."

In a flood of monologue, she let it all spill out. She told him about her two recent panic attacks at work, going to see Dr. Cole, the tests of the last couple of days. "I didn't want to say anything to you until I knew for sure what was wrong. But now—"

"But now what?" he asked. "What can I do to help?"

She sighed. She'd been thinking about this and it was overwhelmingly *her* problem. "Not a lot, actually. I'm the one that needs to change my habits. Sleep for at least eight hours each night. Take Vitamin C…and D…and B-complex. Eat fruits and vegetables." She wrinkled her nose. "Dr. Cole even suggested a vacation."

He kissed her forehead and drew her into the living room so they could sit down on the black leather loveseat. "We could do that. We haven't gone anywhere exotic for a while. I think we're due for a break." He pulled out his iPhone and checked his calendar. "I've got a light week coming up in mid-August. Maybe we can go to Tahiti? It's a long flight, but it would be pretty relaxing once we got there."

She considered this. Tahiti would be really nice, but August was a little too far away, especially given Dr. Cole's sense of urgency. She tried to explain this to Jared.

"Look, Ellen, you don't have to wait for me to take a trip." He slipped his arm around her and squeezed her shoulder. "You know how I had that conference in San Diego in January?"

She nodded.

"And that investors' event in Lisbon back in November?"

She nodded again.

"I was gone for a week both times. So, now it's your turn. Go somewhere you'd like to go, and we'll just pretend you're on a business trip. One where you skip the boring meetings and just practice your windsurfing or something."

"Or learn to knit, if Dr. Cole has his way," she said with a laugh. "But would you be all right?"

"Well, I'll miss you, of course, but I'll manage."

She sent him a disbelieving glance.

"Ellen, I promise I won't starve or stay at work until midnight every night just because you're not home to meet me, okay? I mean, yes, I'll probably order carryout for every single meal and play *Sparkwave* on my phone in bed because you won't be here to stop me, but I can survive for a week or two alone. Really."

Perhaps he could, but could she? She'd gone on a hundred weekend getaways with her husband over the years, but it occurred to her that she'd never gone somewhere just by herself. The idea held shockingly little appeal.

"Maybe I'll just stay home," she said, glancing around the room. There was so much she could do in the house. She'd wanted to rearrange the shelving in the den for months. And spruce up the downstairs bathroom. "I could take time off from work and—and master T'ai Chi." She pointed to her new DVD. "I could probably learn that in a week, with all the time I'd have, don't you think?"

Jared gazed at her with the eyes of a man who knew almost every one of her quirks. Almost every hope. Almost every fear. "Why don't you go somewhere with a friend?" he suggested. "I think you'd have more fun with another woman than you'd have alone."

She thought of her friends. She had a cadre of female associates that she enjoyed meeting up with for the occasional lunch date or happy hour. There was a smaller handful that she'd see outside of the work week. Maybe they'd take in a movie together or chat over cocktails at a holiday party. Not one of them would she go on vacation with for an entire week, though.

"Or what about your sister?" her husband said. "Isn't she at the bungalow right now? You should fly down to Sarasota and spend some time with her."

"What? No!" Ellen said, shaking her head for added emphasis.

"Why not? You like your sister."

"I *love* my sister," she clarified. "Doesn't mean it would be a great idea for us to spend a week together at the beach." She shuddered. How many days would it take—or, hell, how many *hours*—before they were bickering like teenagers again?

"When was the last time the two of you spent any quality time with each other? Not some quick holiday visit," he said before she could mention her trip to Mirabelle Harbor at Christmas to see Marianna and Kathryn. "Think about it. You love Siesta Key. It'll be hotter now than when we usually go but, with you and Marianna together, it would be like a long sleepover party. Or like summer camp. You always told me how much you liked that."

Yeah, she'd liked Camp Willowgreen—a lot,

actually—but it mostly had to do with how much she loved getting away from home and her parents.

"Just think about it," Jared said again. "You're always relaxed when you're on the beach. You could walk every day. And swim. It's a place you know well, so there wouldn't be the stress of trying to figure out how to get around in a new locale. But it's also a place where you wouldn't be as tempted to reorganize the cabinets or anything because there just isn't that much stuff there. Life is pretty pared down in the bungalow. It's uncomplicated."

He had a point.

"And," he continued, knowing he had her full attention, "you and Marianna could help each other if you needed it, or stay out of each other's hair if you didn't. Why don't you give her a call tonight and see how she's doing? Might help you decide if that's something that would work for you both."

Ellen shrugged. "I could, I guess," she said, but she was already warming to the idea. In a blink, she could imagine herself on Siesta Key. Basking in the sunlight. Kicking at the waves. Practicing her new stress-reduction techniques… She supposed if she absolutely had to learn to meditate and to recite absurd positive affirmations to herself, it would at least feel less phony in Florida.

And she had something to celebrate with her sister, after all. She wasn't dying—there was that—at least not at a rate faster than expected. And she wasn't even menopausal.

She found herself squeezing Jared's hand at this thought and leaning closer to him on the loveseat.

Something about the direction of her thinking in the last few minutes prodded at her anxiety, though, and made her heartbeat pick up speed. She forced herself to exhale completely and take in a slow, deep, lungful of air and hold it for a few seconds before releasing it again.

She'd have a lot to think about in Sarasota. Not the least

of which was where this erratic, uneasy, god-awful sucky feeling was coming from and what the hell to do about it.

CHAPTER ELEVEN

Fools Rush In

Until yesterday, I'd never had the occasion to use crimp beads, jewelry wire or nylon and stretch cords, and I could count on one hand the number of times I'd held needle-nose pliers. By Friday at noon, however, those pliers felt like an extension of my right hand, and I could estimate eight inches of cord at a glance, with accuracy. That was about the perfect length for a bracelet, if you left room to tie the ends and snip.

My feeling of accomplishment at this was enormous enough to be almost embarrassing...but also joyous enough that I didn't care.

"You wanna pass me the charms box, honey," Lorelei said, pointing toward the black canister that held most of the sterling-silver endangered animal and insect charms. "I need another panther."

We'd divvied up the different kinds of bracelets between us, so we'd have a good selection for tomorrow's festival. While Abby and I were working on the stretchy ones, Lorelei and Joy were adding the finishing touches to the ones with clasps.

I handed Lorelei the box, marveling at the lovely color

combination she had going on with her current project—an entire bracelet family of panthers that were surrounded by beads that were yellow (like the eyes of a real adult Florida panther), tan (like their coats), creamy white (like their underbellies), and black (like the tips of their ears and tails). Fans of both the living mammals and the famous professional hockey team were going to love those.

Joy glanced at her watch. "How about we break for lunch in about twenty minutes?" she asked, playing with a few slipper shells and a peregrine falcon charm in her palm. "Gil said to give him a call before we ordered out, and that he'd run and get it for us."

Abby sent an arch look in my direction before addressing Joy. "What a nice, thoughtful brother you have," she said, with more than a hint of deviousness playing at the corners of her lips.

Joy's eyebrows shot up. "Well, he's still single, you know. That is, if you're willing to give up dating emotionally unavailable men, Ms. Abby."

Abby giggled. "Nope. Not me. Besides, you know how I feel about our pool guy."

This brought a delighted laugh from Joy and a smirk from Lorelei.

"Your pool guy?" I asked.

"Almost every apartment or condo complex around here has an outdoor swimming pool," Joy explained. "And the maintenance guy in charge of ours is…hmm. How would y'all describe him?"

"Pretty fine," Lorelei contributed.

Abby shook her head. "The phrase you're looking for is 'smokin' hot.' Six foot one. Blond. Abs like a *Playgirl* cover model." She fanned herself. "And friendly. Very friendly."

"And engaged," Lorelei added. "Don't forget that part."

Abby shrugged. "Details, details."

Joy pulled out her cell phone and stood up. "Who was

the one you liked before?" she asked, about to punch in a number when a lady customer walked through the door. "Wasn't it the Gustosa Pizzeria guy?"

"He *always* delivered," Abby deadpanned.

We burst out laughing, and Joy stepped away from the table to help the customer for a few minutes. After the woman made her purchase and left, Joy called her brother and started chatting with him.

In the meantime, Lorelei riffed on the pizza joke and lobbed a few dirty puns at us about the delivery guy's zesty sauce and his spicy Italian sausage. Then she regarded Abby more seriously. "You've still never met Jamison's cousin, Gary," she said, explaining to me that Jamison was her husband and Gary was a thirty-something tax attorney in St. Petersburg. "*So* easy to set you up, little chickadee. Just say the word."

The younger woman smiled, but I could see that lingering sadness I'd noticed the day before. I recognized this particular variety of pain. Someone—and not too long ago—must have really broken her heart. And, because Abby and I shared a hometown and knowledge of the Michaelsen family, it didn't take a genius to guess that Chandler was that someone.

Joy clicked off her phone and returned to the table. "Gil said he's bringing us a surprise. He already ordered it, so he'll be here soon." She glanced at the collection of finished bracelets in a basket on the table. "How close are we?"

Lorelei referred to a list she had near her, scanning it thoroughly and checking off a handful of items. "Looks like we're just about done with the advanced orders. But we still have the extra one hundred we need to keep on hand. If we can each average four bracelets in an hour, we'll be done in—" She paused to calculate. "About six more hours."

Joy grimaced. "Sorry, girls. Next year we'll start

earlier. Like February."

"*Next* year?" Lorelei cried. "You're already thinkin' about next year?" She picked up a translucent blue bead and pitched it at her friend's head.

Joy squealed trying to avoid getting beaned and almost rammed into her brother as he strode into the shop.

"Whoa there, Sis. Careful." Gil was carrying in a large aluminum platter covered in foil with one hand and, in the other, he had a plastic bag stuffed with an assortment of things yet to be seen. "Lunch is served," he told us, setting the platter down on the back counter and pulling out soda cans, paper products, plasticware, and five gigantic oatmeal-raisin cookies from the bag. He then lifted the foil off of the platter and a delicious aroma wafted up at us. Mmm. It was what I'd always imagined a true Floridian clambake would smell like.

"Oh, yum!" Joy said. "You know what I love. Thanks, Gil." She pecked a kiss on his cheek and told the rest of us, "Barbequed scallops with mushroom, yellow pepper, and cherry tomato skewers over jasmine rice and a side of asparagus spears from On The Barbie."

"Our Aussie friends, two blocks over," Gil explained to me with a grin. "They threw in an order of buttered clams just for you, Joy."

Joy covered her heart with the flat of her palm. "Zach's a charmer. He's seventy-two, but I know he's trying to make me fall madly in love with him. He'll probably succeed," she said, handing out plates and napkins to everyone, her brother included. "You'll stay and eat with us, won't you?"

Gil nodded. "I've got a half hour until I have to take over for Carter." He lifted a skewer off of the platter and bit off the grilled cherry tomato at the end. "Mmm. C'mon, ladies, dig in."

I let Joy scoop a few spoonfuls of rice, crisp asparagus, and barbequed scallops onto my plate and plop a vibrantly colored skewer on top of it. "This does look delicious," I said. Even on a plain white paper plate, it looked like a dish ready to be photographed and prominently featured between the pages of a gourmet magazine.

"Wait 'til you taste it, girlfriend," Joy said. "You know I'm a pesco-vegetarian—I haven't had so much as a bite of chicken, pork, or beef in two decades—but I'd order Zach and his sons' seafood every other day if I could. And, oooh, here. Take a clam, too." She transferred a chunky, butter-dripping one onto my plate as well.

Gil then handed me a lemon-lime soda and motioned me over to lean against the counter near him. "So, I see you ladies got a whole bucketful of bracelets finished," he said, around a mouthful of scallops. "That slave-driver sister of mine…"

"Oh, you hush," Joy said, feigning poking at him with a skewer. But then she turned her attention to serving Abby and Lorelei, and Gil lowered his voice. "Thanks, again, for pitching in today. Means a lot to her."

I just nodded. How could I begin to explain to him—without sounding lonely and needy—that it meant far more to me? Even if it were true?

Fortunately, Gil didn't require great depths of conversation from me. He just jabbered casually, while eating his meal, answering a few questions I had about the way the tents would be set up for the arts festival the next day.

I marveled at his seemingly effortless manner. At his level of ease with himself. The assuredness he projected at being comfortable in his own skin.

"The whole circle, the main streets, the sidewalks, everywhere you look is filled with the craft booths. Crafters from all over the state drive in and set up their tents for one-of-a-kind displays." He held up his fingers and started ticking them off. "There's jewelry, soaps, plant holders, crystal and glass items, pottery, quilts, photography, vintage clothing, hand painted greeting cards—"

"Which Gil will have in our booth," Joy interjected. "Right? You've got them packaged?"

"Yes, slave driver. I've got them packaged." He rolled his eyes and I could see a hint of what they must have been like as kids. Maybe arguing about household chores. Or bickering about some instruction their parents had given them. At odds with their words, but not with their true selves. It made me smile to see them as siblings. Their way of being "in relation" to one another. How they seemed to instinctively understand each other's essence...in a way that Ellen and I had always struggled to do, even when we were agreeing aloud.

"Why aren't you selling your larger paintings?" I asked Gil. "Do you need to have a certain number on hand before exhibiting them?"

Gil shook his head. "The festival this weekend is specifically for crafts. Anything like my canvases or our friend Claudia's bronze sculptures are considered 'fine art,' and they're saved for the annual November show, which is dedicated to that. The cards are more craft-like, so I'm allowed to exhibit them at this fair."

"But he's only telling you about half of what's really sold," Abby said. "There are *tons* of food vendors, too. You can get hot dogs, sausages, smoothies, lemonade, kettle corn, Italian ices—"

"Slices of pie, little taster cups of chili and rice, fruit salad, baked clams," Lorelei added. "And don't forget about the music. There are always singers and instrumentalists who play acoustic sets of their music and sell CDs. It's a real festive atmosphere. Like a weekend-long neighborhood block party."

I nodded, unwilling to admit that the neighborhood block parties of my recollection mostly involved charred beef patties, Donny singlehandedly downing a six-pack of Miller Lite, and Vince Jordy blasting nineties-era Britney

Spears from the stereo of his parked car in his parents' driveway. Memorable, yes, but not quite like the fun and classy event my new friends were describing.

I finished my plate while he was talking and unwrapped one of the giant cookies, but I was only able to eat about half of it. I kept thinking about how few real friends I'd had in my life. In high school, I'd hung around a handful of average girls with average grades. Their interest in me was as middling as it was in their schoolwork. And then there was Donny, of course. I'd made him the center of my teenage world—undeservingly, I realized too late. Looking back, I think it was his parents I'd really fallen in love with. They were so much warmer than mine.

Problem was, the reality of living with Donny in his neighborhood didn't live up to my illusion of it. Yes, some of the people I spent time with—like his parents—were genuinely kinder and more concerned about me. Others were just better con artists. The difference between what I'd *thought* I was getting and what I *did* get still haunted me. To be encircled by the warm embrace of "family" was still a persistent fantasy of mine, which I'd only felt in more recent years in the company of Olivia and the Michaelsens.

My college experience wasn't much to speak of, of course. I'd had no time for a social life. And when I began working at the insurance company, my colleagues had been nice enough to me, but everyone at the office had their own lives outside of the job.

Ellen had probably had it great during grad school and at the start of her work life. After getting her undergraduate degree, she'd left home, moved into the heart of Chicago, and was hanging out with wealthy, good-looking, smart people all the time. Like Jared. Never having to worry about rushing home to a fussy baby or to a husband who might've just cleaned out their savings account to fund his latest harebrained "project." Imagine living like that, huh?

With a familiar pang of envy, I wrapped up the second half of my cookie and tucked it in my purse for later, then I watched as Gil and Joy razzed each other some more. Much as I liked this funny little band of Sarasota transplants, and as enticing as spending time with them seemed, I'd learned not to trust my first impressions. These people could be hiding just as much personal dysfunction as I was.

At one point, after Gil had returned to his shop and when Joy and I finally had a moment alone, I tried to broach the topic of their father in Texas and, specifically, Gil's lack of a relationship with him.

The light in Joy's blue eyes dimmed a little at the mention of her dad. "He isn't…a laidback man. He wasn't ever easy to live with for any of us, particularly for Gil." She shrugged. "So there was a rift and, I guess, my brother and I each found different ways of declaring our independence. I became a vegetarian in high school, which our dad considered a serious act of defiance. He's always been a big steak eater." She rolled her eyes. "Gil didn't give up meat, but he gave up something else—his accent. Within a year of Ma moving us to Florida, you couldn't tell he'd ever lived in Texas."

Ah. That explained a few things. I appreciated Joy's honesty, but my new friend wasn't the type to dwell in sadness, and Joy didn't say any more about the situation than that. For me, the most interesting part our conversation was the realization that, with the Canton siblings, a parental rift seemed to bring Gil and his sister closer together. Maybe it had only been a minor kind of family falling out—I couldn't tell from Joy's explanation—but Gil's refusal to set foot in his home state for more than two decades seemed to belie a trivial cause. And despite Joy's warm and accepting nature, there was something uncharacteristically cold in her voice when she spoke of their dad.

Regardless, family estrangement had resulted in a very different sibling experience for my sister and me. Our family "rift," which could be better described as a "major fracture" or, possibly, a "gigantic schism," had pulled the two of us further apart, even though Ellen and I still spoke regularly and professed to love each other. With our family's interpersonal dynamics, especially after I eloped, there was always this unsettling element of anger simmering just beneath the surface for us both. Like the dangerous undertow of the tide.

We finished the last set of bracelets around seven or so, but all four of us continued to hang around and chat. We were tired but, for whatever our own individual reasons, we each seemed reluctant to leave The Beaded Periwinkle.

"I should go home," Lorelei murmured wearily. "The boys are probably at each other's throats, and I won't be able to be in the house to referee this weekend."

Abby nodded and looked unenthusiastically in the direction of her car keys. "I know. Tomorrow will come early, but it's so nice not to have to move."

We all laughed, me the hardest. Every single muscle in my arms was sore, which was to be expected, but my neck, shoulders, and back were aching, too, from all the sitting and working. Still, despite my exhaustion, I felt a wave of contentment.

Joy was passing around a plate of washed green and red grapes when Gil popped back in her shop, along with one of his friends. From what I gathered, this was the man who owned The Golden Gecko. I waved hello to both gentlemen but didn't catch the new guy's name because, just as Gil was introducing him, my cell phone rang. Worried it might be my daughter, I raced to answer it.

But it wasn't Kathryn.

"Hey, there," my sister said. "Lounging on the beach?"

"Oh, hi, Ellen. Um, no. I'm in St. Armand's Circle."

"The shopping district?" Ellen's voice sounded incredulous. *"You?"*

Comments like these from my sister never failed to make me bristle. True, I didn't generally love shopping, but that was largely because I hadn't had the disposable income to spend on frivolous things since before Kathryn had been born. Ellen always made it sound like I thought myself above the activity. "Yes," I replied sharply. "Something wrong with that?"

"Don't get all huffy with me. I just called to see how you are and…uh, to find out what you were doing."

"Well, I'm fine. Mostly." I told my sister briefly about Donny's threat to try to get some of the money from the sale of the house.

"That's bull," Ellen reassured me. "He doesn't have a legal leg to stand on, but I'll call Chelle, who handled the papers originally, just to make sure. Don't worry about it."

"Thanks," I murmured, and I felt drenched in gratitude, yet again, for what Ellen had done for me in the past and, in many ways, was still doing for me. I just wished talking with my sister wasn't always such an emotional rollercoaster. One minute she irritated me, the next I was so appreciative of her generosity, and the next—

"You're welcome," Ellen said. "Hey, who are those people near you? They're so loud."

—she irritated me again.

"They're…nice. They're new friends," I blurted, aware that I was missing a funny conversation with them and resenting being pulled away all the more when the whole group started laughing uproariously at something Gil said.

"Friends?" Ellen asked. "I hear *guy* voices. Who are these people? How did you meet them in St. Armand's? Do you know anything about them?"

I bit my lip to keep from snapping at her. Then I lowered my voice to a hiss and said, "Yes, I know plenty. Stop treating me like I'm twelve."

Ellen snorted. "Well, c'mon. It's not like you have the best track record with men, Marianna. I'm just trying to make sure you don't make any impulsive decisions, particularly with guys you don't know." She paused. "What are they talking about?"

They were talking about the Craft Festival tomorrow, but I wasn't about to explain all of that—and my involvement with the B.E.A.D.S. project—to my nosy sister. "You know, I'm not sure, but I think I'll go find out. Have a great weekend, Ellen. Thanks for checking in. I'll call you in a few days."

"Um…well…" she began. Then there was an awkward pause. "Yeah, sure. We'll talk soon. Very soon." It sounded like she was going to say something else, but she only added, "Just be careful, okay?"

"I will. I promise." *Only fools rush in, right?* "Love you," I told Ellen and then quickly hung up, relieved not to have to deal with my elder sibling's rampant judgmentalism, constant critiques of my life choices and, as of late, aggravating paranoia. At least it was easier to put a swift end to these types of conversations on the phone than it was in person. Thank heaven for small mercies.

I tossed my cell phone into my purse and, quite happily, rejoined my new group of friends.

❀✿❀

Over a thousand miles northeast and staring silently at her cell phone, Ellen clicked it off and set it on her kitchen counter.

"Love you, too, Sis," she said to the empty room. "And, oh, by the way…I'll see you on Sunday."

CHAPTER TWELVE
It's the Singer, Not the Song

On Saturday, the sun rose early and dawn lit the sky in shades of pink, saffron and peach. I knew the Craft Festival would have a gorgeous opening day. I also knew that the excitement coursing through my body was due less to the beauty of the conditions than it was to the delight I felt in having made such lovely new friends.

Speaking of which, Abby and Joy were already in the process of setting up the tent and tables when I arrived at the site.

"What can I do to help?" I asked.

"Hey, good morning!" Joy said, ever cheerful. "We're just arranging the bracelets in loop patterns around the table." She demonstrated. They looked like multiple sets of Olympic rings.

"Okay. I can work on that if you need to do something else." I grabbed a handful of bracelets and began laying them out the way Joy had shown me. She, meanwhile, was able to turn her attention to the task of setting up the earrings she was selling in addition to the B.E.A.D.S. project items. "Everything all right with Lorelei?"

"Yeah," Abby piped up. "She'll be coming in just a few

118

minutes."

"And my brother's already here." Joy pointed in the direction of Castaways. "He's just lugging out his crate of painted cards."

No sooner had those words reached my ears when I caught sight of Gil, striding toward us with the confidence of a sun god. Or, at the very least, The King. Rays of light glinted off of his toned, bronzed body, giving off the effect of golden glow. Maybe the Florida sun did that to everybody, but it was especially noticeable in Gil's case.

"Mornin'," he said to me with one of his broad grins, setting down the crate on an empty spot on our second table.

"It's a beautiful one," I said, nodding at him. He appeared pleasant and friendly whenever I saw him but, during the day, especially early like this, there was something a bit less permeable about him. He was always watchful, but at night, under cover of darkness, he seemed to relax his guard somewhat. In the bright light of morning, his blue eyes squinted at the world with much more serious scrutiny, and I couldn't help but feel that this was due to something more than just the glare of the sun.

I felt his gaze on me more than once during the time we spent setting up. To make him laugh, I picked up one of his packaged postcards. "Ooooh...dreadful," I joked.

A blatant lie. The painted design was positively breathtaking.

He raised one dark eyebrow at me and the corners of his lips quirked upward.

"Oh, that's right. I'd promised to say only nice things today," I murmured. Then added, "You're very talented, Gil. Don't deny it."

He laughed heartily and finally mumbled, "Thanks. Sweet of you to say."

"It's true."

A few minutes later, Lorelei rushed into their tent.

"Parking's already filling up!" She dropped her tote bag and keys on a folding chair. "The first open space I found was down by that English pub."

"The Thames Tavern?" Gil said. "That's over a two-block walk." He glanced at his watch. "The Festival doesn't even open for another half hour. Bet we'll be flooded with customers soon."

"Did you get much of a chance to look around when you arrived?" Joy asked me.

I shook my head.

"Abby, why don't you take Marianna around for a quick spin before things get too crazy here? She should have a sense of where the best vendors are in case she wants to do a little shopping later."

"Or tasting," Gil added. "Be sure to show her the—"

"Clam Pit!" everyone chorused.

I laughed. "Sounds popular."

"Oh, honey, it's the best," Lorelei said. "They come up every year from Miami and we glom onto them while we can. Remind me to pick up a platter for the guys before I go home tonight."

"Oooh, good idea!" Joy glanced meaningfully at Abby, and the latter nodded in agreement. "Maybe put in a couple of carryout orders for us?" Joy suggested. "We can swing by and get them at five."

"For me, too, please," Gil said. "Tell Samuel to make mine a double order."

"Will do," Abby replied.

"Oh!" Lorelei dug through her large tote until she'd unearthed two travel books on Colorado. "Could you drop these off for Nick?" she asked Abby. "I promised to give him these when he was at the shop yesterday."

Abby took the books. "No problem." Then she nudged me. "Hey, we'd better get going before they give us anything else to do."

"Yeah, ladies, could you stop by the bank for me?" Gil

teased.

"I have some dry cleaning to pick up," Joy contributed.

"Uh-huh." Lorelei nodded with faux seriousness. "And about dinner—"

"We're outta here!" Abby said, dragging me out of the tent and into the sunshine, both of us giggling like teens.

"They're funny and…really wonderful people," I gushed. "How long have you known them all?"

Abby pondered this. "I met Joy first. At our condo complex. It's been a little over a year now." She laughed as if not quite believing how fast the time had flown. "Joy introduced me to Gil, of course. And to Lorelei. I work a few hours a week at The Beaded Periwinkle and part time at Floriday Vacations, too. So, it's been nice."

I studied her expression, and she seemed to be very sincere, but there was still that lurking sadness just behind her smile. Courtesy of Chandler Michaelsen, no doubt.

If I didn't know his family or have as much respect for them as I did, I probably would have hated the guy, sight unseen. As it was, I'd never met him, only his identical twin Chance, since Chandler had bolted out of Mirabelle Harbor about five years ago (dragging Abby with him), right around the time Olivia and I were getting acquainted.

I tried to formulate how to ask Abby the questions about her ex-boyfriend that I really wanted to know, but she'd turned her focus elsewhere, pointing out some of her favorite craft and food vendors among the sea of white tents. To my eye, it was part art fair, part tailgate party— with a very willing crowd of participants beginning to infiltrate the edges, ready to partake in both.

"There's The Golden Gecko's tent." Abby made a beeline for it. "Yo, Nick! Got a present for you."

The tall, blond guy, who'd been visiting Joy's shop with Gil yesterday afternoon when Ellen had called, swiveled around and beamed at us. "Ladies! What 'cha got for me? Some luv? Some sugah?" He tapped his left cheek and then his right one, motioning us forward expectantly. Abby snorted, but she kissed him on the left side of his face.

When in Rome...I thought. I pecked him on the right cheek.

Nick stepped back, looking pleased. "That was a very nice gift."

Abby plopped the books down on his front table, between an army of grinning lizards and amphibians. "Well, this is for you, too. Compliments of Lorelei."

The sun-weathered, handsome man in his late-thirties examined the two Colorado travel guides with interest. "Awesomesauce," he said with teen-like enthusiasm. "You give her a big smoocheroo for me. I'll return them to her next month."

"Will do," Abby promised him. With a parting wave, she then dragged me out of his tent and around the Circle.

"I thought you were the go-to person for travel, aren't you?" I asked.

"My travel agency specializes in Florida sites, but Lorelei is our Rocky Mountain expert. She's from Tallahassee, but she went to college out in Denver and met her husband Jamison there. She lured him back here."

I laughed. "Lucky for us."

"Exactly. And Nick could use her help this summer, too, since he's never been out West. He said he 'planned' a driving trip, but I think he employed that term rather loosely." Abby rolled her eyes. "Other than looking at a map and deciding he loves the sound of the names Silver Springs, Bear Lake, and Estes Park, he knows nothing about the area, so Lorelei is just trying to keep him on some sort of beaten path so he doesn't get too lost in the mountains. As you probably guessed, Nick's a great guy, but he's more adolescent than adult sometimes."

"And...single? Someone you might want to go out with...maybe?"

She laughed and elbowed me. "Oh, c'mon. Not you, too? Nick's very sweet, handsome, and fun, but he's ten years older than me and in no way seems like the type to settle down."

"And that's what you're looking for, right? A guy who's ready to commit and settle down?"

"I've been looking for that for a long time, Marianna."

I paused before saying softly, "A guy unlike Chandler Michaelsen, right?"

She nodded. "Yeah, I figured if you knew Olivia that you might also know about that whole situation with her brother-in-law." She took a few deep breaths, pointed out a couple of tents with tasty treats en route to the Clam Pit, and finally said, "I'm nearing thirty, you know? I followed Chandler out here. We meandered our way around the United States and got to Sarasota after *eleven* cities in four and a half years." She shrugged. "The usual routine was that we'd each get a quick job—fast-food chain or another service-industry slot—and a month-by-month rental agreement. Then try to fit in with the locals for however long his interest in the area lasted. Just when I'd start to get used to the new city, know my way around and maybe make a few friends, Chandler's wanderlust would kick in. He'd get antsy, like somebody was tailing him or something. He was going to move on to city number twelve after only five months in Sarasota, but I'd met Joy and Lorelei and realized I'd had enough of being in transit. So he went on—to Atlanta this time—without me."

"I'm so sorry, Abby."

She bit her lip. "Thanks."

I reached out and gave her shoulder a light squeeze. "Couldn't have been easy to choose to stay."

"It wasn't. I loved him...and I think he loved me." She shrugged. "But, when I'm being totally honest with myself, it didn't take long after he'd left for me to recognize that we weren't soul mates. We were too different, and we were both always trying to nudge the other one to change. I kept hoping that if we stayed as a couple for long enough we'd finally grow together, but we were on two very different paths. And, in the end, I realized if he wanted to settle down, it wasn't with *me*. So, I'd been just killing time."

I thought about this. Abby was a decade or so younger than I was, but we shared a common experience. Even though, technically, she'd been single during the years she'd been with Chandler, she'd been living in a dead-end relationship with him. Just as I'd been with Donny, despite our lengthy marriage. Both Abby and I had been waiting for somebody who'd really want to be a permanent fixture in our respective lives. But, sadly, neither of us had found "The One." She hadn't had any more luck with that than I'd had.

I sighed, nodding. "Relationships are hard, no matter which road we choose to take," I admitted. "I was married right out of high school, but I was killing time for a lot of those years, too."

We exchanged a glance—a long look of understanding. And acceptance.

"Yeah, it sucks sometimes," she said. "But the good news is that now you, too, can have a crush on your pool boy!"

I laughed. "Or pizza delivery guy?"

"Exactly. And don't think Lorelei and Joy won't try to set you up with every available man on the peninsula while you're down here, by the way. I've got some blind-date stories that'll make your hair curl."

"Oh, no. Well, forewarned is forearmed, right?"

"Right," Abby said unconvincingly. "But—"

"But what?"

"But, well, you've caught Gil's eye, Marianna. Joy's not going to let *that* go so easily. Just be aware…" Her voice trailed off and she pointed in glee. "Voilà, the Clam Pit! Quick, let's place our orders before the lines start forming. Trust me, you're gonna *love* this."

The two of us returned to Joy and Gil's booth with the promise of baked clams for the evening and a big bag of kettle corn to share with everyone during the morning rush.

"These are addictive," Lorelei said, scooping up a handful of kettle corn after the most recent customer left the tent.

But none of us had a chance to chat or nibble for long.

The bracelets were quickly becoming a big hit—a few dozen sold in just the first hour of the Craft Festival. And the other items for sale were benefitting by the bracelets' popularity. Joy had also sold several pairs of earrings, and Gil needed to replenish his display of painted postcards after a couple of customers discovered and bought his artwork.

I plucked a set of six packaged seascapes from Gil's postcard arrangement and thrust some money at him before he could protest. "I'm buying these *now* before you sell out of them."

He leaned closer and lowered his voice. "Don't be silly, Marianna." He tried to hand the bills back to me. "I'd give these cards to you—"

"I know you would," I whispered. Then loud enough for the new customers entering the tent to hear, I added, "They're a steal at this price. In fact, I want two sets." I forced a little more money into his hands. "He makes Florida come alive on the paper, doesn't he?" I said to the visitors, pointing at the postcards I'd just purchased.

"Wow, that's gorgeous," one of the strangers said. She snapped up a set that looked similar to mine. "Did you paint these?" she asked Gil.

He ducked his head for a second with a surprising

expression of shyness, then he said, "Yes, ma'am," and beamed one of his sun-god grins at the lady.

She looked as dazzled by Gil as she was by his art. "I'll get a couple of sets, too."

I couldn't suppress a little laugh of triumph, and Joy rewarded me with a smile so full of sunshine, pleasure, and pride that she was nearly bursting from it. Gil just shook his head slightly, but I could tell he was pleased. And I hadn't been kidding. As I put the cards away in my handbag, I took a second to study the beach-image card on the top of each set, marveling at his talent. He really *did* capture this beautiful Sarasota coast, with its vivid colors, white sand, and vibrant water and sky. I wanted to walk right into his postcard and wander around.

Soon we were too busy for even a few words of conversation beyond the actual transactions. It took all five of us to handle the customer greetings, the constant restocking, and the many sales, especially of the bracelets. One attractive thirty-something guy in a suit and tie came in late in the afternoon and bought *thirty* of them, along with a couple of pairs of Joy's earrings, and a set of Gil's postcards.

"Wow!" Joy said to the man as he paid in cash for his order. "Thank you for supporting the B.E.A.D.S. project and our other work, too."

The suit nodded. "Of course. I heard about these. You'll be here tomorrow as well, right?"

"Yes," Gil replied. "Ten to five, just like today."

"Good." The man pulled out his smart phone and typed something into it. "You might see me again." Then he grabbed the bag full of items and strode away.

Abby peered curiously out at him from behind the tent's canvas wall. "He's not stopping at any of the other vendors, at least not on our row," she whispered to them. "He almost seemed like he was on a mission."

"I wonder how he'd heard about the bracelets?" Lorelei

mused.

"Maybe he saw some women wearing them in the Circle," Joy said. "In any case, I'm glad he did. Now that most of the advanced orders have been picked up, I can see that, although we've still got a stash of bracelets for the project left to sell tomorrow, we'll be able to make a sizable donation after this weekend's Festival. It's exciting news, isn't it?"

We agreed it was.

As we packed up for the evening, Lorelei said she needed to grab her Clam Pit order and race home to the guys, but Abby, Joy, Gil, and I lingered.

"Oh, I'm so psyched!" Joy exclaimed. "Let's do something fun tonight. What do y'all say?"

"How about baked clams and a movie?" Abby suggested. "Marianna and Gil, are you two in?"

Gil said, "Sure."

"What about you, Marianna?" Abby said.

"I'm open to anything," I said. This was true.

"What are you ladies thinking of watching?" Gil asked.

Abby's grin broadened then she and Joy exchanged some kind of mischievous glance. "Well, nothing goes with baked clams as well as *Clambake*."

Joy giggled and did a little go-go dancing step in place. I chuckled in surprise. Gil crossed his arms.

"Seriously?" he said, his blue eyes narrowing. "Out of *all* the possible film choices out there, you want to see an old Elvis movie?"

"That'd be fun," Joy declared. "But how about we let our guest decide. Marianna?"

As if I were crazy enough to contradict Joy and Abby. Plus, it *would* be fun to see an Elvis movie with an Elvis lookalike in the room. I nodded, laughing helplessly. "Sorry, Gil."

He rolled his eyes. "If anyone asks me to sing along, I will pelt that person with empty clam shells."

"So you know it, then?" I blurted. "That you…um, sort of resemble him?"

"Since I was about sixteen," he said with a reluctant grin.

"And he does kinda sing like The King," Joy whispered loudly.

"I do not."

"You do, too," his sister shot back. "He's really good," she informed Abby and me.

"I am *not*."

"You are, too!"

"Can't you just see them as little kids?" Abby said to me.

"Yeah," I agreed.

"So, it's decided then," Joy declared. "Meet at my condo in a half hour. Baked clams, *Clambake*, and I'll make us a pitcher of margaritas." She rubbed her hands together. "Let's get moving, y'all."

✿❋✿

I followed Gil's car on the short drive to Joy and Abby's condo complex, a warm Clam Pit bag on the seat next to me with an aroma so enticing that it made my empty stomach rumble.

He was waiting for me with his own Clam Pit carryout by the front entrance.

"I'm debating whether or not I have time to scarf down one of these before my sister buzzes us in." He motioned toward our bags. "The scent is killing me."

I grinned. "I know. There was a red light that almost lasted too long for me to stand it."

"The intersection of Third and Willow?"

"Yes!"

"Yeah. Me, too." He pressed the buzzer. "C'mon, Joy."

His sister responded and, soon, we were up on the second floor, where her condo was located, and Abby was waving from down the hall. She met us by Joy's open door, Elvis DVD in one hand, and a quart of ice cream in the other.

"I was thinking Creamy Caramel Swirl for dessert tonight," Abby said.

"Perfect," Gil agreed. "Now, if only I could talk you ladies into a good action flick or, maybe, some light sci-fi/fantasy—"

"Not a chance," said his sister, motioning us all inside.

And before I even had a second to stow my belongings in an out of the way corner, Joy thrust a massive margarita at me, edged with a rim of salt and garnished skillfully with a wedge of lime.

"Drink up, honored guest," Joy said with that impish grin of hers.

I could feel myself beginning to blush at being called that. Thing was, in their presence, they really made me *feel* like an honored guest. Someone special. It wasn't something I'd ever thought I'd need. Nothing I'd craved. And, yet, the pure gift of it couldn't be denied. There was a beautiful sense that I was truly being seen and valued. It was impossible not to appreciate that…or to realize just how long that sensation had been missing from my life.

Abby got the movie set up while Joy finished pouring everyone round one of the margaritas. Gil and I worked together to make space on the coffee table and lay out napkins and silverware for each person present. The table was surrounded by seating on three sides—comfy armchairs to the left and the right, angled slightly to face the TV on the wall, and then a small sofa on the long side of the coffee table, facing the TV screen directly. Plenty of room for the four of us.

It wasn't until Joy and Abby claimed the side chairs and I found myself left only with a space on the sofa next to Gil that I realized the sofa was more like a love seat. Suddenly, this movie thing had a bit more of an intimate feel than I'd expected.

In some ways, the evening felt like getting a taste of what college might have been like for me, had I not already been married, commuting to night classes, and a young mother. Having drinks (potent) and carryout (delicious and still warm) and a movie to watch as a group (a lighthearted romantic comedy) was a fun way to spend several hours just in and of itself.

But I hadn't counted on that sense of hanging out with a couple of girlfriends, who seemed like roommates after just a few minutes, or that hyperawareness I hadn't felt in so long toward an attractive man who was sitting only inches away from me. Every shift of his legs, every change in his posture, every rotation of his torso jostled the airwaves and made me more acutely aware of his presence. His body heat radiated outward from his skin so I could nearly feel it. And the sheer size of him! Gil could take up space effortlessly.

"One of the funny things about the film," Abby said, "is the way the main character that Elvis plays—Scott Heywood—is from Texas." She raised an eyebrow at Gil.

"The son of an oil tycoon," Joy added.

"Clearly, nothing like me then," Gil shot back. "I'm sure he was even from a different part of Texas." He looked relaxed on the outside, but I could feel some genuine tension drifting toward me, half a foot away. I sensed he was tolerating this teasing, but he wasn't entirely enjoying it. Maybe something was hitting too close to home?

"It's been a while since I've seen the movie," I said, trying to pull a little bit of attention away from him. "But I remember that Scott switches places with a very regular guy named Tom, who's supposed to be starting his job as a water-ski instructor at a resort in Miami. Right?"

"Yeah," Gil said, sending me a grateful look. "Much as

I could live without the goofy songs, the premise of the movie isn't half bad. It's like a 1960s version of *The Prince and the Pauper*. I mean, the main guy, who's played by Elvis, just wants to try to make it on his own. To be seen and liked for himself, not for his father's money." He shot a warning look at his sister, who stared knowingly back at him but said nothing.

"A little oil money would be kinda nice, though," Abby said.

Gil shrugged. "Maybe. But, as we're told, the best things in life are free."

True.

While I would have loved to have more of a financial cushion, I counted my blessings like good health and freedom all the time. How grateful I was that Kathryn was doing well. How, despite our differences, I had a sister like Ellen who loved me. And how glad I was to finally be free of the judgment of my parents and the irresponsibility of my ex-husband.

No one was going to like me or want me because of my money (or lack thereof). If any man ever showed real interest in me again, I was fairly confident it was because he liked my personality or maybe even my looks—but definitely not my bank account. And that was liberating. In this way, Elvis had a point.

As the 1967 beach film played, the good-looking cast members went out on water skis or in flashy motorboats, took dreamy strolls along the shoreline or sexy motorcycle rides at twilight, or did some clam baking and wild go-go dancing in the sand. Elvis went smoothly from water sports to roasting seafood. From playing electric guitar to performing chemistry experiments in a nearby lab. (He was developing a special resin formula for racing boats.) Let no one ever claim that Elvis the actor wasn't versatile!

Somewhere in the middle of the film—our Clam Pit carryout long gone—Joy dished us all scoops of ice cream and made us sing along to "But You Don't Know Me" with a crooning Elvis Presley on the screen.

Next to me, I could clearly hear the resonant rumble of Gil's baritone, and I realized his sister had been right. He *did* have a good voice.

But that wasn't the only thing sending tingles down my spine or making my arms dimple with goosebumps.

It was the smell of him—so masculine and compellingly musky.

It was his observant blue eyes and the laugh lines crinkling at their edges.

It was his smooth, tanned skin and the muscular form underneath.

It was his lips. I kept catching sight of him licking the bottom one as if trying to get every last drop of that caramel ice cream. This motion literally made my knees weak. I was relieved to be sitting down.

It was his very presence.

"Did I miss some ice cream?" he asked me suddenly, swiping his mouth with the back of his hand.

Oh, busted! He'd caught me staring. "Um…" I gulped. Then, faking a look of scrutiny, I added, "Yeah. Just a tiny bit, but I think you got it all now."

What a liar I am!

Still, it was better than admitting the truth, wasn't it? That I'd been daydreaming about what it would feel like to kiss him.

"Oh, good," Gil said, hopefully oblivious to my fantasies. "Thanks."

When the father character in the film—Duster Heywood, a.k.a., Elvis's movie dad—said something about how the Florida climate sure does "strange things" to people, I almost laughed aloud.

No freakin' kidding.

How convenient to be able to blame my adolescent thoughts on the sun and surf.

By the time Elvis had won both the big boating regatta and the pretty girl he'd been lusting after for an hour and forty minutes, all four of us sitting in Joy's living room had become almost as boneless as a bunch of baby shrimp, sinking deep into our respective cushions and not at all interested in the prospect of moving.

"I don't wanna get up," Abby moaned. "Should I hit replay? The DVD's not that long. We could watch it again."

"Nope," Gil insisted. "I'm going to fall asleep if I keep sitting here."

"And then he'll start snoring," his sister said. "He sounds like guacamole."

She was serious, but the unusualness of the remark—so very *Joy*—had the rest of us bursting with laughter. And, naturally, a number of avocado jokes and wordplays on her synesthesia-like observations followed.

"Y'all better get out of here," she said, giggling, "before I kick your butts out the door." She pitched a throw pillow at her big brother. He caught it and pitched it right back at her. Joy snuggled up with it, resting her head on it like a toddler, ready for naptime.

Abby pushed herself to standing and yawned. Loudly. She padded over to the TV, retrieved her movie, and blew air kisses at us all. "Tomorrow morning's gonna come way too soon. See you three bright and early."

We all said goodnight to her and then, moments later, Gil turned to me. "Did you want to stay longer and pester my sister? Or would you like me to walk you to your car?"

I grinned. "Well, as tempting as it sounds to pick on Joy for another hour—"

My friend raised her head off her pillow, feigned a look of irritation, and said, "Don't you be taking his side, Marianna. I'll retaliate."

"—given her threats, though," I continued, "I'd better go, too."

Gil chuckled. "Wise choice. That girl can be vicious." Then, belying his words, he walked over to his kid sister and pecked her on the top of her head with such gentleness, as if she were a beloved baby bird. "Just let me grab my keys."

I thanked Joy for the wonderful evening, and the younger woman smiled up at me. "It was my pleasure." I didn't doubt the sincerity of her words at all, but I still couldn't help marveling at it. I had really made some new friends. It felt almost magical.

Moments later, Gil and I strode outside, the heat of the Sarasota night held in the air, like an extra ration of warmth being kept in reserve. We were standing next to my car before my body could even adjust to the absence of air conditioning.

Gil licked his bottom lip again, though there wasn't so much as a drop of ice cream left anywhere. I couldn't even pretend to see a speck, so I glanced away to keep myself from staring.

"This is getting to be a habit," he joked, motioning toward the car.

I forced myself to meet his eye. "It is. But thank you. It's really thoughtful of you to make sure I'm safe."

He waved that off as if it were a given. And licked his lip yet again. Damn.

"So—" he began. Then stopped and took a long breath. "As we were watching the movie, it occurred to me that you might not have seen much of the Siesta Key nightlife, being so new to the area and all. Have you, um, heard of the Sunday night drumming at the beach?"

"No."

He explained something about how a bunch of local folks got together each weekend and beat on their drums to an extemporaneous rhythm of their own making, while people of all ages danced on the sand. "It's fun," he assured me.

"Sounds like it," I said, though, to be honest, I was having a hard time imagining myself at an event like that. Seemed a little hippyish.

"So, after the Craft Festival is over tomorrow, would you like to go with me? Usually starts around six o'clock."

"Sure. Are Joy, Abby, or Lorelei planning to come, too?"

He shook his head and, just to torment me, licked both his top and bottom lips. "I don't, um, generally bring my sister on my dates…and definitely not her coworker or her married friend." He grinned, but there was an endearing look of nervous self-consciousness that he seemed unable to hide. "Still want to go, Marianna?"

Then his words sank in. "On a date? With you?" I had to ask, just to make sure I wasn't misinterpreting his question or anything.

"Yeah."

"Well, yes, Gil—of course." And I nodded for emphasis. Then, in a rare bolt of audacity, I even added, "What took you so long to ask?"

He laughed loudly, the tension in the space between us dissolving. "That's what I was hoping you'd say." And then, ever so tenderly, he brought those wet, luscious lips of his down toward my face and brushed my mouth with a light kiss.

A kiss that, after just a few seconds of our lips touching, turned deeper, harder, wilder.

A passionate kiss that promised so much more…

My breath caught at the surprising intensity of it, and the tension between us returned with a heat that spiked like a fever.

Now I was the one trying to mask my own nervous self-consciousness. "Um."

"Goodnight, Marianna," Gil said, taking a deliberate step back from me and toward his own car. "Until tomorrow."

CHAPTER THIRTEEN
Sunday Drumming

Gil jumped out of bed with a spring in his step and a smile on his lips. The Craft Festival was always a good time, but there was something extra special about it this year. And that something special—or, rather, someone special—had a name: Marianna Gregory.

Kissing her last night... *wowza*. He was rendered almost as speechless as his pet newt when he'd pulled away from her. Hadn't managed to say more than a few words afterward. Could barely remember to breathe.

She'd stolen the oxygen from his lungs and his mouth. But he didn't care. As far as he was concerned, she was welcome to do it again. And again.

God help him if his mother found out about her, though. Ma would have their wedding planned before the evening hit.

He sprinkled some amphibian food into Nancy's tank, bid his low-maintenance pet farewell for the day, and found himself actually whistling on his drive to the Circle.

When he got to their tent, Marianna was already there, chatting with his sister in fevered whispers as they readied the tables for another busy day of sales. When they spotted him, though, both women paused abruptly—too abruptly—and grinned at him. Joy's blue eyes danced with mischievous delight. And Marianna's face was a study in shades of pink.

Hmm.

He knew when he was being talked about. Joy was insatiable when it came to ferreting out information, but he hadn't taken Marianna as a kiss-n-tell type.

"Mornin', ladies," he said warily.

"Good morning," they chorused back.

"Lorelei and Abby are on their way," Joy informed him.

"But we've got almost everything ready," Marianna was quick to say. "So, don't worry."

He met her gaze and held it. "I wasn't worried. In fact, I'm pretty sure this is gonna be a fabulous day."

His sister's eyebrows rose with marked interest and Marianna blinked rapidly. "Me, too," she murmured, and Gil had the satisfaction of seeing her blush deepen.

The other two women came in and, as soon as it was humanly possible, he was cornered by his sister, out of earshot from her friends.

"You and Marianna are going on a date tonight!"

He feigned an indifferent shrug. "So?"

"So? How can you be so blasé about it? I could see a change in her aura right away when she came in this morning. And in yours, too, big brother."

"Ah. You're saying you'd guessed about our date from our auras?"

She planted her strong little fists on her hips. "Of course, Gil. I mean, I had to worm the specifics out of her—when you were going out, who asked whom, and so on—but even though Marianna tried to downplay it, I can tell how much she's looking forward to it. So, don't mess this up tonight."

He laughed. If just the date details got his sister this

excited, he knew he could really jolt her circuits with the rest. "She tried to downplay it, huh?"

Joy nodded.

"She didn't mention our mind-blowing kiss, then?"

His sister actually squealed and bounced in place like a baby kangaroo. "You *kissed* her?" Oh, my goodness, Gil. That's so great!"

"All right, well, now you know, So you can stop pestering Marianna for details. Your enthusiasm might scare her off. And, besides, we all know she's leaving in a few weeks. You can't get too attached, okay?"

Joy wrinkled her nose. "But—"

"But nothing. She and I are just going to the beach drumming tonight and talking. It's a date, yes, but it's a really casual one."

"If you say so," Joy said, but with a distinctly disbelieving tone.

Odd thing was, in quieter moments during the day when he was being honest with himself, he didn't exactly believe his statement either. Every time he glanced at Marianna, his heart leaped. Every time they conversed, he began to fantasize about what a longer-term relationship with her might be like. There was a powerful attraction between them for sure, but there was also a growing friendship and respect. The combination was heady, and it left him breathless at the possibilities.

Why the hell couldn't she stay in Sarasota beyond the summer? He'd come here one June day and had stayed for over twenty years. Based on what she'd told him about her life in Illinois, it wasn't as though she had a lot to go back to in Mirabelle Harbor, right?

He shook his head. No. Home was home. And not everyone found it as easy to cut ties with one's past as he did. That would be a lot to ask Marianna. Plus, this was a damned dangerous line of thinking. And here he'd been telling his *sister* not to get too attached.

Joy's good mood, however, couldn't be repressed and not only because he and her new friend had gotten cozier.

Midway through the afternoon, that suit who'd come in yesterday—the one who already purchased about thirty of the B.E.A.D.S. bracelets—returned. This time with a checkbook and a proposition.

"My name is Peter Barrett," the suit said to Joy, handing her an embossed business card that looked expensive even from across the tent. "I work for a company called Naturalacrity. My employer and I were both really impressed with the jewelry samples I brought back yesterday, and we were hoping we might interest you in a private art event next month. We would, of course, pay for the cost of your materials and the time you and your staff would spend working on the additional bracelets—"

Joy shot Marianna, Lorelei, and Abby an amused grin. Her "staff" consisted of just this small group of ladies, but that Peter dude didn't seem to know that.

"And, naturally," Peter continued, "we would also include one of your business cards with each bracelet and make a sizeable corporate donation to the Florida endangered species fund of your choice." He flashed a check at Joy that had her eyes widening like the many zeroes that followed the number one on that thin strip of paper. "We feel confident that the attendees at our Art Gala will appreciate these hand-crafted pieces as much as we do. We'd like to provide each attendee with one bracelet in their gift baskets, along with a few other delights."

His sister thanked the man, clearly warming to him like an open flower to the sunlight. "Oh, that's... that's just wonderful," she gushed, beaming at the guy. "How many attendees are you expecting?"

Peter Barrett straightened his suit jacket and smiled at her in a way that brought out Gil's protective brotherly instincts. "About two thousand."

Joy gaped at Peter. Then, his sweet kid sister who

almost never swore, whispered, "Holy shit."

❀✸❀

If Saturday at the Craft Festival had been a whirlwind, Sunday was a veritable hurricane. Especially after that handsome businessman came back and made Joy an offer her animal-loving heart couldn't refuse.

"I—I need to check with my staff," Joy had stuttered. "Gil, can you, um—" She glanced frantically at her brother, who just nodded coolly before directing Peter Barrett's attention to the other items in the tent. Meanwhile, Joy motioned for Abby, Lorelei, and me to go outside of the tent with her. We formed a huddle and discussed this surprise proposal.

"We can do it," Abby declared.

"With at least four weeks to work on it," added Lorelei, "we'll get it done on time."

"And I'll help, too," I heard myself volunteer.

Joy sent each of us a very grateful look. "The donation alone—" she whispered.

"I know, sweetie," Lorelei said. "We can't turn this opportunity down."

And so it was agreed that we'd accept Peter's offer and commit to his company's private gala. As he and Joy hashed out the details and the paperwork on one side of the tent, I had a chance to reflect on what I was getting myself into… and why.

Although I believed in the endangered species cause, I'd be lying to myself if I gave that as my sole reason for jumping into this new project. I wanted to help Joy and my other new friends, of course. I wanted to keep doing what we'd been doing these past few days. But, most of all, I wanted to stay in this wonderful cocoon of kindness and warmth for as long as possible. The Art Gala was scheduled for late July. Just a few days later, I'd need to check out of Ellen's bungalow and head home.

Gil caught me frowning. He walked over and whispered, "Is everything okay?"

I shrugged and stole a glance at Joy and Peter, their fair heads bowed together over the legalese of the contract documents. Her radiant happiness almost brought a tear to my eye.

Gil's gaze followed mine over to his sister. "Hey, are you having seconds thoughts about agreeing to this project? The work involved will take up most of your vacation and—"

I shook my head, cutting him off. "Actually, I'm thrilled to be able to help your sister and excited to have a part-time job for a month. It's just that it reminded me that I don't have one to go back to."

"Ah." He paused. "Is the end of July a firm deadline, or might there be some leeway in when you have to leave?"

"My sister's bungalow is rented out for August, so I do have to move out by then. And most of my things are in a big storage unit in Mirabelle Harbor. I might be able to keep them in there for a few more weeks, but not indefinitely."

"Ah," he said again, but nothing else followed. His attention had returned to his sister and the business guy, who looked more than half infatuated with Joy already. Not surprising, of course. She was adorable. But Gil didn't seem too pleased with Peter's overt interest.

"I'm always happy for her when her artistic talent is recognized and supported," he murmured to me. "But this dude seems a little too good to be true. Not sure I trust him."

"Shouldn't you warn Joy, in that case?"

He chuckled softly. "If I say anything to her, she'll prattle on about his warm aura or the colors of his voice and tell me to mind my own business." Gil paused. "So, no.

I'll just have to investigate him behind her back."

I shot him a surprised look. "Really?"

He nodded. "Really."

Gil and I didn't have a chance to talk privately again until well after the Craft Festival had ended. We had last-minute customers to attend to, supplies to take back to Castaways and The Beaded Periwinkle, and the tent to pull apart and pack away.

Joy, who seemed to be running on green tea and elation, said, "What an incredible day, y'all. We'd better relax and get some sleep tonight, though, because staring tomorrow, we've got two thousand bracelets to make!"

Nevertheless, she glanced between me and her brother and broke into a grin that rivaled the sunrise over the Gulf. Out of Lorelei's and Abby's earshot, she added, just to Gil and me, "Have fun tonight, you two. Stay strawberry." Then she flitted away like a water sprite.

Gil and I exchanged a look.

"One of her synesthesia expressions?" I asked.

He laughed and motioned for me to follow him. "Not exactly. Or at least not entirely. My sister always considered fresh strawberries to be one of the best desserts around. They mean pure sweetness to her. So, she was essentially telling us to 'stay sweet.' Not sure how much that's synesthesia or just the uniqueness of Joy."

We walked to where our vehicles were parked, and he instructed me to follow his car to the lot a few miles down the beach, nearest to where the drumming would be taking place.

"The community drum circle isn't too far from where you're staying on Siesta Key," he said. "Every Sunday, about an hour or two before sunset, a group gathers at Siesta Public Beach. It's definitely something worth experiencing at least once while you're here."

And, so, after we'd parked in that public lot, we wandered down to the beach where, already, a crowd had formed. A dozen people had percussion instruments with them—from big bongo drums to small tom-toms, from cymbals and tambourines to wood blocks, claves, shakers, and guiros. And many of the people playing or just attending had formed a large circle on the sand, expansive enough for participants of all ages to dance in the middle.

All along the shore, there were residents and tourists alike enjoying the rhythm of the twilight, as the bright Floridian sun sank gracefully toward the calm waters of the Gulf.

I was mesmerized by the celebratory atmosphere. No national holiday or special occasion needed—just a group of individuals united in their desire to express a beat that was at one with the waves lapping against the shore. At one with our hearts pumping blood through our veins. At one with both the music of the heavens and the pulse of the tiniest sea creature. For a moment, the gargantuan and the infinitesimal stepped in time to the same syncopation and carried me along with their shared rhythm.

"Wanna dance in the middle of the circle?" Gil asked, pointing toward the deeply tanned woman in shimmering belly dancing gear who was currently inhabiting that sacred space.

I shook my head and smiled. "I'm happy right here."

He turned me to face him, held my gaze for a long moment, and then began dancing in place, right in front of me. Silently inviting me into his private circle.

The beat—already a part of me now—flowed through me as I joined him. No fancy footwork or glitzy moves between us, just the kind of dance where our bodies knew instinctively how to flow and sway to the music.

And then, even as the rhythm persisted, Gil stopped, put his arms around me, and brought his lips down to meet mine. The sun slanted beams of orange and gold across the water in its final ray burst before disappearing behind the veil of waves. But I was too lost in sensation to mind the coming darkness. I was—after all—floating above the sand and sea on a virtual wave of exhilaration and infatuation.

When Gil and I finally pulled apart, he swallowed and reached for my hand, his gaze turning again toward the Gulf as we both tried to catch our breath and process this attraction between us.

In broken whispers, he spoke of coming to this beach to get quiet. To breathe in and out with the tide. To center himself when life seemed uncertain.

"I can always count on the water to restore my equilibrium," he said. "We live in a world that's determined to derail our inner sense of balance. I think we need a place where we can go to reclaim it."

"I love the sea, the waves, the shells on the shore, the warm white sand, the breathtaking shades of blue," I told him. "But I'm not sure they can fix within me all of the places where my life went off kilter."

He moved to stand behind me, wrapping his arms around my shoulders, warming me with the heat of his torso, and letting me lean back against his chest.

"It's not that the sand and sun can fix it, Marianna. It's more like you're able to put whatever's been unsettling you into better perspective. You find elements of the natural world that hold meaning for you, and you can cling to the reality of them. It's paradoxical, really, that a place so transitory—with shifting sands and tides—can be so grounding and stable."

"Has it helped you?" I managed to ask, despite being so turned on by having the full length of his body right behind mine. When I leaned back too quickly, too suddenly, and caught him unaware, I could feel the ridge of his erection against my hip. He'd always pull his lower body away again, but his arousal was nothing short of thrilling to me. "Has it made it easier for you to keep things with your dad in perspective?"

I felt him stiffen at once (and not in that fun, sexual

way). "Joy told you about him, huh?"

"Sorry, Gil. I shouldn't have brought it up, but—"

"It's okay," he said. "Truth is, just because I know what to do to be all Zen-like and calm, doesn't mean I always follow through myself. Relationships with real, live people are complicated."

I thought of my ex-husband, my daughter, my sister. "No kidding."

He laughed lightly, his breath tickling my ear. "I'm not trying to distract you or change the subject when I say this, Marianna, but talk of my father can't hold my interest alongside these fantasies I'm having about you… " He held me closer to him and, this time, didn't pull back when my body made contact with his erection. "You must've guessed that already."

There was no way I could have expressed to him just how gratifying his words and his body's natural reaction were to me. After years of feeling unattractive and nearly invisible in the eyes of my ex, to inspire fantasies in a man like Gil rendered me momentarily mute. The physical chemistry we shared was tangible, but my interest in him went beyond his beautiful body.

I'd spent several long days with the man, and I was drawn to Gil's mind as well. To his kindness toward others and to me. To his creativity and artistic talent. Perhaps, our connection had happened too fast to be labeled anything but an infatuation on either side, but I knew more than just lust or an immature crush was at play here—at least for me. All of his wonderful qualities contributed to why I decided to say what I did next.

"Would you like to come to the bungalow?" I blurted. "I have a bottle of wine and a few pieces of fudge." I swallowed. "It's nothing much, really, and I'm not trying to proposition you or anything, but I just thought, maybe—"

I stopped. He was gazing at me strangely, an odd gleam in his clear blue eyes and a growing smile on those warm lips of his.

"What?" I asked.

He leaned in close and then kissed me so gently and, then, so deeply again—even more passionately than our first kiss and so much like a "get a room" kind of lip lock— that I forgot what I'd even asked him. At least until he whispered, "I can only hope that, one of these days, I'll be so lucky as to have you proposition me, Marianna. But, for now, I'm just excited about the wine and the fudge and this conversation with you lasting for a while longer."

"Mmm," I murmured, the delicious taste of him still lingering on my lips. "We can do more of *this*, too, you know?"

"Hey, I don't need any further convincing." He took my hand and led me across the sandy beach to the parking lot and followed my car to the Siesta Sunset complex. I'd never been so glad to be there.

A soft glow emanated from all of the bungalows, giving them a homey warmth. In my imagination, I'd progressed several steps ahead of where we were in time and place. I was already cozying up on the floral sofa with Gil, wine glasses in hand initially, and then carefully set aside on the coffee table, so our fingers could be free to stroke and caress. We would soon sink deeper into the sofa's cushions and begin making out like teens. First base. Second base. Maybe third? I could see it all in my mind's eye. I could nearly feel it happening.

But one of the advantages of not being an adolescent anymore was that I knew a good thing when I saw one. And Gil was a good, good thing.

It wasn't until I'd inserted the key into the door to #26 and twisted it in the lock, that a disturbing thought occurred to me: Why was there a glow coming from my sister's bungalow? Did I forget to flick off the light switch when I left for the Craft Festival this morning?

Gil was right beside me, his arm slung gently around

my shoulders as I pushed open the front door.

"Hi, Sis," Ellen said from the middle of the floral sofa. She smiled one of her triumphant grins at me and then shot a curious glance at Gil. "Who's he?"

CHAPTER FOURTEEN
Two Ships That Pass in the Night

Ellen had never been afraid of making a dramatic entrance but, honestly, this time she'd actually been aiming for low key. From the shocked expression on Marianna's face, though, it looked like she screwed up big time. Seemed she may have overestimated her sister's ability to roll with a slight change of plans.

And then there was the super studly man with his arm draped around her sister. What the hell had she walked into tonight?

Ellen stood up, put her hands on her hips, and leveled her most commanding stare at the Stud Muffin.

Marianna, whose mouth had dropped open like a fish when she'd walked in a moment ago, managed to find her voice. "Ellen, um, wow. What a surprise to see you." Then her sister glanced over at the hottie who was calmly taking in his surroundings. "This is my sister, Ellen Slater," she told the guy. "She's the one who owns the bungalow."

He nodded pleasantly. He had a kindhearted look in his eyes and seemed protective of Marianna. Ellen liked that about him even before she knew his name, but she wasn't sure she liked that Marianna was involving herself with some unknown beachcomber type. Her baby sister had never been a great judge of men.

"And this is Gil Canton, a new friend of mine," Marianna continued.

"Nice to meet you, Ellen," the guy said to her, offering his hand.

She stepped forward and shook it. A good firm grip. Strong and sure. Well, that was something. At least her sis hadn't been hanging out with another weenie like Donny this time around.

"So, w-what brings you d-down to Florida?" Marianna stuttered, her voice sounding a bit breathless.

"To see you, of course," she shot back. "And there are a few other reasons," she added quickly. "It was a last-minute trip. I'll explain later."

"Sure," Marianna said, but there was a brittleness to her tone that Ellen couldn't help but detect.

Huh. Okay, so she was pissed. Well, Marianna would have known all about the visit if she hadn't been so dismissive on the phone. Serves her right.

Mr. Tall and Suntanned, apparently sensing that three people might just be a crowd, gave Marianna's shoulder a quick squeeze and then said, "I don't want to interrupt a sister reunion." He looked her sister in the eye. "Thanks for the fun beach visit and for all of your hard work at the Craft Festival this weekend."

"I *loved* it," Marianna said with feeling.

Ellen raised her eyebrows at this. The Craft Festival? What was Marianna doing there?

"With your sister here now," Gil continued, "you'll probably want to spend some time together this week. If you can't come into the Circle tomorrow, I can tell Joy—"

"No," Marianna all but shouted. "I promised I'd help with the bracelets, and I'll be there as planned." Then she rose up on her toes and kissed her Floridian hottie on the cheek. "Thanks for everything, Gil. I'll see you in the morning."

"Okay," he said to her, grinning as if he was half undressing Marianna in the doorway. What the hell?

He turned to Ellen and added, "I hope you'll enjoy your visit to Sarasota. You have such a wonderful sister but, then, I'm sure you already know that." He was smiling as he spoke, but Ellen couldn't mistake the steeliness beneath his tone. It was as if he were actually issuing her a warning: *Be nice to Marianna, or else.*

Who the fuck was this guy?

"Yep," Ellen said. "I know. Thank you, Gil, and good night." Then, because two could play that game, she sent him a steady look that was in no way casual or sweet. It, too, held a warning: *If you hurt my sister, I'll crush your bones.*

He nodded slowly. Message received.

Then he disappeared into the night.

Ellen crossed her arms and tapped her toes as Marianna watched Gil leave. Once her sister had closed the door, though, Ellen let out a soft whistle. "No wonder you've been so secretive lately. Hoping to get lucky with a hot local?"

Marianna's polite veneer slipped and her eyes flashed with golden fury. Oooh. Maybe she really *had* interrupted a rendezvous between her sister and the Stud Muffin. For a moment, Ellen was actually impressed. She didn't know Marianna had it in her.

"You said you'd explain why you were really here," Marianna began. "I know it wasn't actually to spend time with me, or you would have told me you were coming." She exhaled, like it was taking all of her energy not to implode. "This is, of course, your bungalow, so you're entitled to come down whenever you want, but why now?"

Ellen debated how much to tell her. Her sister had that deep worry gene that would likely kick in at the slightest mention of the truth. It was probably best to delay sharing the actual reason.

She shrugged. "I had a bunch of vacation days. Figured I'd better use some of them."

Marianna narrowed her eyes. "Everything going okay at the firm?"

"What do you mean?"

"You know—with your colleagues and partners?"

"They're fine."

"No... other problems? With clients or anything?"

"Of course not. I rock at my job."

"Naturally," Marianna said coolly, resentment spilling off her in waves. "So you were—what? Just bored at home and figured it might be fun to crash a party, but you couldn't find one in Connecticut, so you thought, 'Oh, my dumb little sister won't be doing anything... '"

Ellen had damn well had enough of this inquisition shit, not to mention her sister's insecurities. "I told Jared that this was a sucky idea," she murmured. She snatched her purse, stepped back into her sandals, and reached for the handle of her carry-on bag. "Never mind. I'll stay at a hotel."

"Oh, for God's sake, Ellen, don't be so dramatic. This is *your* place. You can't stay at a hotel. If anyone should leave, it should be me."

Ellen rolled her eyes. "Who's the one being dramatic now? We both know you can't afford to do that. Besides, I promised you this bungalow for the summer, and I'd never go back on my word. Sorry I sprung an unexpected visit on you. I didn't think you'd get so bent out of shape. I just wanted to, uh... see how you were doing."

"You mean you wanted to check up on me."

"And a good thing, too, or you would've been humping that hot smoldering guy before the night was out," she joked. "Did you notice he has kind of an Elvis look?"

Marianna didn't laugh. She didn't even crack a smile. She just clenched her fists, the same exact way she used to

151

do when she was a toddler. Ellen half expected her to emit that same angry, low-pitched squeal she remembered from their childhood.

"And so what?" Marianna asked, suddenly erupting. "I wasn't going to sleep with him tonight, but what if we did at some point? Seriously, Ellen, what business would that have been of yours? Huh? You already have *everything*. The perfect job. The perfect husband. The perfect house. The perfect life. My life is in shambles and you show up here to… to… do what? To lord your superiority over me again? To judge me for all my mistakes, real and perceived? To prevent me from relaxing, even for a few weeks? And to keep me from getting to know people who aren't constantly holding my past against me? Dammit. Don't you *ever* get tired of proving you're better than me?"

Ellen set down her purse, kicked her sandals off again, and sat back down on the sofa. She exhaled and inhaled half a dozen times before replying, surprised by how much those accusations hurt. "How long have you been keeping that tirade inside you, Sis?" she whispered. "Ten years? Twenty? All your life?"

Tears clung to Marianna's eyelashes, and Ellen could see her trembling. Sure, she'd known her sister's list of grievances against her was long, but it was the intensity of her anger that took Ellen by surprise. Marianna wasn't mildly pissed off at her, in that usual sibling way. Tonight, she was livid with rage.

In answer to Ellen's question, her sister just shrugged and turned away. "Sorry I snapped," she said, bolting toward the hallway. "I'll go make up the second bedroom for you… or for me, if you'd rather sleep in the master." Marianna took several more steps in the direction of the bedrooms.

"Please stop."

Her sister stopped and turned to face her, but very slowly.

Ellen took another deep breath. "I didn't come here to judge you or check up on you or in any way make your life miserable, okay? I came because—" She paused. "I was kinda banished here."

Her sister's eyes widened in alarm. "Are things with Jared—"

"Oh, yeah… no. It's not him. Jared and I are fine. What I mean is that I'm having these, um, odd health issues. And my doctor, my husband, and my partners in the firm all thought I needed to 'relax' somewhere." She grimaced. "So, actually, my *perfect* life isn't so perfect at the moment."

Marianna finally dropped her sullen stare and looked genuinely concerned. "What kind of health issues?"

Much as she didn't want to go into details, Ellen told her briefly about the panic attacks and a few of the symptoms she'd been experiencing whenever she'd have an episode.

"Problem is, I still don't know the triggers," Ellen admitted. "Maybe it's work. Maybe it's my lifestyle. Maybe it's me. But it's been confusing as hell. Only thing I know for sure is that I have some sort of problem. Dammed if I know *why*, though."

"I can see how that would be frightening for you," Marianna whispered. "You should stay here at the bungalow. Okay?"

Ellen nodded. "Just until I get my shit straightened out. But it shouldn't take more than a few days or a week at most, right?"

Her sister eyed her doubtfully.

"Well, anyway, we can coexist peacefully for that long, can't we, Sis?"

Marianna didn't look any less doubtful, but she finally cracked a tiny smile. "To tell you the truth, Ellen, I have no idea… but I hope so."

I shouldn't have been so stunned that my sister barged into the bungalow unannounced and invaded all of Siesta Key with her big personality. That was just Ellen's way.

What surprised me, though, was that—after my outburst the night of her arrival—she gave me a lot more space than usual. I had a work schedule set up with Joy and the gang, and once I'd basically explained to her about the B.E.A.D.S. project, she seemed to accept that I had a role to play somewhere other than Bungalow #26.

And for her part? Well, Ellen was a natural and instinctive leader. She could create order out of chaos simply by standing in a doorway and looking irritated and imposing. Everyone in the room would straighten up and fall into line, like the Von Trapp family children from *The Sound of Music* whenever their stern father, the Captain, walked in.

I wasn't entirely sure what Ellen did while I was at The Beaded Periwinkle making jewelry, but I knew she'd quickly become recognized by the other Siesta Sunset visitors. She inhabited the shuffleboard deck by the outdoor pool and lounge as if she'd built that area herself. I heard from Mr. Niihau that she'd reconnected with a handful of year-round residents who owned their own bungalows in the complex. And I watched her return from vigorous walks along the beach, no doubt frightening any wayward toddlers into submission with her commanding gaze. That formidable presence was my sister's superpower.

She wasn't one to "relax" on cue, though. I caught her sneaking in calls and texts to work a few times, and then telling her concerned husband white lies about how she was "totally taking it easy."

But, thankfully, between Ellen's domain in and around the bungalow and my long daily hours in St. Armand's

Circle with my new friends, my sister and I managed to establish a very hands-off, separate-but-equal routine. We chatted for a half hour every morning over breakfast cereal and, again, in the heart of the evening, after I'd return and collapse onto the sofa next to her, we'd talk for another hour or so, as she flipped through whatever reality TV shows were airing on the networks. We were very much like the proverbial ships that passed each other in the night. And I, for one, preferred it that way.

Gil, too, seemed to sense that I needed a bit of space, although much less in his case. Still, he waited a full week before he officially asked me out again.

We were taking a pizza lunch break from the bracelet making the following Saturday when Gil meandered into his sister's shop and began chitchatting with all of us. He and I had gotten to have several private conversations since Sunday night's beach drumming, but they were relatively short. I knew I wanted to spend a lot more time with him and couldn't keep myself from watching him whenever we were in a room together. I caught him staring at me more than once, too. And smiling.

Today, I detected a purpose in the way he was directing the conversation in the shop. Trying to get at the details of everyone's evening plans.

Lorelei had a family dinner with her husband and two sons—a birthday celebration for one of her boys.

Joy was getting in a delivery of more beads and having a meeting with Peter Barrett about the upcoming Art Gala.

Abby had been invited to be Joy's sidekick for this meeting with Peter, but she could only stay for the first hour or so.

"I have a seven thirty date with Lee, the head chef at the Imperial Mandarin," Abby said.

Gil raised his eyebrows at that.

"Don't judge," Abby told him. "You should see what that guy can do with a pair of chopsticks."

"I'm pretty sure I don't want to know," Gil said with a laugh. "But I thought you were dating Nick's friend, Josh. What happened?"

Abby shrugged. "Josh is a regular customer at The Golden Gecko," she explained to me. "And Nick promised he'd kick Josh's ass if he didn't act like a gentleman. Let's just say, I expect Josh to have a few new bruises this week."

"Ooh, boy. Sorry to hear that," Gil said, his jaw tensing. "He didn't try to push you into—"

"No, no," Abby assured him. "He was just a little too grabby. I could've taken him."

"Well, if you're looking for truly gentle soul, just say the word and I'll set you up with Carter." He thumbed in the direction of Castaways next door. "You just need to be open to the idea of a younger man… "

Abby blushed. "Younger by a year or two, maybe, Gil. But I must be seven or eight years older than sweet Carter. I think of him too much like a little brother."

"It would crush his tender heart if he knew that," Gil teased. "But if you ever change your mind, let me know." Then he turned to me. "Plans with your sister tonight, Marianna?"

I shook my head. Joy, Lorelei, and Abby all knew that Ellen had come to town, but I didn't dwell on how unenthusiastic I was about being alone with her for any long stretches of time. Gil, however, had seen Ellen and me together. I knew he'd immediately recognized the tension between us.

"There are a few nice beaches nearby that you might want to see," he suggested. "Both Sanibel Island and Venice Beach are really pretty and worth a peek, if you haven't been there yet."

I admitted I hadn't been to either.

"Well, clearly, all this work you've been doing at the hands of my slave-driver sister has cut into your Florida sightseeing time. Let me know later if you'd like to trek out to one or both soon. I can drive you."

"Hey!" Joy said, lightly slugging her brother. "Don't talk smack about me, mister." But then she turned to me and I couldn't miss the speculative twinkle in her eyes. "Maybe you should let this big know-it-all drive you to a few places in the area. Sarasota is beautiful, but there are a lot of lovely spots along the Gulf."

The way the Canton siblings were talking made it sound like Gil was simply offering to cart me around to a few nearby towns, the same way he might take a pal grocery shopping or his mother on an errand run. But Lorelei and Abby weren't buying the act. I couldn't miss Lorelei's amused laugh or Abby's quick wink in my direction.

And, the first opportunity I had to be alone with Gil, I decided not to play coy. I let him know that a visit to any beach he suggested would be fun for me. And that I was free that night.

So when we finally knocked off for the day a few hours later, Gil said, "Leave your car here and let me drive. Sanibel Island is a bit of a hike for tonight, but we should get an early start sometime soon and go there." He pulled out his phone and Googled a map of the area. "I'll take you to Venice Beach right now, though," he said, pointing to the spot just a bit south of us. "It's only about forty minutes away. We can grab some dinner there or pick up carryout afterwards and, maybe, take it back to my place."

I was insanely tempted to say, "Let's skip the beach *and* the food and just go directly to your place... " But I refrained. Ellen's comment about me "humping the hot smoldering guy" still rang uncomfortably in my ears. And, besides, Gil and I had lost a bit of romantic momentum after the interruptions of the week. Maybe he wouldn't be quite as interested in picking up where we'd left off.

Before we left St. Armand's Circle, Gil took me on a

quick spin past nearby Lido Beach, and then we hit the road for Venice.

I'd never been to the famed Italian city or even the popular Southern California one, so this was my first Venetian adventure. Like Lido Beach and Siesta Key, the shores of Venice, Florida were stunning and the water was an almost surrealistic blue.

"I'll never get over that color," I told him as we strolled along the shore, barefoot, jumping back and laughing whenever the surf would roll in too close to our feet.

"Have you had a chance to practice those deep breathing techniques lately?"

"With my sister and I sharing a bungalow, anything that invites calm is welcome," I confessed. "But I probably need more than one lesson to master it."

Gil snorted. "You and I both need more than one *lifetime*. Most people would, Marianna. But it's worth practicing, even for those of us who are nowhere near the mastery level yet."

So, for a half hour at least, we breathed in and out with the tide, sharing little stories about our siblings in between our dance with the waves. It was so easy to talk with him. Effortless, really. Like we'd known each other for years and not merely weeks.

After this, we stopped by a little seafood shack a few blocks from the coast—a spot Gil apparently knew well—and picked up a bag of fresh scallops and another bag of raw shrimp.

"I'll cook these up for us with some veggies and butter," he promised, making the return to his place all the more tantalizing.

Gil's place, incidentally, was a newly built and well-constructed brick townhouse in the heart of Sarasota. The inside was tastefully furnished—uncluttered, clear lines, nicely appointed wood furniture—but the artwork hanging on the walls gave his home true character.

"I know some of these are your creations," I said, pointing to a couple of canvases that were marked with Gil's distinctive color combinations and brushstrokes. The way he painted was as unique as his fingerprints. "But some aren't."

He nodded as he moved to the kitchen and began grabbing pans and oils and veggies and spices. My mouth was already watering before he even pulled the scallops and shrimp out of their respective bags.

"I've been influenced by many different artists. Salvadore Dali, of course, but also far less famous visionaries." He paused. "There's a local cartoonist who's been working the shopping areas for years, and I just loved the caricature he did of Joy and me."

My gaze followed his to the framed pencil sketch on the far left kitchen wall.

"And then there's that Lithuanian mask maker." He pointed toward a carved wooden mask hanging all the way across the room in his den.

"And this?" I asked, motioning toward a drum-like object we'd passed in the hallway en route to the kitchen.

"That's a *doumbek*—a Middle Eastern clay hand drum that I got on a trip to New York about ten years ago."

"Ever bring it to the beach drumming on Sundays?"

He laughed as he tossed a few handfuls of scallops into a sizzling skillet. "I probably should have, but no. I've never been gutsy enough to bring a percussion instrument and actually play it there. Can't think of what kept me from it, though."

For me, the answer would have been easy—I was simply too self-conscious. But I hadn't gotten that impression for Gil. At least not with the confident way he came across in public. It didn't strike me as plausible that there was anything he wasn't gutsy enough to do. But I should know better than most how easy it was to put on a mask.

Tonight, though, I felt I needed to somehow project real gutsiness, even if I rarely ever felt that way. Tonight, I wanted to prove—if only to myself—that I was no longer that wimpy divorced woman who'd arrived in Florida so wearily just a few weeks ago.

I watched in awe and appreciation as Gil prepared dinner for us.

And then we ate. Buttery deliciousness. The plump scallops and succulent shrimp were perfectly cooked, and the vegetables added a crunchy lightness to an already fairly healthy meal. But, good as it all was, it wasn't nearly as good as my memory of Gil's lips on mine. I wanted more of *that*.

So, when Gil asked what I'd like for dessert—fresh fruit, ice cream, or both—I decided it was high time to put boldness into action.

"Option D," I proclaimed. "It's not on the list, but I'd rather have a kiss from you." I feigned a heavy sigh and hoped he wouldn't be able to hear the crazy thumping of my heart. "I've been feeling deprived since last Sunday, and I'd like to pick up where we left off."

Whether or not I'd fooled him into thinking I was being genuinely gutsy, it didn't matter. He grinned at me with a devilish twist of his lips. "We do have some unfinished kissing time from last weekend. But, if we pick up where we left off, my body will betray my desires again." He was still smiling, but his look turned more serious when he added, "Just know that the fact that I want you doesn't constitute *any* pressure to go further than you want to go or feel comfortable with tonight, okay?"

He was being entirely sincere, and I appreciated that more than I was willing to admit. His respectfulness gave me an extra burst of courage. Enough so that I added, "That is a really thoughtful disclaimer, Gil. Now, please, *please* kiss me."

He immediately rose from the table and held out his

hand.

I took it and he led me to the sofa in his den, passing a pet tank on the way with a little black creature in it.

"We can do formal introductions later," he said, tugging me deeper into the room. "But for now, I'll just tell you that this is my newt Nancy. She and I have been living together for three years. My longest relationship to date."

"Then Nancy knows a good man when she sees one," I said.

"Oh, you sweet talker. Let me taste those words." He put his mouth on mine and, suddenly, I wouldn't have been able to speak a complete sentence if my entire future depended on it.

He nudged me toward his sofa, which was made of a soft brown leather. "Imagine being seventeen and making out on your parents' couch," he joked as he pulled me onto the cushions.

But I didn't have to imagine that. I'd lived it... and lived to regret it.

Thoughts of Donny were, of course, an instant mood killer, so I pressed for an immediate change of subject.

"I'm not one of those women who misses adolescence, Gil. I lived with someone who was very juvenile for a long time. Now, I'd like to be with a *man*, not a boy." I paused. "And you're that man."

It was impossible to see much of a blush under Gil's deep tan, but I still detected a hint of rising color. "That's flattering to hear," he whispered, "but it's also a pretty big leap of faith. I'm not known for my commitment readiness, you know. What if I disappoint you?"

I chuckled as I tugged his body closer to mine. Close enough so he was half on top of me. So I could feel his belt buckle against my abdomen, the weight of his chest on mine, the ridge of his erection at the apex of my legs. God, it had been *so* long. I let my hips rise to meet his. Scandalous behavior, my mother would have said, had she been around to judge me on this. And my sister, of course, would have been full of her usual criticisms and sarcastic commentary. But, dammit, for once I didn't care.

This was *Gil*. And I'd witnessed enough bad male behavior up close and personal to recognize its opposite.

"You won't disappoint me," I assured him. "And I know this probably isn't true of every woman you've ever met, but I'm not looking for a commitment right now. Truly. I just want to explore this connection we share. I want to spend these next few weeks with someone I really like... *you*."

I heard him exhale, heavily, almost like a moan, before he started to systematically press every square inch of his body against mine, as if stamping me. Limb to limb. Mouth to mouth. Hip to hip. We moved together as if we had but one skin.

And one moment flowed so naturally, so effortlessly into the next that there was no sense of struggle or second guessing. Our kisses not only connected our bodies, but it synched our breathing and, possibly, even our pulse. So, later, after we'd been making out for what felt like hours, and after all of me had come to be tuned in to all of him, the next step seemed not only natural but inevitable.

Gil removed his jeans, pulled out a condom, and looked at me in question.

I nodded. "Oh, yes," I murmured.

Then, when he slid it on, helped me get rid of my shorts, and thrust himself deep inside me, I said those same words again—only much louder. And all I could think was that this was how it always should have been. That, thank goodness, I'd lived long enough to finally get *something* right in the relationship world.

Sure, there was a soft voice crying within me, who remained sad that I'd wasted my youth on someone like Donny. Resentful of the innocence I'd traded for a man who'd betrayed me. But I was also grateful that I'd gotten to experience the difference now. Being with someone like Gil, who was as warm and passionate and generous in his lovemaking as he was in his life, was significant for me.

And while I hoped he and I would get a few more nights like this one before I had to head back to Mirabelle Harbor, I knew I'd always be incredibly thankful that his fiery touch wiped away the memory of Donny's indifferent one—at least for tonight.

"It's been a long time for me," Gil whispered sometime later, covering both of our half-naked bodies with a cream-colored throw blanket that had been draped over one arm of the sofa.

"Longer than three and a half years?" I asked.

He winced and hugged me tighter. "No, not quite that long. But it wasn't just a couple of weeks ago, either. It's been a few months since I was even dating anyone and… well, more than a year since I was with a woman who made me want to cook her dinner or stay up half the night talking and kissing and—"

"Wait. You mean I'm not the only woman you ever wanted to cook dinner for? And here I thought I was special." I kissed the tip of his nose and winked at him.

He laughed. "Believe me, Marianna, you're plenty special. You are, in fact, a far more unusual woman in my life than you could begin to guess." He reached to brush the hair from my eyes, his hips angling toward me. It'd been less than an hour since our first time together, but I could feel the stirrings of his arousal again.

Practicing boldness, I decided, had its advantages. It got easier to be gutsy with a little experience. "I want to hear about all the ways you think I'm an unusual addition to your life, Gil." I paused for dramatic effect, running my fingertips up the backside of his thigh until I felt him quiver beneath my touch. "Or you can just expound upon a few of my better qualities through nonverbal language."

"I'm more of a show rather than tell kind of guy," he

divulged in a low, sexy tone.

"Then by all means, feel free to start showing… "

I wouldn't have thought it possible, but making love with Gil was even better the second time around.

It was well after one a.m. when he drove me back to my car.

"You know you can stay with me tonight," he'd said. "Nancy won't mind."

I was tempted. "Your newt may not have a problem with it—or, maybe, she just wouldn't tell us—but Ellen might worry if I didn't come back to the bungalow. Plus, I could use a toothbrush and a change of clothes before showing up at your sister's shop tomorrow morning." I glanced at my watch. "Or, rather, today. In about eight hours, actually."

"Joy's making you work on a Sunday morning?"

I nodded. "And she'd probably be suspicious if I came back in the same outfit I was wearing all day Saturday."

He chuckled. "Trust me, Marianna, she's gonna be suspicious anyway. The girl can sense things like a gypsy woman, I'm telling you. Hope you won't mind being at the center of a good-natured inquisition."

I shook my head. "I know your sister's heart is in the right place. And, whether she asks me directly or just guesses, I'm not hiding from her how much I like you, Gil."

He gave me a long, lingering kiss by my car. "She definitely knows I like *you*. But Joy can be dangerous with too much information. I give you permission to downplay tonight's events with her, or she'll likely have us engaged and planning a fall wedding before you can say, 'Here comes the bride… '"

We both laughed at that. Then with a final peck on my forehead, he tucked me into my car and I drove dreamily back to the bungalow.

The lights were off at #26, so I carefully slid my key

into the door lock and let myself in. I'd taken only two steps when I heard my sister's angry voice cutting into the darkness.

"Where the hell have you been?" she demanded. "It's 1:42 a.m., Marianna. I was worried you were dead or abducted or some bad shit like that."

"I just had a date," I said, feeling my defensiveness rising. "And, for the record, Ellen, you're not my mother or my court-appointed parole officer—not that I have one of those. I don't have to let you know every place I'm going or every person I'm seeing."

"Ah. Screwing Elvis, were you?"

My brain flashed red and my temper snapped like a Chinese firecracker. "For heaven's sake, can't you just shut up and mind your own damn business for a change?" I heard myself shout. My eyes, having begun to adjust to the dark, could see Ellen's outline on the floral sofa, curled into an angry ball and clutching a pillow like she was trying to strangle it.

When I'd left Gil in the parking lot, I didn't think anything could dampen my mood. Clearly, I hadn't counted on my bossy sister waiting up to badger me.

"I texted you *four* times," she shouted back.

I grimaced. I'd muted my cell phone earlier in the day and hadn't remembered to undo that. "You know I don't have that thing glued to my hands, like *some* people."

But she wasn't distracted by my not-so-subtle insinuation that *she* was one of those people.

"If I knew anything about these new 'friends' you've been hanging around with every fucking minute, maybe I wouldn't have been so scared out of my mind about your safety. But I only met your hot beachcomber once, and you won't tell me hardly any details about him or these hipster jewelry makers you're supposedly 'working' with. It could be a cult, for all I know. But you don't care about what anyone who knows you and loves you thinks anymore, do you? I mean, what would things be like for Kathryn if something bad had happened to you? Did you even think about her while you were out running around tonight with that stranger?"

"Gil's not a stranger." *Certainly not anymore.* "And don't you dare try to guilt trip me. I've done nothing but be there for my daughter every single day of every single year of her life. Be honest, Ellen, you weren't thinking of Kathryn tonight. You were thinking of *you.* You probably just wanted someone to yak at while you channel surfed, but you didn't have anybody at your immediate disposal. Not with your employees and your colleagues and your husband hundreds of miles away from you, and probably relieved to have a couple of weeks off from your constant demands."

I glared at my sister who was, in turn, glaring back at me with a ghostly white cast to her face, illuminated as she was by only a sliver of moonlight streaming into the bungalow. So very pale.

I expected her to immediately argue back. Tell me I was full of bullshit. Or claim she wasn't as condescending and irritating and demanding as I knew she was.

But she just stared back at me with an oddly haunted expression on her face, which somehow telegraphed both discomfort and surprise. She swiped at her forehead repeatedly, as if trying to brush away a pesky bug.

"What's wrong?" I asked.

She didn't answer me, but I sensed a new movement from where she was sitting on the sofa. She almost looked like she was shaking.

I reached over to the wall and flipped on the light. Her pallor wasn't just from the cast of the moon. She really *was* ghostly white. And she was trembling like a frightened animal. Fresh sweat beaded up on her forehead the second she'd managed to wipe it away, and she was struggling to catch her breath.

This freaked me out.

I raced over to her. "Ellen? Are you okay? What's happening?"

She clutched her chest above her heart and grimaced. "I think—" she began, and then stopped.

"You can tell me," I said, suddenly flooded with shame that I'd left her alone for the whole night and come back so late, only to argue with her over petty things. I'd had no idea she was so sick, but what kind of flu or virus was this? I felt her forehead. I couldn't detect a fever, but there was no denying she had other symptoms of illness. "Do you need a doctor?"

She nodded. "Pretty sure I'm having another panic attack. But this is worse than the last one. You'd better take me to the ER."

CHAPTER FIFTEEN
Revelations Unexpected

If Ellen had been annoyed by that pain-in-the-ass Dr. Joseph Cole back in New Haven, this Sarasota doctor—Dr. Kristy Sutterfield—had brought Ellen's irritation to a whole new level.

"Ms. Slater, can you try to remember what you were talking about and thinking about just prior to this latest episode?" the doc asked at the hospital an hour later.

She shrugged. "I was arguing with my sister. But that's nothing new." Hell, she and Marianna had spent over four decades disagreeing on nearly everything. Hadn't given her a panic attack before.

"Was there anything *different* about your conversation with your sister this time?" the doc persisted. "Anything that irritated you in particular?"

"In particular?" Ellen repeated. Shit. Everything irritated her right now. Her inability to go to work without worrying about sweating through her clothing. Her longstanding family dynamics with all of the same old dysfunction, which always reared its ugly head when she and her sister fought. Her aging body and being in her forties or whatever.

"Look," she said to the woman, "all I know is that I was fine until Marianna came back to the bungalow tonight. I mean, I was ticked off at her for getting in so late, but I wasn't panicky or anything. Not right away."

"Had your sister promised she'd be back at a specific time?"

Ellen shook her head. "She didn't tell me a time, although I think she should have. It would've been more considerate. Living with her has never been easy, though. And I knew that before I came down here and surprised her last week. She's not typically a huge fan of the unexpected, but… " She shrugged.

Dr. Sutterfield glanced at her sharply. "So, you came down knowing that? Were you purposely trying to anger her? Throw her off kilter?"

She glared at the doc. "Of course not. I just needed a place to go for a bit. But when I tried to tell Marianna on the phone about my plans to fly down for a visit, she was too busy to listen to me."

"Hmm." The doc jotted some notes down on her clipboard and frowned.

"Hmm… what?"

The lady doctor inhaled slowly, as if she were gathering a supply of much-needed patience, and then she exhaled even more slowly before she spoke. "Would I be correct in surmising that being the one in control is important to you, Ms. Slater? That you're a Type A personality?"

Ellen rolled her eyes. "Do I look like one of those laidback, I-live-for-yoga types?"

The doc cracked a smile. "You do not."

"Then there's your answer."

Dr. Sutterfield regarded her thoughtfully for a moment. "Your sister asked to see you after I'd had a chance to conduct my exam and chat with you privately. But after you visit with her for a few minutes, I'm going to instruct her to go home. The nurse is going to run a few tests and, given that it's so late, I'd prefer to keep you here for observation tonight—"

"What? I have to stay—"

"You do. I'd like for you to get a restful sleep, ideally away from whatever trigger set off this latest panic attack. And I'm going to give you just one small assignment." She pulled a pocket-sized spiral notebook from one of the drawers and handed it to Ellen, along with a ballpoint pen. "Write down, in chronological order, the conversational progression you had with your sister earlier tonight. Everything that you remember saying to her or hearing her say. Every thought you can recall that ran through your head or emotion you experienced. Pay particularly close attention to how your body feels as you revisit the dialogue from the evening. The way your conversation escalated into a full-blown argument. Do you think you can do that?"

She nodded. "Should I talk with my sister about this? Tell her I'm supposed to write it all down? She might remember something I don't."

"No. Not this time. The exercise is about you, not her. It's your memories and reactions that we need to pinpoint, okay?"

"Okay."

Then with a competent, kind, and—in Ellen's opinion—utterly exasperating nod that signaled the end of their discussion, the doc left her in the hospital room alone.

Fifteen seconds later, Marianna rushed in.

"Hey, how are you feeling?" her sister asked, her face flushed with heat and creased with worry, exhaustion, and guilt.

"Don't look at me like that," Ellen told her.

"Like what?"

"Like it's your fault that I'm in here."

Marianna shook her head and held up her cell phone. "I read all of your texts in the waiting room. If I would've just let you know I'd be late, we wouldn't have been arguing and—"

"And nothing. Listen, you were sort of right. You *are* almost forty, and I'm not your mother. You'll always be my kid sister, though, so there's a part of me that's forever going to want to tell you what to do. Seriously, Sis, when are you gonna get used to that?"

Marianna smiled slightly, which was Ellen's reward. But it was a short-lived victory. Her sister was soon frowning and shaking her head again. "I was never a very obedient kid sister, was I?"

Ellen laughed. "Actually, until you ran off with Donny the A-hole, you played by the rules more often than I did. I was supposed to be the rebel of the family." *And you took that away from me*, she added in her head.

Funny, she hadn't thought about that in ages. But it was true. Until Marianna's defection, Ellen had been on a wilder path. Taking her time getting through college. Navigating boys, beer fests, and the occasional bong. She hadn't gotten serious about school or her career until after her sister's surprise marriage, when their parents' gaze turned toward her to make up for their disappointment in her younger sibling. Then she began working on her profession in earnest.

"What? You were always so reliable and so certain of what you wanted to do, Ellen. Our parents' favorite child by a long shot," Marianna said, with only a tinge of her usual resentment. Tonight, it came across more as resignation.

"Nope. Not until after you eloped. Don't tell me you honestly don't remember? All the family patterns changed after that. Swiftly and suddenly."

Marianna shrugged, but Ellen didn't buy the disinterested act. It had been like an immediate rewriting of history with their parents, and the sisters had remained complicit in their screwed-up family mythology even after Mom and Dad had passed away. That was one of their dirty little secrets. After her elopement, Marianna had become the black sheep overnight, and Ellen had been made over as the good girl, when they all knew it had been the reverse for eighteen years. Marianna was judged forevermore by their parents a deviant, despite having chosen a very traditional domestic life as a wife and mother, along with a "safe" career. (She'd gone into *insurance*, for cripes' sake. The girl craved safety.) While Ellen had been all but forced by their parents to subdue her natural rebellious streak, and she was only allowed to take out her love of arguing in heated tax meetings. And, occasionally, with her sister.

Could that be part of why she was having these damned panic attacks now? Had her mind finally reached its saturation point, unable to placate her parents' wishes anymore, especially from beyond the grave? The only praise she'd gotten from them in decades had been for being a successful career woman—not for her marriage to Jared or, heaven forbid, for any maternal instincts she might possess, however remote. Not that she'd ever wanted to taint a new generation with the residual dysfunction of her nuclear family anyway.

She felt the sweat beading up on her forehead again and the shortness of breath returning. Shit.

"I don't want us to dwell on all of that now, Ellen. No matter how it happened. And, besides, I can tell it's upsetting you. Why don't we wait until after you're back at the bungalow before we start revisiting the unhappy past?"

Her sister had a point, and Ellen readily agreed to let it drop for the time being. But she had the uncomfortable sense that she was getting really close to the source of her panic attacks. In the relative vicinity, at least, though she still hadn't quite nailed it. Perhaps the dark truth was that she wasn't sure she really wanted to know.

The nurse came in to usher Marianna out of the room and to run the tests that Dr. Sutterfield said were coming.

"You may come back in the morning," the nurse

informed her sister. "After nine a.m. We'll be able to give you both a more thorough update then."

Marianna squeezed Ellen tight before she left. "I'm so sorry about tonight."

"Me, too," Ellen whispered. "But go to the bungalow and get some sleep, would'ya? Otherwise, they just might end up admitting you here, too." Her sister chuckled. "Oh, and please don't call Jared to tell him about this, um, episode. I'll talk to him tomorrow."

"Are you sure? Because I could—"

"It's after three in the morning, Marianna. Yeah, I'm sure. A phone call now would scare the crap out of the poor guy." Plus, she needed time to think of exactly what to say.

After her sister finally left and the nurse had poked and prodded her for fifteen minutes, she was finally left alone with her thoughts and instructed to "rest." Like that was gonna happen.

So, she pulled out the little spiral notebook that the doc had given her and began writing down the moment-by-moment rundown of everything that'd happened since Marianna had walked into the bungalow after her late date. But try as she might, she couldn't isolate the trigger. Maybe she was forgetting some important detail or overlooking a tidbit of dialogue that would illuminate the problem. Hell if she knew.

It wasn't until several hours later—at a quarter to nine, to be precise—that Ellen finally figured it out.

Her bedside phone rang. It was the nurses' station, telling her that her niece was on the line, hoping to speak with her. "Shall I put her through to you?" the nurse on call asked.

"Of course," Ellen said. She *loved* Kathryn. She always enjoyed talking with her, although she'd never chitchatted with her niece from a hospital bed before.

"Aunt Ellen?" Marianna's college-aged daughter said softly.

"Hey, sweetie," she replied, her throat tightening up a bit. Weirdly overemotional for her, but she'd been running on roughly four hours of sleep.

"My mom told me you were at Sarasota Memorial when I called this morning. I had to worm the details out of her, but I had to call. I've been thinking about you a lot, and I just wanted to hear the voice of my favorite auntie."

That last bit was an old joke between them. Donny the Deadbeat was an only child, so Ellen was Kathryn's only aunt. But, nevertheless, tears sprung to her eyes and her heart began to race at her niece's loving words.

"Aw, thanks, Kathryn," she said, forcing herself to sound upbeat, even though she was crying, her throat was tightening, and she could feel a trickle of sweat dripping down her back, beneath her thin hospital gown.

The truth settled over her like a blanket. All of the childhood memories that had been dislodged from her mental vise grip recently—not to mention all of these panic attacks—were leading her to the one realization she'd never expected to have. Not at age forty-four, that was for damn sure.

Did she really want to be endearingly called something other than "auntie"? How would it sound to her heart... to her soul... if she actually wanted to be someone's "mommy" instead?

Oh, God. I need to talk to Jared. Now.

I had to cancel out on my friends for the first time that morning, but there was no way I'd be able to function—let alone work pliers and crimp beads—on so much emotion and so little sleep. As it was, I could barely drag myself out of bed to answer the phone when my daughter called. But, after talking with Kathryn, I figured I'd better tell Joy what was going on.

"I'm so sorry I can't come in today," I said to her on the phone. "There's been a little emergency… " I explained about Ellen's panic attack the night before, carefully omitting the reason for our argument. Joy was, of course, very understanding.

"You take all the time you need, lady," she said sincerely. "Just tell me, what we can do to help. Bring you and your sister dinner? How about some fudge?"

I laughed. "Nothing right now, but thanks. I'm not sure if the doctors are going to prescribe a special diet for her, so we'd better not tempt her with Fudge Fantasia until after we know it's on the approved list."

"Oh, I can bring her a pretty assortment of veggies," Joy informed me. "The fudge—that'll be for *you.*"

After I hung up with her, I texted Gil. I didn't know how early he'd planned to get to Castaways, but I was pretty sure Carter was the one opening the shop this morning, and I didn't want to wake Gil unnecessarily. Last night, he and I had made tentative plans to grab a drink together after we were all done with work for the day. Clearly, that wasn't going to happen.

I briefly explained the situation to him, too, and was surprised to get an immediate text in reply.

"This isn't some awkward morning-after avoidance thing, is it?????? ;)" he texted, complete with half a dozen question marks and a goofy winking emoji.

"LOL. No!" I immediately typed in return.

He didn't text back. He called.

"You sure, Marianna?" he asked, his voice joking, but there was a hint of concern beneath the humor.

"Oh, Gil. I am *very* sure." I told him a few more details about my sister than I'd told Joy, but not any of Ellen's comments about us. Still, he seemed to guess that my late return to the bungalow had been an issue.

"I'm sorry I kept you out 'til the wee hours." He

paused. "Well, I'm not, really, but I'm sorry if that created discord between you and Ellen. Once your sister recovers—and quickly, I hope—I'd love it if we could take a full day off, just the two of us, and go down to Sanibel Island. I'd like to show it to you, and—" He hesitated.

"Yes?"

"I know our time together is limited. I want to make the most of it."

"Me, too," I said, and I meant it with my whole heart.

The past twenty-four hours had been a rollercoaster of thoughts and feelings, but just about the only thing I knew with absolute certainty was that I was going to miss Gil like crazy when I went back home. And Joy and Lorelei and Abby, too. Mostly, I was going to miss the *me* I'd become when I was with them.

Gil and I said our goodbyes, and I glanced at the clock—it was just after nine a.m. Time to go back to the hospital and find out where things stood with my sister today. She'd been so intent on unearthing the secrets of our family's past that, I had to confess, I was nervous to be alone with her. I didn't want to relive all of that crap.

But, no doubt about it, it was partially (maybe even primarily) my fault we were dealing with all of this now. I needed to face it.

So, I splashed some water on my eyes, brushed my teeth, got dressed, and tried to make myself look less like a human zombie. One glance at the mirror told me I hadn't come close to succeeding. Nevertheless, I grabbed my keys and a granola bar for the road and got in the car.

When I walked in to Ellen's hospital room, her cheeks were streaked with fresh tears and a nurse I hadn't met yet was standing next to her, handing her a box of tissues. I felt my anxiety spiking. Oh, no. Now what?

"Did the tests come back?" I blurted. "Was there a problem?"

The nurse glanced at Ellen first, then at me. "No. Dr.

Sutterfield will be in with the results in a couple of hours. Your sister is just, uh… "

"Sad," Ellen said. "And moody. Like I have a bad case of PMS. Got any chocolate?"

"Um, not with me." I thought about Joy's fudge offer. "But it could be arranged."

My sister smiled wanly. "Good. I may need some later."

"Have you talked with Jared yet?"

She nodded. "Briefly. But we'll be talking for longer later in the day. He's in a big meeting right now, so we've got a phone date planned for four-ish this afternoon."

A meeting on a Sunday morning?

But I knew Jared was a workaholic, just like my sister, so all I said was, "Okay. Hopefully, you'll be back at the bungalow by then and can take the call from your favorite spot on the sofa."

She almost laughed. "Thanks, Sis. We'll see what the doc says."

As it turned out, the doctor said the tests didn't show any other problems and that the panic-attack diagnosis seemed to be right on. Dr. Sutterfield requested a few minutes to talk privately with my sister, so I stood outside the room while they had their discussion. I had no idea what they were saying in there, but I was more than a little surprised to see Ellen actually give the doctor a hug before she was discharged. Since when had my sister become so weirdly emotional? Was there something more to this panic-attack thing than she was telling me?

Probably. It wasn't as though she hadn't kept secrets from me before.

By lunchtime, we'd return to the bungalow, and I'd gotten Ellen set up like the queen bee she was in the middle of her floral command post. I handed her a cup of green tea, which she sniffed at in mild disgust ("This doesn't have caffeine, Marianna. What's the point?"), along with the remote control to the TV, a stack of magazines, and some extra pillows for the sofa.

"You can watch a show, read an article, or just take a nap, if you'd like," I told her. "I'll figure out something to make us for lunch, okay?"

"Sure," she said, apathetically flipping through the magazine on the top of the pile. "Thanks."

To be honest, I would've given her whatever form of entertainment might keep her occupied and not interested in rehashing the past today. But, despite how she'd professed her desire to talk about our parents in the early morning hours at the hospital, Ellen seemed unusually tightlipped this afternoon. I couldn't account for the change, but I was grateful.

Before I had a chance to even look through the refrigerator and pantry for food options, I got a text from Lorelei.

"Are you and your sister back home now?" she asked.

When I replied that, yes, we were, she wrote, "Excellent. Expect us in about 20 minutes. Joy already ordered the meal, so there will be no arguments."

Standing in the kitchen, holding my cell phone, I actually laughed aloud at the words on the screen. No, there was no point in arguing with Joy. Or with Lorelei and Abby, for that matter.

"Looks like we're going to have some company soon," I warned my sister.

When the ladies arrived at our door less than a half hour later, it was like inviting a funnel cloud of love and delight into the bungalow, and it swept both Ellen and me into its whirlwind. I'd gotten used to their energy and enthusiasm—more or less—over these past few weeks. But Ellen, who was usually so imposing and commanding herself, looked comically railroaded by my new friends and the way they simply took over the place.

Joy bounded in first with a platter of seafood skewers.

"Shrimp and veggie kabobs from On the Barbie," she informed us. "Very healthy!" She put the platter down on the kitchen counter, skipped over to Ellen, and thrust out her hand. "It's so great to finally meet Marianna's sister. I'm Joy."

Ellen, staring wide-eyed at her from behind a large sofa pillow, slowly reached out to shake it. "And I'm Ellen."

Joy pumped her hand. "I know!" Then, to me, "Wow. You two have seriously different auras, though." She waved her palm in Ellen's direction. "So much orange. Who knew?"

Ellen squinted at her in confusion, and I couldn't help but laugh. But I didn't have even a second to explain before Lorelei plunked two wine bottles onto the coffee table in front of my sister, and Abby came into the room, too, bearing a Fudge Fantasia bag and a devilish grin.

"Joy's seafood and Lorelei's wine might be heart healthy," Abby said to Ellen, "but I got you covered on the dessert."

My sister grinned back, and I could sense Ellen finally giving in to what I knew would be a lively introductory lunch with my Sarasota friends.

"We're taking the afternoon off to spend it with you two," Lorelei said.

"Yep," Joy concurred. "We closed the shop for the next few hours, and we're taking a break from the bracelets. This is more important." She shot me a significant look, and my heart soared at their kindness.

When I explained to Ellen that these were the women I was working with on the B.E.A.D.S. project, I saw the light of understanding dawn on my sister's face. She could hardly help but notice how vivacious and spirited they were. And if she'd been lost in pensive thoughts and on the verge of glumness prior to their arrival, she didn't have the opportunity to dwell long in that mood. Not in the presence of such dynamic company.

Soon, she was laughing just as loudly as the rest of us at the stories that were being shared, and even contributing several of her own.

In the midst of this, the phone rang. Olivia Michaelsen's number. I picked it up.

"Hi, Olivia!"

Across the room, Abby twisted her head in my direction.

"I heard through the grapevine that your sister was in the hospital," my lovely Mirabelle Harbor friend said. "How is she doing?"

"You heard through the grapevine?" I repeated.

Abby's gaze caught mine, and she winced. "Guilty," she mouthed at me.

Ohhh. I nodded.

"Just because I'm not a few blocks away this summer doesn't mean that I don't still keep tabs on you," Olivia said lightly.

I laughed and let her know that Ellen was definitely doing better and back at the bungalow now. While Olivia and I were busy catching up on the phone, I could overhear Ellen asking Abby about how she knew the Michaelsens. (Because, even though Ellen hadn't resided in Mirabelle Harbor for years, *everyone* who'd ever lived on Chicago's North Shore seemed to know the Michaelsens.) Abby explained that she'd grown up in the area, too, and she gave my sister an abbreviated account of her relationship with Chandler.

Soon, the two of them were comparing notes on all of the families in town and giggling like schoolgirls, along with Lorelei and Joy, with the help of several glasses of wine. It allowed me to slip into the bedroom for a few minutes, so I could answer the questions Olivia was asking me.

"What's been happening with that hot man you met at the beach?" she asked me. "Gil, right? Have you seen him again?"

When last we'd spoken, I'd only just been formally introduced to Gil. He'd walked me to my car and we'd chatted by the shops. But that was all before the Craft Festival. Before our growing friendship. Before he'd kissed me. Before the beach drumming... or the visit to Venice Beach... or making love at his place. I suddenly realized there's been a *lot* of things I hadn't told my good friend.

"I'm crazy about him," I admitted to her, after giving her a quick but still fairly comprehensive rundown of the highlights. "He's just a wonderful man, Olivia. And these weeks here are going by so fast."

There was a long pause as she took in everything I'd been telling her. Then she said, "For purely selfish reasons, I'm really looking forward to you coming back to Mirabelle Harbor. But I know how rare love is. How hard it can be to find. Do you think your relationship with Gil could be special like that? Or is this just an exciting, life-affirming summer fling that you'll always cherish? Because that's a good thing, too. It's just—" She paused.

"It's just what?"

"Well, with a fling, you take a bunch of pictures and make a lot of memories, but then you pack them up, go home, and get on with things. With love, Marianna, you move heaven and earth to keep it in your life."

I closed my eyes and felt tears forming behind my lids, but I didn't try to fight them. Olivia was asking me something both valuable and wise, and I needed to let myself feel my real emotions when thinking about this. She was being a true friend and forcing me to look honestly at my relationship with Gil. At who we both were, where we belonged, and what we truly wanted from our lives.

Nothing he'd ever said in all of our conversations—or even in the heat of our lovemaking—indicated that a long-term love story was part of our future. We'd both gone into this relationship insisting that commitment wasn't going to be a factor. Knowing that our connection was intended to be, at most, for a passionate few weeks. Maybe a month. I fully expected us to go our separate ways after I left Sarasota at the end of July.

Sure, we'd probably call each other a handful of times after I was back in Mirabelle Harbor. Exchange Christmas cards for a year or two. "Like" some random posts on the other person's Facebook page. Or catch up on each other's lives through emails Joy would send us.

But even if I extended my stay by a few weeks so Gil and I could be together for a bit longer, once I left Florida for good, he and I would drift apart. It was inevitable.

"Thanks, Olivia," I whispered. "You're right. There *is* a distinction between the two, and I appreciate that you reminded me of it. This thing with Gil... it's a fling. It's gotta be. But it's a really fabulous one. It's going to be hard to let him go."

"All right," she said. "That's important to know. But, don't forget, I'm here for you. I might be a thousand miles away at the moment, but I've always got your back. And if you need to talk any of this out—at *any* time—please call me."

"I will."

There was another knock at the front door, but I was in the bedroom, so I couldn't see who was outside.

"Hey, I've got to go," I told her. "We'll talk soon, okay?"

"We'd better," she said, before she rang off.

I went back into the living room and—*Ohhh!*

"Gil?" I said, my heart fluttering at the mere sight of him standing in the doorway, dressed in a brightly patterned Hawaiian shirt and cargo shorts.

Joy had let him in, and he was holding a bouquet of flowers in one hand and a CD in the other.

"Marianna." He grinned at me with a look that left me utterly breathless. We both just stood there for a second and stared at each other.

Out of the corner of my eye, I saw my sister grimace and narrow her eyes at Gil. And then I saw *his* sister glance between Gil, Ellen, and me with her mouth agape. Joy's face was so expressive, she couldn't hide her surprise.

"Ellen, I see you've met my big brother." She turned toward Gil. "Why didn't you tell me?" she asked him, incredulous.

He cleared his throat and quickly thrust the floral arrangement at my sister. "Uh, it was a very brief meeting." Then, to Ellen, "These are for you. Glad to see you're doing better."

The expression on my sister's face was less than welcoming, but she managed to reply, "Thanks. So, you're Joy's brother, huh?"

"Yep," he said.

"I'm starting to understand all of this now," I heard her murmur.

But Gil had returned his focus to me. "And this is for you," he said, handing me the CD.

Seashore Instrumental was the title. I skimmed both covers and read the insert. Relaxing island music. The soothing sounds of waterfalls and rippling waves. The flow of the tide on swirling sands.

I laughed. "This looks very calming."

"That's the idea," he said. "It's for deep-breathing practice."

It was all I could do not to kiss him. "Thank you, Gil."

He nodded sweetly at me but kept his physical distance. For my part, I longed to fold myself up in his strong arms, slip my fingers beneath the Hawaiian fabric, and be warmed by his embrace. But there were four pairs of very curious eyes watching our every move. Not that we were fooling anyone with our restraint. I had no doubt Joy had already magically intuited everything that'd happened between her brother and me and was busy processing it all in her active little brain. Ellen had guessed as much last night. And, from the matching grins worn by Lorelei and Abby, they more than suspected Gil and I had moved beyond a platonic friendship. Into *what*, however, was the question I could almost hear them both asking themselves.

But friends don't push each other into revealing things they're not ready to reveal and, so, Gil and I were able to get through the next hour without any overt teasing.

And it was fun. Even Ellen soon started laughing again, relaxing into the company of my friends with an ease I found gratifying. I was proud to know these wonderful people and show them off to my sister. Pleased to see that she appreciated them, too.

Only one thing—aside from my growing closeness to Gil—seemed to nag at Ellen. Four p.m. came and went with no phone call from Jared, and my sister was getting antsy waiting for him to reach her. She texted him twice. No answer.

"That's not like him," she whispered to me in worry.

"Did you know what kind of meeting he had going on this morning? Maybe it was something that took longer than most," I said.

"It's possible," Ellen replied, but she sounded skeptical.

Not more than ten minutes later, though, there was yet another knock on the door.

I glanced at my friends. "Is anyone else coming over? Carter or Nick, maybe?"

They shook their heads.

"Hmm." I got up to check to see who was out there.

Jared.

"Oh, my goodness!" I swung open the door and welcomed him with a hug. "Come inside."

When my sister saw him, she covered her cheeks with her palms and let out a small squeak. "You came in person?" she asked him with astonishment. "From Connecticut? Are you crazy?"

He wearily dropped his carry-on bag and walked over to where she was sitting on the sofa. He threw his arms around his wife and kissed her. "Well, you left out a few important details, honey. When you said you wanted 'to talk' this morning, you didn't mention you were asking from a hospital bed. I just came from Sarasota Memorial, but they said you'd been released."

"I didn't want to worry you," Ellen told him. Then, "Hey, how did you know I was there?" She shot an annoyed glance at me. "Did Marianna call you and—"

He shook his head and thumbed behind him.

Ellen and I exchanged a look in confusion.

There was yet another knock on the door. I opened it and almost keeled over in shock.

"Kathryn?" I stared at her. "What are you doing here?"

"Hi, Mom," she said, breezing into the bungalow without bothering to answer my question. She gave me a quick side squeeze that was supposed to pass for a hug, scanned the faces of my friends, and broke into a smile. "Whoa, it's a party."

She, too, walked over to my sister, kissed her on the cheek, and said, "Glad you're feeling better, Aunt Ellen." Then, to the room at large, she turned to introduce herself. "I'm Kathryn Gregory, Marianne's daughter," she said. "And this is Sid O'Connor—" She pointed to a lanky, dark-haired guy who'd slipped through the door amidst all of the confusion.

I studied him with immediate interest. I'd never met her college boyfriend before. Hadn't even spoken with him on the phone. I'd only heard stories about the guy from my daughter's point of view. Seen a few social-media pictures. That was it.

"He's my fiancé," she announced.

CHAPTER SIXTEEN
One Thing Leads to Another

Ellen watched her sister's face turn an interesting shade of pale at Kathryn's pronouncement. She'd spoken with her niece only that morning, and there had been nothing in the conversation indicating that her sister's nineteen-year-old daughter was contemplating marriage.

But, for a dozen reasons at least, Marianna didn't seem inclined to think near-future nuptials were a good idea. Hell if Ellen did either.

She, however, had her own surprise visitor to deal with. Jared.

Oh, damn. Now she'd have to have this baby discussion with him face to face.

"Are you saying that Kathryn called you this morning?" Ellen asked her husband. "She was the one who told you I was in the ER?"

He nodded. "She'd left a message on my cell asking about when you were planning to return home. She'd assumed I knew you were in the hospital." His lips curved upward, but there was a shadow of hurt behind his smile.

"I'm sorry for not telling you, Jared. I hadn't wanted to worry you."

He shrugged off her apology. "Anyway, I called Kathryn back right away and she told me about your conversation. She sounded concerned, so I asked if she wanted to fly down to see you, too. I'd made the decision at once to come myself, but I didn't want her to travel alone from Michigan, so I offered to buy a ticket for her boyfriend as well." He lowered his voice. "The *fiancé* bit is a new one on me, though."

"It was new to all of us," she replied.

Both she and Jared turned to look at Marianna, who was bolstered on either side by the Canton siblings. Joy was on her left, Gil on her right, and both were supporting her by their presence. They both looked ready to physically hold her up, too, if necessary.

As it was, it didn't look as though Marianna was having an easy time staying upright, not with the one-two punch of the surprise visit and the engagement details Kathryn was relaying to her mom in that blasé manner only teenagers can effectively pull off. Plus, unless Marianna had been elusive about sharing, Ellen suspected this was the first time she was meeting this Sid guy.

"The kids are actually staying for a whole week," Jared told her, nodding toward Kathryn and Sid. "Although I'm afraid that might be news to your sister, too. I'd wrongly assumed Kathryn would have told Marianna earlier today. Both kids managed to score some vacation time from their summer jobs. I, unfortunately, was only able to take off the next couple of days, but I figured we could offer for them to stay here at the bungalow with Marianna, and you and I could check into a nice hotel and have some time together—just the two of us." He looked at her tenderly. "I was insanely worried about you, Ellen. We need to talk, as you'd suggested, and we'll have to do whatever we can to get to the bottom of these attacks."

She nodded at him, her heart filled with love for this man and, simultaneously, with fear that her newfound needs might push him away. But she had to trust that he would be fair about it. That he would at least listen. Just because they'd both sworn off the notion of becoming parents years ago didn't mean that revisiting the idea now was definitely a dead end.

"Thanks, Jared," she whispered. She reached out and grasped his hand. The two of them worked so well together as a team. They always had. A baby would throw every relationship pattern they'd shared out of whack. Neither of them were especially good with change, and what she was about to suggest to him tonight was one helluva change...

She glanced around the living room. Pure chaos. Although, given the hurricane of emotions that had been raging inside of her for the past few weeks, especially these last several days, all the loud talking and gesturing and general ruckus inside the bungalow—which wasn't designed to hold a party of *nine*—wasn't quite as jarring as it might have been.

Poor Marianna, though. She looked like she needed a sedative. Or some more wine and fudge at the very least.

As soon as Ellen could spirit her away from the group for a few minutes, she pulled her sister into the second bedroom and closed the door. "First of all, I'm so sorry Jared came down here without a word of notice to you—or to me, for that matter—and that he flew down Kathryn and Sid without telling you either. Thinking back, I'm not sure why I thought it was such a great idea to just show up unannounced either, but I got a taste of my own medicine today. And, honestly, I wouldn't blame you for wanting to beat up both of us for orchestrating so many surprise visits since you've been here in Florida."

Marianna winced but she still managed to laugh a little. "You've both certainly made things interesting."

Ellen hugged her sister close and could feel Marianna's body trembling. "Hey, it's gonna be okay. We'll make sure of it. Just hang in there and let's tackle one issue at a time."

She stepped away from her sister and began gathering up her clothing to toss in her carry-on bag."

"What are you doing?" Marianna asked. "You're not leaving, are you? You shouldn't be traveling so soon after—"

"Relax. I'm not going far. Jared's making a reservation for us right now at a hotel near the hospital. His idea. He wanted us to be close by if I should need any other medical attention." *Although, he's probably going to be the one who'll needed to be revived by doctors after we have our little chat.* "He figured you were already going to have your hands full with your daughter and her... erm... guy, so it would be better if we left the bungalow all to you three."

She sank to the mattress. "Oh, my God, Ellen. Can you believe her? Getting engaged? What am I going to do with that child? She's only nineteen."

"You were married at eighteen."

"Yeah, and look how well that turned out."

"It's going to be all right, Sis. You're a good mom. A wonderful one. Incredibly supportive of her and very strong. You really listen to her—in a way our mom never did for us. Kathryn doesn't realize what a gift that is, and she probably doesn't come close to fully appreciating all the things you've done for her. But someday she will. Sooner rather than later, I hope. You brought up a beautiful daughter—" Ellen paused as tears sprung to her eyes and her sister looked over at her in concern. "I don't think I've ever told you this, but I'm a bit envious, actually, of what you and Kathryn share. You two are so lucky to have each other."

Marianna stood up and hugged her. "Seriously, Ellen, are you going to be okay? Is everything with Jared—"

She nodded. "Yes. I mean... maybe. At least I'm hopeful." She bit her lip and shook her head. "I have no idea. There's been a lot on my mind lately, and I need to discuss it all with him. But I love him and I trust him and I think we'll be able to get through it. I'll tell you more tomorrow, after Jared and I have a chance to talk things over."

"Okay."

"Now, help me strip this bed," Ellen said, tugging at the top sheet. "My niece is welcome to stay in this room. It's your call, though, if you're going to let the fiancé stay in here with her. My vote is for Sid on the sofa."

Marianna laughed aloud at that. Good.

"Yeah, we'll have to see about that. But thanks, Ellen. Please let me know if you need to talk later tonight about any of the things that have been going on. You can call me anytime, you know."

"Thanks. I know. And, by the way, your new friends are pretty awesome. Joy is a hoot. Abby and Lorelei are both so sweet and fun. I can totally see why you love hanging out with them. As for Gil—" She paused.

"What?" Marianna's brow creased with her usual worry. "You don't like him, do you?"

"I like that he cares about you. A lot. His feelings toward you seem genuine." Ellen squeezed her sister's hand. "So, I guess the guy is growing on me. And if Joy has her way, she's going to make you an honorary member of the Canton clan before the summer's out."

Marianna smiled a little. "Maybe I could be their Midwestern cousin or something. Not sure there'd be a point in anything more since I'll be back in Illinois soon, but they've both been very good to me here."

"They'd better be." Ellen winked at her and grabbed her things before heading out into the living room again. "We'll talk," she whispered to Marianna. "Tomorrow for sure. But don't worry about me, okay? Jared can take over that task—at least for tonight."

Then, after saying goodbye to her sister, her sister's friends, her sister's lover, her niece, and her niece's new fiancé (oh, dear God), Ellen and her husband slipped out of the bungalow, into the car Jared had rented, and drove away from the chaos that had buffered her so effectively from her thoughts for the past few hours.

Couldn't stay that way forever, though, could it?

"So," Jared said, once they'd settled into the luxury hotel suite he'd reserved for them. "What was it you wanted to talk with me about, Ellen?"

In Gil's opinion, Marianna's sister had departed the bungalow with a well-honed sense of the dramatic. The parting stink eye she'd leveled his way didn't go unnoticed by either him or by his perceptive sister, although Ellen paired her latest warning gaze with a mischievous half smile that left him wondering at the mixed signals. Did she approve of him for Marianna, however reluctantly? Or was she letting him know that she had every intention of trying to separate him from her kid sister?

As for Marianna herself, once Kathryn arrived on the scene, her whole demeanor had changed. The lightness and the laughter he'd gotten used to seeing in her expression, particularly when they were walking hand in hand along the shore, had been muted. It was as if a brightly painted canvas had been treated with a dull brown wash, as if to purposely age it or dull its luminosity. The effect was unsettling.

With Ellen and her husband gone, his sister and her two other friends began to pack up the party, so as to give Marianna and her daughter some privacy.

Joy pulled him aside while Marianna was trying to get a few other details out of Kathryn and this Sid character. Marianna looked even more shaken now than when Ellen had surprised them after their beach drumming evening, and that was saying something.

"Abby, Lorelei, and I need to head back to the Circle," Joy told him. "But I think you should stay here for a little longer. Marianna needs you."

He shrugged. "I'm not sure I'm the one she needs right now. She's juggling a lot of family stuff. Old baggage. New issues. Lots of change in her life. Many unresolved things. She probably needs space and an opportunity to work through future plans with her daughter more than she needs time with me."

Joy shook her head. "You're selling yourself short and underestimating her, too, Gil. Not sure what you did to piss off her sister, Ellen." She raised a brow at him. "But Marianna's eyes play Mozart when they look at you, which is something new. She's always liked you, but I can tell that things have gotten more intense between you two recently." Joy studied his face with a laser-beam gaze that was almost accusatory. "If you back away from her now, you'll hurt her."

He considered this. Of course he didn't want to hurt Marianna. He was crazy about her. But he wasn't the optimist his sister was either. Joy probably still believed in Santa Claus, the Tooth Fairy, and the Easter Bunny. Hell, she probably *was* the Easter Bunny in her free time. Or, maybe, just Cupid's charming young assistant. In any case, much as he adored her, Joy danced around in wistful, wonderful fantasy land, and he didn't intend to do the same.

"I'll talk with her," he said to his sister. "I'll ask Marianna what she needs."

Joy responded by grimacing at him in that girly way, which indicated that she thought he was a clueless male. Gil didn't have the energy to argue with her.

After she, Lorelei, and Abby reassured Marianna not to worry about the bracelets for a few days—they'd make up for lost time—the three of them dashed out of the bungalow, and Gil was left with the woman he was falling for, her sullen daughter, and some college dude, who looked like he'd been plucked from the pages of *Super Slacker* magazine.

He tried to decide what the best course of action would be. Stay and help Marianna through any conversational awkwardness with the two kids? Or leave for a while, perhaps inviting the boyfriend/fiancé with him for an hour to give Marianna a chance to have a one-on-one talk with her daughter.

Turned out, Marianna had a completely different plan in mind.

She thrust her car keys and her debit card at Kathryn, whose eyes widened in surprise, and then said, "Why don't you and Sid go to the Publix in town and pick up some groceries?" She gave them the directions quickly and then nodded at Sid. "I'm not sure if you have any food allergies or sensitivities, but I'd like to make sure we have some things on hand that you'd like to eat, and I know we don't have a lot in the fridge right now, aside from leftovers that my friends brought this afternoon."

"Thanks, Mrs. Gregory," the boyfriend/fiancé said with a heartening degree of politeness. "That's very thoughtful of you."

Marianna smiled kindly at him. "Well, I'd like you and Kathryn to feel at home while you're here."

Her daughter inclined her head appreciatively, but there was a glint of wariness in the teen's expression. Like she suspected this was still part of the calm civility before the all-hell-broke-loose storm ahead. From the shuttered, careful look on Marianna's face, Kathryn had probably called it right.

"Okay. We'll be back soon, Mom," Kathryn said, as she and Sid edged away from them and toward the door.

"Take your time," Marianna replied, locking the bungalow's front door behind them and, then, sinking to the floor in an exhausted heap.

"Hey," Gil whispered, kneeling down next to her and slowly stroking her hair. "I know you had a rough night and a crazy day today. Are you doing all right?"

She nodded, shook her head, and then shrugged. "I'm not sure." She covered her face with her palms and then collapsed her upper body onto her bent knees.

He continued stroking her, like a little kid who'd fallen off a bike or something. "What can I do for you right now? Do you need a shoulder rub? A stiff drink? Time alone to process all of this? You just tell me, and I'll make it happen."

She laughed and raised her head just enough to meet his gaze. "I kicked them out because I wanted to be with only you for a little while, Gil. Even if it's just for a half hour. I'm getting the feeling that my family members are conspiring to annihilate any possible shred of a social life I may have here in Sarasota. And, well... I can't stop thinking about making love with you." She paused and swallowed. "Can we do it again?"

"What—you mean here? Now?" Gil blurted. "They could walk back in at any minute."

"No. Kathryn's a picky shopper and, besides, this door is locked and I didn't give them the key to the bungalow. They'll need to knock. Still—" She glanced between the doorknob and him. "We'd better be quick."

"Marianna, you've had a lot of upheaval today. Are you sure you don't just need a friend right now? Someone to talk to about—"

She pushed herself up and wrapped her arms around him. "Gil, I need *you*."

And something in his heart broke open at those words. Maybe this was some bizarre reverse psychology game his mind was playing on him. Maybe he was just being contrary and wanting what he damn well knew he couldn't have. But against all logic, all experience, and all self-preservation, he could see himself making a commitment to a woman for the first time in his life. Specifically, with *this* woman.

Nothing had changed about their situation—except for him and what he'd begun to hope for, which made it all the more futile—but he wasn't going to fight it. If she wanted, no... *needed* him for now, and if she'd let him rub and kiss away the dull brown wash that was covering her and bring back some of her brightness, he sure as hell wouldn't turn her away.

"I'm all yours, Mariana." He shot a glance around the room. "Floral sofa?" he suggested.

She stood and took his hand in hers. "My bedroom. And Gil?"

"Yes?"

"Lose the shirt."

CHAPTER SEVENTEEN
Relativity

My daughter and Sid returned to the bungalow only about five minutes after Gil slipped out. I'd somehow managed to get dressed and was in the process of making a full pot of coffee (I figured we'd be up talking for a while), when they knocked on the front door, seven bags of groceries between them.

As we all pitched in to put away the perishables, I studied Kathryn's significant other and tried to take his measure. I had—not surprisingly—a lot of questions about the guy. But not all of those could be answered with words.

What kind of a young man was he?

What did he see in my daughter… and love about her?

Would he be faithful? Kind? Supportive? Not just now, but in the decades ahead?

Would he be a good father someday, if they decided to have kids—

Oh, my God.

"You're not pregnant, are you?" I blurted to Kathryn before I could stop myself. "That isn't why you two got engaged… "

But my daughter was looking at me with a horrified and

embarrassed expression, and Sid was shaking his head as vigorously as he could. He was the one who spoke first.

"Uh, no, Mrs. Gregory. I asked Kathryn to marry me because I love her. We've never, um, slept together."

I blinked at him—grateful, relieved and, admittedly, stunned. "Really?"

Kathryn looked mortified. "Yes, Mom. Really. Now can we drop this?"

"Well, okay, in a sec... I just—why the rush to get married then? I mean—" I was stumbling over words but I had to ask. "Please don't be offended by this, Sid," I said, turning toward him. "But I just met you less than two hours ago. I don't know a whole lot about your background or your educational plans or your life goals, but I remember Kathryn telling me that you were still in school, right?"

"I'm two years ahead of her," Sid said calmly, showing none of the agitation my daughter was displaying or I was feeling. "I'll be graduating with my business administration degree this coming May."

"That's great." And I meant it. He didn't entirely sell himself as a business guy—what with the faded t-shirt and smudged sneakers and droopy jeans—but I was reasonably impressed with his collegiate perseverance and his good manners. Still, these qualities hardly guaranteed a job upon graduation, explained how the two of them intended to support themselves, or even offered an excuse as to why getting married in the near future was desirable. So, I added, "When were you planning the wedding?"

"Right after I graduate," he said.

Too soon, although at least it wasn't next week or anything.

"But Kathryn needs to finish her degree as well, and it's still early days for her. Unless I missed something—" I glanced at my daughter. "I don't think you've even declared a major yet, have you, Kathryn?"

She shot me a dagger look, but she also shook her head.

"With jobs to look for and classes to finish, there are still quite a few things in each of your lives that will need to be figured out. I really think you should wait until the dust settles after college for both of you before getting married. Although—" I tried hard to think of something that was honest yet, simultaneously, conciliatory to add. "It's wonderful to see how strong your commitment is to each other."

Sid, who dressed like the poster child for the skateboard generation, shoved his hands into his pockets and smiled at me with a vague sense of pity. "It is," he said, and I knew they would, of course, do whatever the hell they wanted, no matter what I advised.

My daughter just continued to glower at me.

"Well, um, I'm going to get some fresh linens so we can make up the bed in the second bedroom, as well as the sofa bed," I said with fake cheerfulness. "Kathryn, could you please help me with that?"

While I had no illusions that she was pleased with me, having not reacted to her engagement announcement with shouts of delight and a show of confetti, I'd thought our conversation had remained rather civil, and that it'd gone fairly well under the circumstances. The look on Kathryn's face, however, told me otherwise.

She followed me in silence into the bedroom where, until recently, her aunt had stayed. Ellen and I had stripped the bed sheets, but her presence still hung in the room as a reminder.

I closed the door behind us, hoping for a bit more privacy for my daughter and me, but it was a moot point since she was actively avoiding speaking to me.

Finally, I exhaled slowly and said, "Look, sweetie, Sid seems like a very nice boy, but you're barely nineteen. You haven't had many relationships yet. Trust me, you don't want to get married this early in your life. Even taking out the possibility of motherhood while you're still in college, it's hard to be a wife and go to school at the same time. Not that it can't be done, but I know from personal experience that it isn't easy, and why complicate things for yourself? If he really loves you, he'll wait another couple of years for you to finish school, too. He won't pressure you into—"

"He's not pressuring me," she snapped. "Sid loves me, and he *promised* me he'll stay with me forever. He won't leave like Dad did. Sid won't go back on his word." She crossed her arms. So indignant. So young.

"Kathryn, honey, promises—even when they're made sincerely—can sometimes be broken. What you or Sid think you want right now might not be—"

"I'm not *you!*" she shouted. "This is my life, okay? And just because you failed at your marriage and you made a gazillion mistakes, it doesn't mean I will. So stop judging me and telling me what I should be thinking. Stop trying to control everything I do. You can mess up your own relationships as much as you want, but stay out of *mine*."

She dropped the pillow case she'd been holding, pushed open the door, and marched through the bungalow, clomping loudly with every step. "I'm going for a walk on the beach," she called out, slamming the front door.

I wasn't sure if this angry announcement was for my sake or as some kind of invitation for Sid.

He called out, "Hang on! I'm coming with you," and I heard his feet sprinting after her.

Kathryn didn't reply to him, but when I looked out the front window, I saw that he'd caught up and was keeping pace with her as she made her infuriated beeline to the water.

I sighed and finished making the bed alone.

The next morning, I awoke to find my daughter talking

on her cell phone to my sister.

Kathryn was in the kitchen, hunched over a bowl of breakfast cereal, while Sid had folded up the sofa bed I'd fixed up for him last night and was watching *The Today Show*. He waved pleasantly at me from across the room. My daughter, by contrast, merely glanced indifferently in my direction and then continued her conversation with her aunt, who'd always been "the fun one."

"Oh, c'mon, Aunt Ellen," she said with a derisive laugh. "Now you're starting to sound like my mother."

Good heavens, kid. Anything but that, eh?

There was a pause. Then Kathryn rolled her eyes and said into the phone, "I know, I know... Um, sure. I guess that makes sense." Another pause, longer this time. I was just about to grab a granola bar and return to the dark cave of my bedroom when she said, "Yeah, she's finally up." She thrust her phone at me. "Your sister wants to talk with you."

I swallowed. "Thank you, Kathryn." She shrugged and wandered into the living room to be with Sid. To Ellen, I said, "Good morning."

"Good morning, yourself," she replied cheerily. Ah, that was a good sign. "So, I've been chatting with your daughter for the past half hour and thinking about the three of you over there. And I have an idea."

"Should I be worried?"

She laughed. "Probably. But what I'm going to suggest is actually something fairly innocuous."

I raised an eyebrow at that. What Ellen considered to be innocent or harmless was likely different from my definition. Then again, it was still so rare for the two of us to be in sync on anything. The fact that we'd had "a moment" of sisterly bonding yesterday remained surprising to me. For some reason, though, I sensed I could trust her on this one.

"I'm listening," I told her.

"I want you and Kathryn and I to have lunch together tomorrow. Just the three of us. Here at my hotel."

"Are you feeling up to—?"

"Oh, yes. I'm feeling great," she insisted. And, in fact, she did *sound* great. But a voice on the phone could be deceiving.

"What about the guys?" I asked.

"They can bond. Jared was looking for an excuse to go out deep-sea fishing for a few hours. He was hoping Sid might like to come along with him. Today, Jared and I are spending the day together. He'd like to keep an eye on me himself. But tomorrow, if I'm here with you and Kathryn, I think he'd be all right leaving me for a few hours. He's got to head back to New Haven the day after that, and I'll probably go home myself later this week, so I want to make the most of these last few days in Sarasota, okay?"

"Okay," I said. "I'll talk with Kathryn and Sid about it, but it sounds like a lovely plan." I lowered my voice. "About Jared, how did your talk with him go last night?"

"So far, so good," she said cryptically. "But he and I have more to discuss today, so I'll give you a full update tomorrow. Pretty sure I finally nailed the panic attack trigger, though."

"That's good news, right?"

Ellen hesitated. "Right." Then, "I gotta go. My husband is insisting that we take a 'very relaxing stroll' along the beach. So, I'm going to be relaxed today if it effing kills me." She sort of laughed. "Tell your daughter and her guy that we won't take no for an answer. I want your butts over here by eleven thirty tomorrow morning. The hotel has a fab restaurant downstairs. I'll order us up a feast and we can eat on the balcony. Deal?"

What else could I say? "Deal," I replied.

And, thankfully, neither Kathryn nor Sid objected to Ellen's proposal, and Sid even professed an interest in fishing with Jared. To be honest, I was looking forward to being with my sister and having her offer an attractive distraction from the tense mother-daughter-fiancé dynamic we had going on here.

I used the day to catch up on messages and phone calls I'd gotten from Olivia, from Joy, Lorelei, and Abby, and from Gil.

Joy kept insisting that they were making progress with the bracelets and that she knew I'd help more later, whenever I could, but that I was needed by my family for now.

It was hard to disagree with her on that.

While Kathryn and Sid were technically legal adults and semi-formally engaged (she didn't have a ring yet, and I was still holding out hope that I could talk her out of the whole blasted thing), it wasn't a comfortable relationship for me. Plus, I wasn't sure I should leave them stranded at the bungalow on their first full day in Sarasota, since I had a car but they didn't, and neither of them were familiar with the area.

When I called Gil, he backed up my intuition.

"How well do you even know this Sid guy?" he asked. "No, Marianna. You're right to be there with them today, if only to watch to see how Sid treats your daughter. There's nothing like having a visual when it comes to all of those nonverbal signals. It's harder for a man to hide his genuine nature face to face."

"That's true for women, too," I said. "It'll be good for me to watch Kathryn's behavior with Sid as well. She says she loves him, but it's been impossible to get a clear read on her emotions, especially with her being so frustrated with me—her overbearing and overprotective mother."

He laughed. "I have no direct experience with raising kids, but it's gotta be a damn hard job. Just do the best you can and, please, give me a call later and let me know how it's going."

I agreed and clicked off. What I'd neglected to mention

to Gil, though, was just how much it helped to have him as a sounding board. It'd been too long since I'd had that kind of support from a man in my life. Even longer since it had been a man with good judgment.

And I appreciated, too, that Gil didn't try to step in and parent. He recognized that I was the one who needed to make the decisions, but he shared his perspective candidly and, even through the phone lines, I could feel he had my back.

In short, I'd known from the day I met him that he was a man of character, but I hadn't realized just how much I valued his honesty and trustworthiness. How reliant I'd become on his integrity over the few weeks we'd known each other, and the confidence I placed in the way he reasoned. How I, in fact, trusted myself more when I was with him.

This reminded me that I needed to be diligent about putting those qualities at the forefront in my own life. In my own interactions with those close to me. Like my sister. And my daughter. I wanted to be just as honest with them as Gil was with me.

Which was why, after a full day and night of watching my daughter with her significant other and studying his every reaction to her—his body language whenever she spoke or moved or laughed, his facial expressions whenever he glanced her way or vice versa—I couldn't help but reach the conclusion that, yes, he truly loved her. It was obvious in everything he did.

And Kathryn, in her more unguarded and less angry moments, projected a similar degree of affection toward Sid. Perhaps without as much mature conviction as I would've liked, but certainly her emotions hovered in the general vicinity of "love." For all of Sid's slacker-boy façade and the Millennial Generation vibe he radiated to the world at large, he'd been setting a good example for Kathryn. And much as I was loath to admit it, I might have been wrong about them as a couple.

I'd be interested to hear Ellen's impressions on the subject after our lunch date. My sister had always had a strong bullshit detector. I imagined if I'd missed some important signal between my daughter and her young fiancé, Ellen might well be able to pick up on it.

The following day, I drove the three of us over to the Gulf Shores Resort & Spa, where Jared and Ellen were staying, just a few miles down from where we were on Siesta Key. Lovely as the bungalow was, though, this hotel was a whole new world. Gorgeous balcony with decorative iron railings and an unobstructed view of the beach. A spacious and expensively furnished suite with every imaginable amenity. Close proximity to the hospital and dozens of other services, but the kind of place its residents would be reluctant to leave unless absolutely necessary. I felt like I was walking into a brochure that Abby and the Floriday Excursions staff would show to affluent tourists who wanted the "Lifestyles of the Rich and Famous" vacation package.

Jared and Sid grabbed a few sandwiches to go from a platter on the mahogany table, along with a selection of beverages and easy-to-pack desserts, to sustain them for a few hours on the boat. Then the two of them headed off on their fishing expedition, while Ellen, Kathryn, and I relocated to the balcony for a delectable lunch of maple and pecan-encrusted salmon, mashed sweet potatoes, grilled asparagus spears, and slices of Key Lime pie.

Even my daughter was in good spirits after that.

For the most part, Ellen was the one who kept the conversation flowing, and she appeared to be at her energetic best. It was stunning how much of a transformation had occurred in just a day and a half. I was dying to ask her about these conversations she'd been having with her husband and what she'd discovered about her panic attacks, but I knew my sister well. She was adept at strategy, and she was biding her time on the subject for some reason.

"I like this young man of yours," Ellen said to Kathryn. "Can't say he's a trendsetter as far as metro fashion… " she joked, and even my daughter laughed at that. "But just these couple of times that I've talked with Sid, he seems very respectful of you and goodhearted."

"Thanks." Kathryn shot an arch look at me. "Sid's awesome. I think even Mom is starting to like him."

I acknowledged this to be true. Because it was. But I was surprised by the next words my daughter said.

"Yeah, I know the whole engagement thing had to be kind of a shock," she said. "Especially knowing your history with Dad." She paused. "But Sid's really been there for me this year. We were friends first. We met in a lit class my first semester and just kept running into each other around campus." She glanced over at me. "I didn't tell you, Mom, but I actually dated a few guys during the year before Sid and I started going out seriously. He's the only one that seemed like a man, not a boy."

I blinked back a little emotion at these words. It was exactly what I'd felt about Gil versus most other guys I'd met, including, of course, my ex-husband.

So, I nodded. "I know what you mean. And, yes, Sid definitely seems more mature than most college kids his age."

This earned me a small smile. "He was especially great after you'd told me about what Dad really did with my gold locket. He helped me understand your point of view better and why you needed to draw the line with Dad's behavior."

"Wait. Are you talking about the locket Jared and I gave you for your twelfth birthday?" Ellen asked.

Kathryn nodded reluctantly. "It's a long story, Aunt Ellen, and I'm sorry. I never told you about it because I felt so guilty. For years, I thought I'd lost it, but Mom explained a few weeks ago that this wasn't exactly what happened."

She narrowed her eyes. "What happened?"

So, between the two of us, Kathryn and I told her about how Donny had pawned it. Ellen already knew about dozens of incidents of Donny's greed and his many attempts to badger me into giving him more money, but this story made her particularly livid.

To her credit, though, she didn't go off on a rant about "that bastard" in front of Kathryn, the way she had with me so many times in the past. She did, however, regard us both with a deep sympathy, as if some of the pain and tension and fear that my daughter and I shared were, somehow, more understandable now.

"You two are stronger and more resilient than even I realized," Ellen whispered to us. Then, to her niece, she added, "You're an incredible young woman, Kathryn, and you're sharpening your judgment and strengthening your perceptiveness all the time. I'm glad you have someone like Sid on your side. But you also have a tremendous gift in having a mother like yours. She really cares about you. She really listens to you. I know for a fact—because your mother and I grew up with the same parents—that we didn't have that same gift. Our mother was... well, not exactly the support system either of us needed as teens." She glanced over at me, reached across the table, and squeezed my hand. "Maybe you can understand now why your mom is a little more cautious sometimes than you might like. Why she tries so hard to have calm conversations with you, even when she's worried about something you're doing. She's trying to offer you the perspective of her experience, which was hard-earned, and give you a gift she'd had to work to attain all by herself."

"Not all by myself, Ellen," I said. "You've always been there for me. Even when I didn't think I needed your help."

My daughter turned to face me—her eyes bright with a sheen of tears—and she grabbed my other hand and then reached for her aunt's hand, too, so that all three of us were connected around the table. A live family circuit, joined by love.

"I *am* lucky," Kathryn whispered. "And I love you both. Thank you."

The three of us had dried our tears and were laughing again by the time Jared and Sid returned, slightly sunburned, exuberant, and in possession of a bunch of fish pictures on their iPhones, although, thankfully, they didn't return with the actual fish—it was a catch-n-release experience. After they shared their favorite photos with us, my daughter joined her uncle and her fiancé (it was getting *slightly* easier to think of him that way) inside the hotel room, while Ellen and I remained on the balcony.

I observed Ellen watching my daughter as she walked away. It was a peculiar look. Something different. A fierce love, yes, but also an odd brittleness. I couldn't figure out the reason for it, but it appeared to be some strange mixture of longing, adoration, and fear, and it had frozen on my sister's face like the expression on a porcelain doll.

"What is it?" I asked her.

Ellen met my gaze, paused, and then started babbling on a tangent that seemed completely unrelated to her facial expression from the moment before. At least that was what I thought at first.

"You know Anne Morrow Lindbergh's *Gift from the Sea*?" she asked me. "I have a copy of it on the shelf at the bungalow."

I said I'd seen it. That I'd flipped through it and read several passages.

"Good, good. You should read it all. In fact, you should take that copy with you. It's a beautiful book. So many apt analogies and reflections. Like the way different sea creatures inhabit different kinds of shells, much like we do with our homes. And how a shell covering, which might be perfect for certain creatures during one period in their lives, can grow too small and they need to relocate. Or how the sea itself can help us to find joy in the now. It can teach us patience, faith, simplicity, openness—"

"Where are you going with this, Ellen?"

She gulped down half a glass of water. "I've been struggling to be open to what life is trying to teach me, Sis. And I've been trying to find 'joy in the now,' which isn't exactly my nature. But lately I've come to realize that I'd outgrown a mental house—one I'd lived in for a long, long time. A part of my body must've realized it before my mind did, which was why I think I was having panic attacks."

I nodded at her, encouraging her to continue.

"I know for years you and I have lived very different lives. I know for a lot of that time you probably thought I had it easier. Maybe, in some ways, that was true. But the deeper truth, Marianna, was that I was jealous of you, too. You might've had a lousy first husband, but you also had a beautiful child, who's grown into a remarkable young woman." She inhaled, then exhaled. "And I know your relationship with Kathryn hasn't always been smooth, but I've been scared out of my mind that I'll never get to do what you've done. To be a mother."

I stared at her, mute. For years she'd insisted that parenthood was the *last* thing on earth she'd ever want. That the coldness of our parents, especially our mom, had left such a bitter taste in her mouth that she'd vowed never to inflict such a relationship on a future generation. Where the heck was this sudden maternal instinct coming from?

"I'm forty-four, though," she continued. "By the ticking of a lot of biological clocks, that's really pushing it. But I'm not super picky, Marianna. If I can't get pregnant, I'd love to adopt. And I don't begrudge anyone else the decisions they've made in their lives. For lots of people, having kids will never be something they desire. In my case, though, it was... but I'd just buried the hell out of it. For decades."

"I had no idea," I murmured.

She laughed. "Me either."

"What about Jared? How does he feel about all of this?"

Ellen pursed her lips and shrugged. "To say he was 'surprised' would be a fucking understatement. Honestly, I don't blame him. And he and I are still in the discussion-slash-negotiation stage of this whole idea. Neither of us are really big lovers of change, but I know my panic attacks scared him. And they terrified me. So, when I was finally able to isolate why my brain and body might be reacting the way they were, that helped a lot. Plus, it's in Jared's nature to be supportive. His exact words when I first managed to spit all this out on Sunday night were, 'I have no real objection to becoming a father. I just have no idea how good—or bad—I'll be at it.'" She grinned. "So, although it's definitely more my dream than his right now, it hasn't been a deal breaker as far as our marriage. And that had been one of my biggest fears, as well as one of the main reasons why I'd stuffed down the urge to face this for so long."

"Jared's always been really good with Kathryn," I said. "And he and Sid seemed to hit it off pretty well today. He might not realize it yet, but I think he has the potential to be a wonderful dad."

"Yeah. I think so, too."

"And *you*—" I got up and hugged her. "You are going to be *amazing* as a mom. I pity anyone, from preschool age on up, who so much as dares to try to cross a child of yours. You'll be strong and confident, proficient and fair, and you'll teach your baby to do the same."

"You don't think I'm too old to do this? To be a first-time mom?"

She looked really afraid of what I might say, but I could only tell her the truth. "It's hard no matter what the age, Ellen, but if anyone is capable of handling the task, it's you. Particularly with a man like Jared by your side. And

I'm here for you as well. Always. Whenever you might need me."

She nodded. "I know you are. And I'm gonna need you a lot. I mean, seriously. A freakin' *lot*. As it is, this still fictional kid of mine will probably be so screwed up that he or she will need to go to therapy every day of the week and twice on weekends." Ellen mimicked a child on a psychologist's sofa, bitching about his or her crazy mother. "What if I don't do anything right?"

I couldn't help but chuckle. "Oh, please. Don't you know that *every* mother worries about that at some point, and some of us worry about it constantly?" I hugged her again, even harder this time, and she held onto me with a tightness that reminded me of Kathryn as a toddler, frightened and clingy after she'd had a nightmare. "Hey, it'll be okay, Ellen. Really. Don't be scared."

"Well, if you're wrong, I'm going to blame you—*for years*—for encouraging me during this vulnerable time." Then she kissed my cheek and whispered, "Thanks, Sis."

"You're welcome." And then I told her something I'd been mulling over for a while, especially during these past few weeks. "Maybe our mom did the best she could with what she knew about parenting, Ellen. It wasn't what we always needed, but I don't believe she set out to try and mess up our lives. Even so, I think you and I are both capable of doing better. And, really, that's all our kids can ask of us."

"I hope so. I will say that Jared found the silver lining in this immediately."

"What do you mean?"

"The sex, Marianna. Lots and lots of extra sex. He's already enjoying that bonus. It can take a *ton* of tries before a woman my age gets pregnant. Although, we can't know our fertility level until we test it, right? It might happen sooner than we think." She pointed at me. "And you'd better watch yourself as well, especially with that stud muffin of yours."

"Ellen! I'm not planning on having another bab—"

She cut me off. "Never say never. Plus, I suspect you're going to spending a lot of time in bed with Gil before you leave Florida. Don't try to deny it." She crossed her arms and struck that know-it-all big sister pose that I remembered so well from our childhood. "I saw the way he looked at you, Marianna. And the way you looked back at him. The two of you practically steamed up the living room windows and you weren't even touching. So don't act like it couldn't happen to you, too… "

CHAPTER EIGHTEEN
Expanding the Circle

While I wasn't about to deny that Gil and I had remarkable chemistry, discussing the intimate details of my sex life with my sister was *so* not going to happen. At least not this soon into my relationship with Gil. But there was something else I was willing to share—not just with Ellen, but with Kathryn, too.

The following day, Jared flew home, but I promised him as he got into the taxi to head to the airport that I'd keep an eye on my sister. That she and my daughter would be spending the entire day with me... and with my friends.

"Joy, Lorelei, and Abby have been working tirelessly on the B.E.A.D.S. project and have been struggling to get enough bracelets made for the Art Gala, which is coming up at the end of next week," I told them. "Since I've been AWOL for the last several days and couldn't work on it with them, I think it would be wonderful if we had a ladies' day today and chipped in to help them catch up. Are you two game?"

They were.

So, immediately after we waved goodbye to my brother-in-law, the rest of us went to The Beaded

Periwinkle, dropping Sid off at nearby Lido Beach for him to explore that area, along with the Circle, at his leisure. He was invited to join us all later in the day for dinner at Joy's shop, though, which satisfied Kathryn. And Ellen confessed that she was looking forward to getting in a little more time with my friends before she, too, had to return to Connecticut. Her flight home was this weekend, and she said she was ready for it.

"A two-week vacation once every few decades is plenty for me," she joked. "God knows what other major life changes I'd make if I had more time off."

"Yeah, it's definitely safer for you to be a workaholic," I replied.

"I know you're mocking me, but it's kinda true."

"If you're a fan of working hard, Ellen, trust me, you'll have a chance today."

My friends whooped with delight when Ellen, Kathryn, and I walked into the shop and demanded to make ourselves useful.

"I'll give 'em a quick lesson on how to use the tools, "Lorelei offered. "You go join Abby and Joy." She grinned at me. "It's great to have you back, Marianna."

"It's great to be back," I said. And, oh, how true that was. If I felt such a strong sense of missing them after an absence of only four days, how hard would it be to be away indefinitely?

But I pushed that thought from my mind, grabbed a handful of beads and charms, some nylon string, and my pliers and got to work.

With the six of us making bracelets steadily for over eight hours, we made some serious progress. Plus, it was a *blast*. Even my daughter thought so.

"Your friends are really chill, Mom," Kathryn confided after a few hours, giving me one of her rare full hugs and a quick kiss on the cheek. "I'm glad I came today."

"I'm glad you did, too, sweetheart." I smiled at her and

hoped she could see my tremendous love for her in my gaze. She bobbed her head before turning and skipping toward Abby, where the two of them were creating a beautiful series of butterfly-themed bracelets.

Dinner time came and, with it, so did Sid, who'd amused himself around St. Armand's for most of the day and had ended up at Castaways, chatting with Gil and Carter during the late afternoon.

"Kathryn, you gotta see the insane t-shirts and towels these dudes have at their shop," Sid said with a grin, thumbing in the direction of Gil, who'd come into The Beaded Periwinkle soon after closing with a couple boxes of pizza, and Carter, who was toting a twelve-pack of sodas. Sid himself was carrying a tub of caramel corn and a handful of napkins, clearly impressed with all he'd seen during the day. "They're crazy clever," he added.

"Thanks, man," Gil said with a laugh.

And Abby, inhaling the aroma of the warm pizzas, said, "Oh, my God... carb heaven has arrived. I could kiss you guys."

Gil just grinned, taking it as the joke it was. Sid was too busy telling Kathryn about the wild and wacky items for sale at Castaways to hear her. But Carter looked hopeful that Abby would make good on her comment.

Too bad I knew she thought Carter was too young for her tastes. The guy had such an obvious crush on her. But the heart, unfortunately, didn't work according to convenience. I knew that well enough.

If the day had been fun, the night was even more so. We sat around the shop talking, laughing, eating, and tallying up the number of bracelets we'd made.

"I thought we were going to barely make it by the deadline," Joy said. "But we're actually ahead of schedule now."

We simply enjoyed being together until the leftover pizza was cold and the tub of caramel corn was just a container of crumbs.

At one point in the evening, Gil spirited me away to his shop for a few minutes, just so I could secretly help him choose a few gifts for Sid, Kathryn, and Ellen.

"Your daughter's young man is actually pretty funny," he whispered. "He had about a million questions for me about good business practices in Florida and what I thought made the shops in the Circle so successful. The guy has got a lot of drive, and he also seems very attached to Kathryn."

"I know. He's growing on me. Although, I can't help but hope they'll wait a few more years before tying the knot."

Gil nodded. "Agreed. But I learned something interesting about Sid today. He's a child of divorce, too. Like Kathryn. And like Joy and me." He paused. "Sid told me his parents split when he was still a preschooler and that it was a particularly nasty breakup. Yet, he somehow maintained his optimism about love and marriage. I gotta give the guy props for having the courage and determination to try to make a committed relationship work, especially in the face of what he witnessed growing up. He's earned my admiration for that. Kathryn has, too."

I could appreciate what he was saying but, at the same time, what he *didn't* say rang loudly in my ears. That Gil wasn't somebody who had that kind of courage. That he wouldn't be likely to take a leap of faith like that himself. That he hadn't been able to overcome the bad memories of his own parents' divorce and no one would be calling him an optimist when it came to love and marriage.

Nor would they say any of those things about me.

Maybe Gil had the excuse of being an artist. Someone extra sensitive to the world and even, perhaps, a little idealistic about it. But I didn't have that. For me, it was all just emotional baggage and a fear of being burned so badly again.

At the end of the night, when Gil gave Kathryn and Sid

their t-shirts (both with highly witty sayings that Sid had commented on earlier in the day), there was much laughter and appreciation. Gil gave a specialty towel to Ellen, which I'd been the one to select, and she, too, was surprised and grateful.

She actually snorted when she unfurled it and turned it around to show off to the group. It featured a woman standing in the middle of a palm-tree-lined Florida intersection, who had clearly just stolen a police officer's cap, and she was demonstrating to him how to more efficiently direct traffic to the beach.

"This is perfect," she said, smiling warmly at Gil for, perhaps, the first time. "I love it. Thank you." To me, she whispered privately, "Okay, he's a nice guy, as well as being a stud, but I'll still kill him if he hurts you."

"To serve and protect, eh?" I murmured.

"You know it, Sis."

The next morning, Sid and Kathryn had plans to take a bus tour down the coast and visit a few new places, including Sanibel Island.

"I still haven't gone there myself," I admitted with a pang of regret. I wasn't sure if Gil and I would have time to do that now, especially since my departure date was looming. "But I know you two will have a wonderful day. Wear lots of sunscreen!"

"We will," they promised.

Once they'd left, I drove over to Ellen's hotel to pick her up and drive her to the airport in Tampa/St. Pete.

"I'm actually going to miss you, bossy girl," I said, nudging her.

She elbowed me back. "Not as much as I'm going to miss you, little brat."

We laughed and then teared up, and then wiped our eyes and laughed again.

She hugged me fiercely before she headed toward Departures, and I watched my sassy, nutty, intense, and oh-so-loving sister as she walked down the long hallway that would, eventually, lead her home.

A part of me wanted to follow her—to talk with her in person for even a few minutes more—so I could tell her again how much this time away from my old life had meant to me and how thankful I was for all she'd done for me and how glad I was that, in spite of everything, we were sisters.

But I didn't go racing after Ellen. I knew she knew all of that already, and more.

Instead, I drove myself to the Circle and spent another gloriously busy day with my Sarasota friends, trying to wring out every last bit of time with them that I could. It was much like watching the sunset over the Gulf. How I always tried to keep my eye on that last ray of light, which seemed to linger in the sky extra long, just so we could treasure and remember it.

I made the return trip to the airport once more, a few days later, when it was time for Kathryn and Sid's flight back to Michigan.

"Be careful," I said reflexively. Once a mother, always a mother, right?

My daughter rolled her eyes, but there wasn't any genuine irritation behind it. Just amusement. "Of course, Mom," she said with feigned exasperation. Once a daughter...

As Kathryn made a final run to the washrooms before she and Sid entered the Security line, Sid and I were briefly alone. He shoved his hands into his jeans pockets—now a familiar gesture—and thanked me for my hospitality to him while they were here.

"And I've been thinking a lot about what you said, Mrs. Gregory. About waiting until after Kathryn graduates to get married. We've been discussing it and considering that idea seriously. I just wanted you to know that your approval is very important to both of us, especially to your daughter, even if she doesn't always tell you that." Sid shrugged. "That's really why she wanted me to come down here with her. She said she needed for me to meet you and your sister."

Kathryn returned to find me hugging Sid. And when I hugged her goodbye, she whispered, "Love you, Mom," in my ear.

My heart trailed after her and her fiancé, whispering, "Love you more," with every step they took. I watched until they were out of sight.

But though my heart would always be with my daughter, the rest of me seemed to have firmly rooted itself in the Sarasota sand. For the week that followed, Joy, Abby, Lorelei, and I spent our days in a final frantic push to finish the bracelets and deliver upwards of two thousand of them to Peter Barrett, so he could get them into the Art Gala gift bags.

"He's been absolutely wonderful," Joy gushed.

"Just about the B.E.A.D.S. project?" Lorelei teased. "Or, perhaps, there's something more… "

Joy blushed. "We've only gone out a few times—"

"More like seven," Abby interjected. "She *likes* him."

"Maybe a little," Joy admitted, but she glowed whenever she mentioned his name.

During those long, hot evenings, Gil and I spent whatever hours remained together—strolling on the beach, watching old movies, eating meals that one of us cooked, and making love late into the night.

Peter had sent Joy, Lorelei, Abby, and I beautiful gold-leaf-on-linen invitations to the Naturalacrity Art Gala, and I'd planned to bring Gil as my guest. On Thursday night, he asked me the location details—Saturday, West Whelk Country Club in Sarasota, six p.m.—and I pulled out the invitation to show him.

On the back of the envelope was an embossed company logo, which Gil kept staring at all through dinner and beyond. I watched as he repeatedly traced the design with his fingertip—a half circle, like part of a sun on the left side, with a tree sprouting up on the right side. Simple, but not a logo I'd seen before. The same didn't seem to true for Gil, who insisted he recognized it from somewhere.

I'd dozed off on his sofa and woke around midnight to see him typing like mad on his laptop. I yawned, got up, and wandered over to him. "What'd you find, Gil?"

Despite the lateness of the hour, his eyes were wide open and he practically vibrated with an odd, anxious energy. "I had my suspicions," he told me, "but I couldn't find a direct link to anything definitive. Until now." He tapped the screen with his index finger, drawing my attention to an online image that looked identical to the embossed seal on the envelope.

"What's that symbol mean?" I asked. "The sun with the tree? Is it bad? Is Peter part of a disreputable organization or something?"

"The symbol doesn't belong to Peter, nor does the company. I'd seen this emblem years ago, but it's been decades since it was in use. He'd been so careful... " he murmured.

"Peter has been careful?"

Gil shook his head, his jaw tense and his mouth pulled into a tight, unforgiving line. "It's not about Peter. At least not directly. And the logo isn't a sun, Marianna. That half circle is the letter 'C'—which stands for 'Canton.'" He exhaled heavily and rubbed his temples. "It seems Peter Barrett works for a branch of the company that belongs to my father."

CHAPTER NINETEEN
Seasons of Change

Joy was going to flip out when he told her about this. Gil knew that with a certainty and an apprehension that settled deep in his bones. But he sure as hell didn't want her to find out from anyone else.

Naturalacrity, was it?

Now that Gil knew what to search for specifically, he was able to verify through family and legal channels that it was, indeed, a hidden subsidiary of the Canton Corporation.

Oh, shit.

"Do you have any reason to think your dad has been trying to hurt Joy? Or that he wanted to upset her by offering her this Art Gala opportunity?" Marianna had asked him. "Because it seems kind of… well, supportive of him. The type of thing a parent might do to help his child if, let's say, said parent was convinced his direct help wouldn't be welcome."

Gil took this in, nodding slowly. He liked the goodness of spirit and intention that this explanation showed—about Marianna and *her* nature—but she didn't know his dad.

"You might see it that way," he said. "My dad might

see it that way, at least I hope he would. Even I might sorta-kinda-maybe see it that way. But my sister? I know Joy. And she will *not* see it that way. Believe me. For her, this is pure intrusiveness, not support."

Marianna looked at him with great empathy, yet another quality he appreciated about her. "How long can you reasonably delay telling her, Gil? Long enough for us to make it through the Art Gala on Saturday? She's been working on this project nonstop for weeks. We all have. But it's an especially huge night for her. I'd hate to see it ruined after all the time and passion she's put into it."

"I know." The knot that had formed in his stomach when he made the connection had only grown. "And the crappiest thing is that, usually, anyone who lends Joy a hand—anyone who encourages her creativity and her causes—is someone I'd back up without question. Someone I'd see as an instant ally." He shook his head. "But these are special circumstances."

"Would it help to talk with Peter, perhaps? Maybe call him? I know you were never his biggest fan, but perhaps he could explain… "

He almost laughed. He just couldn't quite bring himself to it. "Whether or not I'm his fan is, sadly, irrelevant." He turned away from the computer and sighed. "But it's a necessity. Any chance you've got the suit's phone number? I don't want to have to ask Joy for it."

Peter Barrett was as hard to reach as a rattlesnake hiding out in the Texas brush.

Gil left him several voicemails and sent a couple of urgent emails, too, but Peter responded to none of them.

He finally managed to corner the guy just as the Art Gala was set to begin on Saturday night. Fashionable guests had begun arriving in designer clothing, sparkling jewels, and expensive vehicles. The lot of them could have fit in at the freakin' Oscars, if they were so inclined. There was even a red carpet in the entryway.

In little clusters, the guests meandered into the country club's ballroom, where pricey artistic displays were arranged for silent auction and with museum-like meticulousness. Gift bags were distributed by the hostesses to everyone officially on the guest list, and their names and invitations were checked with precision. Security guards manned each entrance like royal sentinels who'd be quick to remove any interlopers.

Since Marianna had the invitation and was coming separately, Gil had to wait until he could catch Peter walking out of the ballroom. The guy was in ultra-professional mode, greeting guests and schmoozing with them, completely engrossed in the pageantry of the event.

Gil wasn't.

He waved Peter over. "We need to talk."

"Of course," Peter said, gazing distractedly at an older woman wearing a floor-length evening gown and enough jewelry to open her own branch of Tiffany's. "But it'll have to be a bit later. Part of my job is to officially welcome our Golden Tier donors, and make sure—"

"Yeah." Gil cut him off. "That's going to have to wait. This is important and it involves my sister, so let's go someplace private. Right now."

The suit eyed him warily. "Er, I... um, I'd really like to, but I'm sorry. I need—"

Gil's patience snapped. "You need to stop deflecting me. And you need to tell me, is he coming?"

"Is who coming?"

"Gilbert Canton, *Sr.*" He put a sharp emphasis on that suffix and finally managed to garner Peter's full attention.

The guy's face turned an unusual shade of purple—a cross between plum and puce, actually, if Gil were to try to paint it. "You know?" Peter whispered.

"Just answer my damn question, Barrett. Do I need to worry about him showing up here tonight or not?"

"Worry about who showing up?" said a voice both he and Peter recognized at once.

Crap.

His sister was standing directly behind them. She must have just entered the building. Gil sighed and turned around.

Peter winced, but he turned to face her, too. "Oh, don't you look lovely, Joy," he declared.

Not that this wasn't true, but Gil knew better than the suit that his sister couldn't be redirected with flattery. Gil almost felt sorry for the guy as Joy's eyes narrowed dangerously and she crossed her arms, waiting.

When neither of them immediately spoke, she took a few steps forward, leaned in close, and whispered, "Y'all should know I don't like secrets—especially *you*." She poked Gil in the chest and then leveled a suspicious glare at the two of them. "And I recognize a pair of guilty looks when I see them. What's. Going. On?"

This wasn't going to be good, but Gil was helpless to stop the train wreck this late in the game. If their dad suddenly showed up and Joy had no warning, there was no telling how she'd react. She could be very unpredictable that way.

Unfortunately, with what he knew about the connection between Naturalacrity and the Canton Corporation, there was nothing uncertain about what his sister's reaction to that news would be—infuriated. The only damage control he could summon on the spot was to keep this private rather than public.

He motioned with his head toward one of the small rooms down the hallway, away from the ballroom entrance.

Peter took the hint and said, "Joy, let's, um, go somewhere a bit quieter." A very pained expression crossed his face. "I've got a story to tell you… "

❀❁❀

I was running a little bit late.

I'd been on the phone with Ellen, checking in on how things were going for her, which was fine, thankfully (no new panic attacks), but it took me longer to get to the country club than I'd thought. I knew Gil had planned to be there before six, to see if he could finally get ahold of Peter, and it was ten minutes after the hour when I arrived at the Art Gala.

After scanning the lobby and seeing no one I knew, I checked in with the hostess at the table, entered the ballroom, and looked around in there. I felt woefully underdressed. Peter had told us it would be a "formal" occasion, but I'd expected wedding-guest attire, not Hollywood-esque glitz.

Truth be told, though, I might have blended well enough with the crowd if only I'd upped my application of makeup and the amount of bling I had on. My single strand of pearls and my dangling gold earrings weren't going to cut it in this crowd. These women were decked out in rocks that rivaled the Crown Jewels.

I tried to catch Abby's eye from across the room. She was wandering by a table filled with bronze statuettes, all with "nature" themes, that was set up for silent auction. She sipped from a flute of champagne and sampled a mushroom and caramelized onion appetizer pastry, which I tried, too, when the waiter came near enough to offer me one. Delicious!

Finally, Abby spotted me waving at her, and she made a beeline toward me.

"Have you been here long?" she asked.

I shook my head. "Just walked in the door. And I feel

like one of the scullery maids who accidentally stumbled upon the Prince's private party."

"I know. Same here. Did you check out the gift bags already?"

I hadn't yet, but I'd been given one when I entered. They were small and silver and filled with a variety of treats. Our handmade bracelets, of course, with one of Joy's business cards attached to each one and a description of the B.E.A.D.S. project printed on the back. A twin pack of gourmet French cookies—*macarons*—freshly made by a nearby bakery. A tasteful sterling silver bottle stopper with the name of a local wine shop engraved on it. And more.

"It's like we're celebrities," I whispered. "Getting spectacular gifts whenever we walk into a room. I could get used to this."

"Yeah, seriously." She glanced around the room. "Have you seen any of the others? Lorelei told me she wasn't going to be able to get here until six thirty, but I'm really surprised not to see Joy or Peter around. And where's Gil? I thought he was coming with you."

"I should probably text him in a minute, if he doesn't send me a message first. He was planning on coming here early to talk to Peter, but he and I were going to meet in the lobby at—*oh*."

I stopped.

Peter Barrett had just walked into the enormous ballroom, looking very serious and a little sweaty. Not at all like his usual cool and confident self.

Ohhh. Had he and Gil already had their chat?

As we approached him, Peter pulled at the sleeves of his suit jacket, straightened his tie, and wiped his brow.

"What's wrong?" Abby asked him at once.

He cleared his throat but didn't answer that question.

Oh, no.

"I have to be in here right now, but, um, Joy and Gil are in the staff lounge next to the coat room. She—they—I mean, um… " He shook his head then pointed vaguely in the direction of their location.

"Is one of them sick?" Abby asked, confused.

But, given what I knew about Peter's employer, I more than suspected what the real problem was.

"Is their father here?" I asked him.

Abby looked at me like I had two heads. "Their *father*? Neither of them have spoken with that guy in years. Why would he—"

"So, Gil told you?" Peter asked me.

"Just that the Canton Corporation is the parent company for Naturalacrity," I replied.

"What?" Abby cried.

"I tried to explain that he just wanted to give his daughter a little boost. Help her out." Peter rubbed his forehead, his lips in a grim line. "She wasn't buying it. She didn't accept my apology for my part in 'deceiving' her, as she put it. I'd planned to introduce her to the crowd, but she says she won't come back out here tonight. She said a lot of other things, too." He exhaled and inhaled again, rather unsteadily. "I'm not allowed to *ever* talk to her again. Anywhere. At any time." He looked genuinely hurt by this, and I felt for him. I could tell that, ever since they met at the Craft Festival last month, he'd been falling for her.

"I'm so sorry to hear that, Peter."

He shrugged. "Thanks."

"We need to go to her," Abby said, tugging at my arm. "C'mon, Marianna." Then, to Peter, she added, "Joy's relationship—or lack thereof—with her father isn't something Joy talks about openly. But she feels everything quite deeply. Her reaction isn't all about you, but people who know her don't ever go behind her back. For one thing, she always figures it out. And for another, it insults her terribly." She shot him a sympathetic look. "It's not impossible that she'll get over this, though. Eventually."

Peter swallowed and nodded toward the door. "Please

just tell her I'm sorry. Again."

We intercepted Lorelei in the lobby and filled her in on the situation en route to the staff lounge.

"Damn, that's not good," Lorelei said. "This is one of those times when friends just have to be there for each other. She's gonna need us tonight. All of us." And she wrapped an arm around my shoulders and Abby's, as the three of us went in search of Joy.

When we found her in the small side room, Gil was holding her and she was sobbing uncontrollably, as if her heart had been shattered.

I wanted to rush up to them and help hold and comfort her, too, the way I would Kathryn or Ellen or someone I loved like family, but she looked inconsolable, even for Gil.

He gazed at me from over her head, a sad half smile on his beautiful lips, as Lorelei, Abby, and I surrounded the two of them to offer our shoulders to lean on as well.

"We're here for you," Abby whispered.

Joy sniffled, glanced at each of us, and broke into a fresh round of tears. "We worked so hard," she sobbed. "And it was all *fake*."

Gil kissed his sister's forehead and stroked her hair. "It wasn't *all* fake," he murmured. "The guests love the bracelets in their gift bags. I watched several people pull theirs out and exclaim how lovely they were. Their positive reaction is real. And Peter's admiration of you—"

"I *hate* Peter," Joy snapped so vehemently that I almost took a step backward. Sweet, generous, loving Joy sounded downright murderous. "That interfering, condescending, sneaky ass! I can't believe I actually almost let myself like him. That I thought for ten seconds that he was a kindred jade-green." She huffed with the expectation that we knew what this meant. "I was fooled... and I just feel so stupid." She leaned against Gil's chest again, crying some more, until she suddenly pulled back and punched her brother in the upper torso, hard enough that all of us gasped. "And I can't believe you *knew!* He lied to me and you knew, Gil. How could you know something like this—even for a couple of days—and not tell me?"

Gil pulled her even closer. "Sorry, Sis," he whispered, smoothing her hair again. "I was only trying to get a handle on Peter's intentions before talking with you. He was definitely doing our dad's bidding and, maybe I'll regret saying this, but Peter might not be such a bad guy. It's clear he doesn't know much about our family history. You heard his explanation. When Dad approached him about this project, Peter thought he was just being a helpful go-between. Neither of us were even supposed to find out that Dad's corporation was behind it. So, if I hadn't stumbled upon the logo—"

"That makes him all the more devious and contemptible, in my opinion," Joy declared, wiping her eyes with an angry dab. "He willingly helped our dad control and manipulate me, and under the guise of pretending to support something I truly believe in and care about. That's just—just so infuriating. And it hurts me so, so much."

"I know," he said. "But I don't think Peter anticipated that. And even Dad—God, Joy. You have to know how freakin' hard it is for me to defend him on anything, but I don't think he *meant* to hurt you. Not this time. He did anyway, and I want to strangle him for it, but I can't help but doubt that was his intention. And you know better than anyone all of the reasons why I haven't spoken to him in practically two decades. This thing with Naturalacrity, though—it seems different. It could be as simple as the fact that he knew you'd never accept his help any other way. Maybe he thought he'd finally found something he could do to support you as an adult. A way to feel less guilty for all the ways he didn't support you as a kid, you know?"

Joy glanced up at him and then back at all of us. "So,

friends, what do y'all make of this psychoanalysis? Do you think what my brother is saying could be true?"

Lorelei shrugged. "Doesn't matter what we think about it, or even if it's true or not. What matters now is figuring out what you need to do to find peace within yourself so you can move on."

Abby nodded. "You always told me that we were family. Family we'd *chosen*. And that meant a lot to me, Joy, since I was so far from home and didn't have anyone here after Chandler left." She reached out to squeeze Joy's arm. "It works both ways."

"Family. That's how you all made me feel," I heard myself admitting aloud. "Just because you haven't known me as long as everyone else in this room, Joy, it doesn't mean I'm not here for you, too." I paused. "And, for the record, I know a little something about very difficult parents. I should've owned stock in about a dozen ice cream companies for all the gallons I've eaten as comfort food in my lifetime. So, I say we start with a few pints and go from there."

"Agreed," said Abby.

"And there's nothing wrong with a few bottles of booze," chimed in Lorelei. "My vote is for some hard brandy tonight."

All of us laughed.

Gil said, "I'd love to join you ladies, but I'm going to hash out a few things with Peter Barrett." He gently swiped a few remaining tears off his sister's cheek and exhaled. "You go get yourselves out of here, and I'll see you all tomorrow."

Joy hugged him one more time, and then she and the other two women started heading for the door. But I hung back just long enough to ask Gil privately, "Are *you* okay?"

He shrugged. "Been better. This thing stirred up emotions neither Joy nor I like remembering, but I know she can't calmly talk with Peter about what's been going on behind the scenes—not at this point. And not when it involves both the guy she's been dating this summer and the father she's been estranged from for years. Surprisingly, though, I think I can have that conversation now." He smiled at me. "Getting to know you and understanding a bit better the struggles of a parent… well, it's helped me to see the emotional rollercoaster from the other side."

"I'm glad for that. I aim to be useful."

"You're more than *useful*, Marianna." His smile turned into a full-on grin.

"Is he here?" I asked. "Your father?"

Gil shook his head. "Not as far as I know. And it's better that way for all concerned. I'll have to make sure Peter understands that." Then he leaned down, kissed me softly on my mouth, and gazed at me, somewhat sadly, I thought. "But hanging out with this Barrett dude wasn't the way I was hoping to spend tonight."

"Me either," I said. "We've still got a few more days after this, though. I'd like them all to be with you."

He nodded and kissed me again. Then he sent me on my way with his sister and our friends, while he headed off in search of Peter.

By the end of the night—and thanks to four half-gallons of premium ice cream (we each chose our favorite flavors and shared), plus topping (let's just say we went kind of wild with those), and a large bottle of imported brandy— we'd managed to restore some of the brightness to Joy's eyes again.

But I couldn't help but think that, much as I adored these women and felt accepted by them, I didn't know them nearly well enough yet. I knew the essence of them—their good hearts, a few of their quirks—but not the details a person gathers from regular contact. Day in and day out interactions. One of the reasons why I treasured my friendship with Olivia so much was because we'd built that kind of knowledge about each other.

She'd been on my mind an awful lot lately, and tomorrow I planned to call her, fill her in on everything, and hear all about what had been going on for her in Mirabelle Harbor. We'd have to have a real catch up over coffee when I got back to Illinois next week, but I missed her and didn't want to have to wait that long to hear her voice.

During our post-ice-cream coma, while Lorelei and Joy were channel surfing in hopes of finding a program that would make us all laugh, Abby mentioned my upcoming return to Mirabelle Harbor. She admitted she missed home sometimes. "My parents are still living there. My brother Allan, too. A handful of friends." She looked wistful. "On certain days in October, I daydream about seeing the way the trees lining Main Street are on fire with color. During Easter, there's nothing as funny as watching those little kids do their egg hunt in Eastman Field. I miss burgers at Sloppy Joe's. On rare occasions, I even miss the snow."

"You *are* homesick," I said with a laugh. "But, yes, the seasons are beautiful in the Midwest. I've always loved that about it, too."

"And being near Chicago is great. The Art Institute. The Magnificent Mile. All of the amazing theaters downtown." She grimaced. "Just listen to me getting all sentimental about it. I probably drank too much brandy. Maybe if I had someone waiting back there for me, I'd return. I'd need a good reason, in any case, and I don't have one." She shrugged.

"Any chance that you and Chandler might ever—"

"No." She paused. "Well, it's very doubtful. First step would be to chain the guy down long enough so that he'd stay in one place. And, then, we'd have to work through all the reasons why we broke up." She picked up her nearly empty brandy glass, finished the last drop, and shook her head. "It's especially hard when a relationship is *close* to being right, but not quite, you know? Chandler and I had a lot of things going for us, just not enough. Or, I guess, the things that didn't work between us were issues that could pull us apart. But there were other qualities that brought us together. Things I loved about him and haven't found in any other man. It's because of those things that a part of my heart still clings to him."

I thought about Abby's comments for the rest of the night. How they related to Gil and me. As was the case with his sister, I knew the essence of him as a person. The kind of man he was—generous, warm, creative, intelligent, sexy—but I didn't know the day in and day out details. The specific events that had shaped his relationship with his father, their subsequent estrangement, the past lovers Gil had alluded to, or why none of those girlfriends ever became his wife.

He and I had talked about thousands of things, but there were thousands more we hadn't so much as touched upon. There were questions about Gil that I knew I hadn't even thought to ask. How could I leave Sarasota with so much still unresolved here? I didn't even know yet if Gil and I were "close but not quite close enough… " Heck, it'd taken Abby five *years* of being with Chandler to determine her answer to that question. Gil and I had scarcely had five *weeks* together as a couple. Quite simply, we needed more time.

The next day, I called Olivia. It wasn't even eight o'clock in the morning and she was already bubbling over with ideas she had that might help me.

"Hey, Marianna! I've been thinking about you and some great places you can check out when you return. There are these super cute apartments for rent on Spring Street, near where my brother-in-law Blake lives. Let me know if you want me to send you the links to their web listings, or I can ask Blake to scope them out for you. And, oh, this goes without saying, but you know you're welcome to stay with us for as long as you need until you find the perfect place, right?"

I grinned into the receiver. "I do know that. And, Olivia, I can't tell you how much I appreciate your offer and all you're trying to do for me. You and your whole family are the best. But—I think I found a condo complex that I might like to move into."

"Really? That's fantastic! I know there were some condos in Shar's building, just off Crescent Lane. Were those the ones you were thinking of?"

"The place I'm thinking of is further south. A lot further south, actually. I'm—"

"You mean like Evanston? Or Lincoln Park? There are some lovely northern Chicago neighborhoods near the—"

"I mean more like Sarasota."

She squealed. "What? Seriously? Is this about that hot guy—Gil? You're thinking of staying?"

When she finally stopped shooting questions at me long enough to give me a chance to answer, I told her about how things had definitely progressed with Gil. How I still didn't know if our relationship would last forever—I'd been so wrong about Donny and, really, Gil was only my second serious boyfriend, ever. I needed to be more mindful of all of my decisions this time, but I felt Gil and I had a good chance.

"Maybe it's too soon to say," I said, "but I'm falling for him for sure. It wouldn't be the wisest thing for us to move in together just yet, even if he'd asked me, which he hasn't. But I've been thinking a lot about it and, if I'm able to get a job down here, even something part time to help me get started, then renting an apartment or a condo in the building where a couple of my friends live might not be too insane of an idea, would it?"

She sighed. "Not insane at all… although, dammit. I'm going to miss you if you stay in Florida."

"Well, if things don't work out, I might be back in Mirabelle Harbor before you know it." I paused. "To be honest, Olivia, other than being geographically closer to my daughter, the only part of my old life that even makes me consider returning home is your friendship. I'm not willing to let that go."

"Oh, Marianna. I wouldn't let you. We'll have a strong friendship always, whether you're living in Mirabelle Harbor or in Siesta Key or in a frozen dome on Pluto. Although, I'm going to have to lobby the staff at Not the Same Old Grind to sell their coffee in bean form, so I can ship a few bags of it to you at your new address. We can each brew a pot and have our coffee dates over the phone."

"Deal. And I've got the perfect treat to go with our coffee! There's a shop nearby called Fudge Fantasia. I'll have to ship some of that up to *you*."

She laughed. "Then let's hurry and set up our first long-distance coffee date. I'm already seriously excited to try that fudge… "

CHAPTER TWENTY

Sandcastles in the Air...and Gifts by the Shore

Gil pulled out his paints.

He'd been raised to be a corporate suit, but he'd turned his back on that lifestyle for the freedom and creativity of being an artist. In the end, though, he found his surprising professional niche by combining unique artistic creations with sales and business. If anyone knew it was possible to bridge two very different worlds and be successful at it, he did.

But it took balance.

Tonight, he needed to stop everything, find that quiet center within, and just paint.

It'd been late when he returned from the Art Gala and from talking one on one with Peter Barrett. He'd dragged every detail he could wrangle from the guy about his father and the directives his old man had given Peter with regards to Joy's bracelets.

Yes, their dad had specifically sent Peter in search of them.

Yes, once Peter learned of the B.E.A.D.S. project, he'd been instructed to offer Joy a deal she couldn't refuse.

And, yes, the promised donation really was made to her

endangered species cause.

But, no, Peter wasn't supposed to date her, let alone fall head over heels for her.

And, no, he wasn't going to hide the fact that Joy and Gil had found out about their dad's involvement in all of this, even though Peter said he'd probably lose his job as a result.

"My discretion was one of the biggest rules of this assignment," he admitted. "Even though using the logo had been your father's choice—and that was what tipped you off—it had been my responsibility to ensure neither you nor your sister learned about Naturalacrity's origins. If one of you guessed or even had suspicions, I was directed to lie, which was why I avoided you and ignored your calls and emails before the Art Gala, Gil." He frowned. "Sorry, man."

Gil didn't immediately accept his apology but, eventually, he offered to buy Peter a beer at the nearest bar. The two of them sat there for hours, getting to know each other for real for the first time and, after a bit, their talk turned to women.

"Don't give up on Joy," Gil found himself telling the guy. "She's gonna need some space for a while, though. She's always had a forgiving heart, but these machinations of our father's… well, they've taken their toll." He shrugged. "No matter how good you say his intentions might have been—and the jury's still out on that verdict— his interference took something valuable from her. The pride she has in her work, for instance. Being a respected and recognized craftswoman on her own merit. The sense of accomplishment in 'making it' by herself. Some people might welcome having a relative with tons of money who could buy their way to the top. Joy's not one of them."

"Yeah. I figured that out."

"Also, she's my kid sister. And, be advised, I *will* be watching your every move. Especially now, after all of this."

"Yeah. I figured that out, too," Peter said with a laugh. He raised his beer to Gil and the two of them clinked bottles and drank.

They ordered another round. And then one more.

Sometime after the third beer, Gil shared with Peter a little about his relationship with Marianna. How he didn't want her to leave, but he couldn't offer her anything definite to make her stay. He wasn't about to promise her something he couldn't keep.

Peter thought about this. "Could you tell her what you *are* able to promise? And do you even know yet what that is? Like, maybe, you know it's not getting engaged or married or anything that serious yet, but it's more of a willingness to be open to her ideas or to spending time with her, you know? You should figure out what you can realistically promise and offer her that."

The cut-to-the-chase simplicity of Peter's suggestion stayed with him through the evening. And when he walked into his townhouse, he fed Nancy, changed into his painting clothes, and got to work.

He might, if he was lucky, be able to stumble through some sort of lame speech to Marianna about how much she meant to him. And, eventually... hopefully... convey a fraction of his feelings to her. But wouldn't it just be better to show her?

After all, everybody knew that a picture could paint a thousand words. And Gil was good at painting pictures.

But the pressure was on. He needed this one to be perfect.

I had so much to plan, arrange, and reorganize—and only a few days to do it—so taking time to stroll aimlessly on the beach and practice breathing calmly should've been about the last thing on my day's agenda. But Gil had reminded me incessantly of the importance of taking time to center myself and listen to my inner voice.

His words—like the rest of him—had left a lasting impression on me.

And, since I was about to take a life-altering step, it was probably wise for me to make sure I was making these decisions for the right reasons, yes?

My conversation with Olivia had helped a lot, though. If she didn't think I was insane, then I must not be. At least not entirely. I knew there was still quite a lot to reflect upon, however.

"Hey, there, girlie," Vivian called. She was dressed in her usual white-on-white attire, complete with a hat, pausing in her power walk to downshift to my tortoise speed. "Haven't seen you out here for a while. Thought, maybe, you'd already gone back to your home."

I shook my head and began to explain to her about Joy's B.E.A.D.S. project and how I'd gotten involved with it, about my friends in St. Armand's Circle, and about meeting Gil. "The experiences I've had here are changing my life and the dreams I had for it." I picked up a small banded tulip shell half-buried in the sand, wondering where its original inhabitant had gone. Perhaps, like me, the sea creature had just needed a new place to call home.

"Nothing wrong with having new plans and big dreams, girlie." She squeezed my arm with surprising strength and winked at me. "Just build them on something solid. You know, make sure your sandcastles have a good foundation."

We chatted for a while longer about nothing much—the weather, the pretty shells—but there was a profound pleasure in this seemingly mundane exchange. A comfortable rapport that I knew I could easily slip into again and again without tiring of it.

Vivian soon headed on her way down the beach,

moving at a clip that would have left me winded and wheezing. I hoped I could be a bit like her when I got a few decades older.

I splashed at a significantly slower pace through the lattice edges of the water meeting the sand, trying to match my inhales and exhales with the movement of the waves. And, naturally, thinking of Gil.

Seven weeks ago, I never would have thought my life could feel so open to possibilities, but being here reignited my desires, in more ways than one. As I gazed out across the Gulf—another brilliant, blue-sky day—I felt the intoxicating gratitude of being given a second chance at love and at life. I was thankful for the physical passion Gil stirred in me, of course, but, even more, for the mental and spiritual reawakening he and my friends helped to facilitate.

Perhaps Gil didn't have much faith himself in love, commitment, or marriage—I could understand that—but his honesty, compassion, and kind treatment toward everyone gave some of that faith back to *me*. Restoring that belief had been my most secret and long-held fantasy, so Gil had given me a truly priceless gift.

As if summoned by my imagination, I could almost hear his voice calling my name. Weird. Then, a few seconds later, I heard it again and realized it wasn't just my brain playing tricks. Gil was really here at the beach, too.

I scanned the faces of all the strangers on the shore, and then I saw his now familiar form, jogging toward me across the glinting sand.

"Hello, you," I said, picking up my pace so I could meet him halfway.

"Marianna." He beamed one of his gorgeous grins at me. "I stopped by the bungalow first. No answer when I knocked, but your car was still parked in front, so I'd hoped you might be wandering around down here."

"Good guess. And, oh, you'd be so proud of me. I've

been mindfully breathing along with flow of the tide."

He laughed and leaned down to kiss me. Warm, lovely, but far too short. I wanted to protest, *Please, keep going... or at least give me a sign, Gil, that I'm making the right choice. I think I am, but—*

"I've got something to show you," he said. It was then that I noticed he had a large tote bag with him, slung over his shoulder and across his back. He pulled it off and handed it to me. "I made what's inside for you."

I reached into the bag and lifted out the item it held—an art canvas with a stunning seaside picture painted in radiant shades of blue, turquoise, white, and cream and featuring a couple that looked a lot like us, walking hand in hand along the white-sand beach.

"Oh, Gil. It's beautiful! Is this... *us?*"

"It is. And I painted it in acrylics so it would dry overnight. I wanted you to have it right away. I'm so glad you like it."

"I *love* it. Thank you."

"Marianna." He paused. "I'm not sure how to say this. I was kinda hoping the picture would do the talking for me but, ever since we met, I've been thinking a lot about optimism." He reached for my hand, which had begun to tremble at the seriousness of his tone and my worry over what it might mean. I hoped he wouldn't notice.

"My mom couldn't have had a more disastrous marriage and devastating divorce," he told me. "But, yet, she never stops trying to help Joy and me find that special someone. She still very much believes in the power of true love and wants us to have that magical experience ourselves. I had my doubts about love's power or even its existence." He swallowed a few times. "Until I met you. Now, you've got me rethinking everything. There are so many new sensations I'm trying to understand. I'm feeling like a Dali painting on the inside—my heart's melting and time has changed shape. You've made all the world's colors brighter and, maybe, a little stranger." He grinned at me, but there was tremendous emotion in his eyes. "But I like it that way, and I just—I just really, *really* wish you'd stay."

A few tears slipped down my cheeks before I could stop them. Gil had given me far more than "a sign," but that was so like him. To give me so much more than what I'd asked for, even if he didn't know I'd made a request. I knew I didn't need to second guess my decision for even a moment longer.

But Gil saw me crying and immediately jumped to the wrong conclusion.

"Oh, no," he said. "I'm so sorry. I didn't mean to pressure you or make you sad. I just was trying to expla—"

I cut him off with a kiss. A much longer one this time.

Then, when we broke apart for air, I whispered, "I *am* staying, Gil. I was afraid to make you the sole reason for that decision because I know it's still early in our relationship. That there are no guarantees what we've started will last. So I have other good reasons lined up for wanting to stay in Sarasota for a while, but the truth is that you're the main one."

I took a few deep breaths before I continued, a bit more confidently. "A very wise friend of mine told me that I needed to decide if what we shared was just a summer fling, or if it was something more. She said with a fling, you pack up the memories afterward and go home. But with love—or the real possibility of it—you move heaven and earth to keep it." I looked at Gil, letting him see me with all of my passions and vulnerabilities. Hoping he could feel just how much I cared for him. "So, I'm moving. Here."

He didn't immediately speak, but the excited twinkle in his blue eyes, the bright smile that graced his lips, and the warmth of his body as he pulled me closer to him, all let me know this was what he'd hoped to hear.

A second later, he whooped loudly, successfully scaring a few nearby seagulls into flight. He lifted me up and twirled me in the sand, the waves lapping at our feet and the sun streaming down on us as we kissed and hugged, laughed and danced.

And then we walked together on the shore—hand in hand—talking about the future and sharing new dreams.

EPILOGUE

A Month Later in Early September

Thanks to the help of Olivia and the Michaelsen men—who'd loaded up a big truck with my belongings from the storage unit in Mirabelle Harbor and had it sent down to Sarasota—I would soon be officially moved into my new place.

Joy and Abby had been instrumental in finding me an unfurnished condo in their complex that I could sublet for the next six months.

"Not that we're going to let you leave Florida in March," Joy informed me. "But we'll help you move wherever you want to go next."

"As long as it's within a twenty-mile radius," Lorelei added.

"Exactly," Joy agreed, grinning.

All of my friends were there to lend a hand when the truck arrived. Gil, Carter, and Nick did the majority of the heavy lifting, but Abby, Lorelei, and Joy scurried around like mad, carting in boxes and helping me get things set up. Between the seven of us, the move was done in record time.

Ellen and Jared had sent me a beautiful "Welcome to Your New Home" basket, overflowing with sweet goodies that all of us could enjoy after we'd gotten everything into the condo. My sister wasn't pregnant yet, but the two of them were hopeful, and I was keeping my fingers and toes crossed for them.

Kathryn and Sid had been quite supportive of my decision to stay in Sarasota, and they were already planning a visit over their Christmas break. They told me they were going to drive down and we'd get to spend at least two weeks together. I couldn't wait. They were still happily engaged and I hadn't heard any talk lately about having the wedding at the end of the school year, which was a relief. So all was going well in that regard, too.

Joy had refused several of Peter's invitations to meet for lunch or even a drink, but she was at least willing to speak with him (briefly) again. (Sometimes.)

"That's big progress," Gil said about the situation.

And thanks to Abby, I'd gotten a part-time job at the place she worked, Floriday Excursions. Mostly organizational tasks, data entry, and answering the phone, but it kept me solvent enough to cover rent. The owners said there might even be more weekly hours available soon, and I really enjoyed getting to talk with new people and work in the Circle near my friends.

As for Gil, he and I had been together throughout all of August, and I felt our relationship was continuing to progress steadily. He understood and agreed with my reasoning for needing my own place initially, but he'd already hinted that my next move should be with him. We'd take it one season at a time. I liked where we were headed, though.

"This was left in the foyer. Is that where you want it, Marianna?" Lorelei asked me, holding a mid-sized cardboard box.

Even from half a room away, I could hear the faint but familiar ticking coming from inside. I smiled. "No. Bring that one in here. Thank you."

She did. I peeled off the packing tape, opened the box, and removed the top item—my peachy conch-shell clock that Ellen gave me so long ago. Now it was back on the Sunshine Coast, where it had been made. I released it from the bubble wrap and set it in the middle of the kitchen table—a perfect decoration for my new place.

"It looks at home here," I told my friends.

Gil put his arm around me, pulled me near him, and whispered, "It does. And so do you."

~END~

UP NEXT: Look for Sharlene Michaelsen's unexpected romance with Declan Night, as well as Abby's return to Mirabelle Harbor, in *One Night Love Affair*— coming soon!

THE SERIES

If you enjoyed *STRANGER ON THE SHORE* (Book 4) from Marilyn's *"Mirabelle Harbor"* series, check out this excerpt below from *TAKE A CHANCE ON ME* (Book 1), and the story summaries for *THE ONE THAT I WANT* (Book 2) & *YOU GIVE LOVE A BAD NAME* (Book 3), all of which are available now...

And please keep an eye out for other stand-alone stories in the series, including *ONE NIGHT LOVE AFFAIR* (Book 5)—coming soon!

Description and an Excerpt from TAKE A CHANCE ON ME (Book 1) - Out Now!

Welcome to Mirabelle Harbor! In this scenic suburb on Chicago's North Shore, overlooking the sparkling waters of Lake Michigan, the Michaelsen family has made their home for generations. Although their parents and grandparents are now gone, siblings Derek, Blake, Sharlene, and the twins—Chandler and Chance—all have fond memories of growing up in town, and most still live there.

Chance Michaelsen, the youngest member of the family (by two minutes) and the quietest (by far), is a dedicated twenty-eight-year-old personal trainer at the local gym. While he might not say much, Chance has made it clear that he's not a fan of toxic people, unhealthy habits, or sharing too many of his emotions. With anybody.

Enter Antonia "Nia" Pappayiannis—the prettiest member of the loudest and most overly demonstrative family in town. They're also the owners of The Gala, a Greek restaurant and bakery known for its decadent pastries and located just a few steps from Chance's gym. He considers their entire family business to be the enemy of good health, but he can't quite shake his attraction to Nia, who doesn't seem nearly as impressed with him or his sculpted physique as most of the women around Mirabelle Harbor.

Unfortunately, between her doctor's orders and the interfering ways of Chance's crazy-making ex-girlfriend, who just happens to be one of Nia's long-time friends, Chance gets assigned to be Nia's fitness coach for the month. Pure torture. And if his ex weren't already causing enough problems, he also has to deal with Nia's current boyfriend—some hotshot Chicago CEO who talks big but, in Chance's opinion, is as fake as a Styrofoam barbell.

The road to romance is going to be a rocky one, and though Nia has her doubts about getting involved, Chance has a well-developed competitive streak and might just be willing to give it a shot...if he can convince her to do the same.

In matters of the heart, would you risk it all? TAKE A CHANCE ON ME, a Mirabelle Harbor story.

From the Novel:

I couldn't dismiss Chance's gaze. He was watching my every movement, noticing each inch of exposed skin, which wasn't much on my side, really. The white towels gave comprehensive coverage. They were jumbo sized, so only my shoulders, arms, lower thighs, calves, and feet were visible.

But Chance took in every bit, and I squirmed under that

level of scrutiny.

We sat in silence for a long time.

Finally, he cleared his throat. "So, Nia, is Grant Jordan still your boyfriend?"

I shook my head. I hadn't said any official breakup words to Grant, which would really be more like, "Hey, I don't think we should hang out for a few hours during the weekend anymore." Our relationship had hardly been the stuff of soulmates. But, after tonight, I knew I didn't want to go back to Grant's large but lonely mansion.

"My parents liked him a lot, though," I explained to Chance. "They'll be disappointed."

He narrowed his eyes. "Are *you* disappointed?"

"No."

He abruptly stood up and walked over to me. With no shirt fabric as a shield, there was nothing that could camouflage his incredibly buff upper body. Bet he did more than torso twists to get that six pack, huh? Even more than wanting to touch him, though, I wanted to know what he was thinking. My attention kept getting drawn back to his face. To his inquisitive hazel eyes.

He stood in front of me and pulled me to standing. "Turn around," he whispered.

"Why?" I murmured, glancing at the door. There was an oval sliver of a window where people walking by could peek in on us, if they were so inclined.

"I'm going to rub your shoulders," he said simply. "Don't worry. I'll stop anytime you want, but now's the best time to loosen those tight muscles. You can lean against the wall for balance."

There was almost nothing in the world I wanted more than to feel Chance's hands on my skin. Between his nearness to me, my anticipation of his touch, and the blazing temperature of the sauna, I could only take quick, shallow breaths but, nevertheless, I turned around.

From the very second his fingertips connected with the

top of my shoulders, it was all I could do not to gasp or moan. He had magic hands, that man. A grip that was strong, firm, but not pinching. My neck and shoulders had never felt better.

I could only imagine what he could do to my back if I were to throw the towel on the floor and let him rub whatever he wanted, or wherever he wanted. Aunt Helen would be evoking all kinds of prayers to the blessed Virgin if she knew what I was thinking.

"You really missed your calling," I managed to say.

Chance made that low chuckling sound that sent a bolt of desire from my ears to my toenails. "I have some background in deep tissue and Swedish massage," he told me. "Board certified, actually. But I'm very selective in choosing my clientele for that service."

The air in the sauna must have hit about three thousand degrees when he spoke. I was burning up. But he continued to rub only above the towel line. Nothing remotely inappropriate. And his self-control made me want to scream, "Go lower! Push the towel down, Chance. Tell me you want me half as much as I want you."

Instead, I just sighed, and his fingers stilled. *No!*

He very gently turned me around to face him, lowered his head until his lips were millimeters from mine, and whispered, "Number 127 Arpeggio Avenue. Apartment 3."

"What?" I asked. There was steam all around us and, more than that, my brain was in a fog.

"That's my address. Just two blocks south of here." He paused. "It's your choice, Nia. But remember your question when we were texting tonight? When you asked if I was propositioning you?"

I nodded. Oh, yes. I remembered. *If I were propositioning you, I'd say to meet me at my apartment...*

"So," he said slowly, "if you would like, meet me at my apartment." Then Chance smiled, stepped away from me, and walked out of the sauna.

~*~

About THE ONE THAT I WANT (Book 2) - Out Now!

The summer after her beloved husband died in a car accident, Julia Meriwether Crane is still picking up the pieces of her life in Mirabelle Harbor and trying to help her ten-year-old daughter adjust to this difficult new reality.

After her best friend Sharlene—one of the well-connected Michaelsen siblings—talks her into finally going out on the town again, Julia finds herself stunned to be the object of interest of several different men: The boy who'd broken her heart back in high school. The college ex she'd left behind. And most surprising of all, the movie actor she'd always fantasized about but had never met in person...until now. Can one woman have more than one "great love" in the same lifetime? And, if so, how can she be sure which man that'll be?

Sometimes the person you think will be best for you isn't the one you really want. THE ONE THAT I WANT, a Mirabelle Harbor story.

~*~

About YOU GIVE LOVE A BAD NAME (Book 3) - Out Now!

"Nothing but love, 24/7" is the slogan of Mirabelle Harbor's only radio station, 102.5 "LOVE" FM. On the

verge of turning thirty-five, local DJ Blake Michaelsen is well-known for several reasons: his very sexy on-air voice, his omnipresent family, his eligible bachelor status, and his reputation as one of the most impulsive men in Chicago's northern suburbs.

High-school French teacher and lifelong romantic Vicky Bernier is not at all wild about people who exhibit reckless conduct. (Blake.) Or men who have gigantic egos. (Blake.) Or grownups who still act like teenagers. (Blake, again.) She deals with enough adolescent behavior during the school day. Unfortunately, she's the staff advisor to the Homecoming Committee, and they've chosen him as their DJ for the big fall dance.

What happens when a man whose job it is to play love songs for a living is forced to admit his deepest secret—that he doesn't believe in true love—only to discover that the one woman who might capture his heart is the same woman who distrusts him the most?

No matter what you call it, with love there's an exception to every rule. YOU GIVE LOVE A BAD NAME, a Mirabelle Harbor story.

Learn more about the Mirabelle Harbor books on Marilyn's website page for the series: http://www.marilynbrant.com/books/the-mirabelle-harbor-series/

ABOUT THE AUTHOR

Marilyn Brant has been told she writes with honesty, liveliness and wit (descriptors she's grown terribly fond of) about complex, intelligent women—like her friends—and their significant personal relationships. Although her favorite pursuits undoubtedly involve books, she proves she's not just a literary snob by confessing her lifelong fascination (read: obsession) with popular music, especially from the '70s and '80s, most flavors of ice cream, and a variety of sensuous body lotions/oils.

As a former teacher, library staff member, freelance magazine writer, and national book reviewer, Marilyn has spent much of her life lost in literature. She is the *New York Times* and *USA Today* bestselling and award-winning author of twelve novels and three novellas to date, and a lifetime member of the Jane Austen Society of North America. The Illinois Association of Teachers of English (IATE) selected her as their 2013 Author of the Year.

Her debut coming-of-age novel, *ACCORDING TO JANE* (Kensington, 2009), featuring the ghost of Jane Austen giving a young woman dating advice, won the Romance Writers of America's prestigious Golden Heart Award and the Booksellers' Best, and it was named one of the "Top 100 Romance Novels of All Time" by Buzzle.com. Her second novel, *FRIDAY MORNINGS AT NINE* (Kensington, 2010), was a Doubleday and Book-of-the-Month Club pick in women's fiction. *A SUMMER IN EUROPE* (Kensington, 2011) was featured in the Literary Guild and BOMC2, and it became a Top 20 Bestseller in Fiction and Literature for the Rhapsody Book Club. The Polish translation of the novel was released in June 2013.

She's also a #1 Kindle bestseller, who writes fun and flirty romantic comedies, like her stories in *THE SWEET TEMPTATIONS COLLECTION*, that involve sweet treats, unexpected love, and large doses of humor. *THE ROAD TO YOU*—a coming-of-age romantic mystery—was selected as one of the Top 20 Best Books of the Year (December 2013) by The Reading Frenzy. Now she's at work on the "Mirabelle Harbor" romance series: Look for books *TAKE A CHANCE ON ME, THE ONE THAT I WANT, YOU GIVE LOVE A BAD NAME, STRANGER ON THE SHORE,* and more! And be sure to check out her short story, "When Life Imitates Art," in RWA's upcoming anthology, *SECOND CHANCES* (tentative title), edited by international bestselling author Sylvia Day.

Marilyn currently lives in the Chicago suburbs with her family. When she isn't reading her friends' books or watching old movies, she's working on her next novel, eating chocolate indiscriminately, and hiding from the laundry.

Please visit her website: www.MarilynBrant.com.

www.ingramcontent.com/pod-product-compliance
Lightning Source LLC
Chambersburg PA
CDIIW020333180626
46810CB00007B/2491